ryan *and* avery

Also by David Levithan

ryan
and
avery

david levithan

Alfred A. Knopf
New York

THIS IS A BORZOI BOOK PUBLISHED BY ALFRED A. KNOPF

Visit us on the Web! GetUnderlined.com

Educators and librarians, for a variety of teaching tools, visit us at RHTeachersLibrarians.com

Library of Congress Cataloging-in-Publication Data is available upon request.
ISBN 978-0-399-55309-7 (trade) — ISBN 978-0-399-55310-3 (lib. bdg.) —
ISBN 978-0-399-55311-0 (ebook) — ISBN 978-0-593-71003-6 (international ed.)

The text of this book is set in 12-point Adobe Garamond Pro.
Interior design by Michelle Crowe

Printed in the United States of America
10 9 8 7 6 5 4 3 2 1

First Edition

*To Noah, the reader who
suggested I write this*

and

*To Andrew, who loves
a queer love story*

Snow Day

(the fifth date)

On the day of Avery and Ryan's fifth date, it snows.

This is not out of the ordinary—it snows a lot in the towns where they live. But this is the first snowfall, and that always occasions a certain amount of surprise. Winter is no longer deniable, even though there are still some leaves that refuse to abdicate from the trees. The days have already been shortening, a minute or two of sunlight leaking away each evening, but that isn't as noticeable as the sudden shift to snow.

If Avery and Ryan lived in the same town, the snow wouldn't have much impact on their date. Their progress toward each other would be a measure slower, a measure more thoughtful, but everything would go as planned. As it happens, Ryan is driving to Avery. They might have met midway, but for them there is nothing midway, nor is there anything, really, within a fifty-mile radius. A pair of movie theaters. A few diners. A mall that has seen better days. A

1

Walmart where you were sure to bump into at least three people you didn't want to see while out on a date. Places you could hang out, but you wouldn't necessarily want to, at least not for a special occasion. And at this point, for Avery and Ryan, each date is a special occasion.

They met at a dance—a gay prom—the blue-haired boy (Ryan) and the pink-haired boy (Avery) spotting one another and filling one another's minds with music and color, shyness and an inexplicable but powerful urge to overcome shyness. It has progressed at a pace neither Ryan nor Avery has any reference point for. Are they going fast? Slow? The speed limit? Ryan has now met Avery's parents; Avery has yet to meet Ryan's parents, but at least he knows the reason has nothing to do with him and everything to do with the fact that Ryan's parents aren't quite ready for their blue-haired son to bring home a pink-haired boyfriend (or a boyfriend with any other hair color, for that matter).

Avery's parents have always been understanding—even before he realized he was a boy and should be recognized by the world as a boy. When he shared this truth with them, they didn't dismiss it or try to persuade him otherwise. And when Ryan appeared in Avery's life, and Avery let him appear in his parents' lives as well, they were nothing short of welcoming. Avery isn't particularly surprised by this, even if it still feels like he's sharing a new chapter with them as it's being written, and he's a little nervous about how they'll read it. Ryan, meanwhile, is unfamiliar with this level of acceptance. He doesn't know how to act around anyone's parents, because his own are so negating.

Ryan does not check the weather forecast as he grabs his keys and leaves his house. There might have been murmurs about snow at school, but Ryan has learned to tune out all murmuring when he's there; most murmurs are nastier and less important than the weather report. When the first flakes hit his windshield, it's so gradual that it looks as if small, translucent spiders are dropping from the sky, filaments in their wake. It's only when he's ten minutes from Avery's house that the wipers need to be turned on and the truck needs to slow. The snowflakes have begun to crowd the sky, and Ryan can't help but smile at the way something solid can materialize from air, as if it has been summoned by a gentle spell.

He feels he already knows the route by heart . . . but sometimes the heart makes wrong turns. He could call Avery to ask for directions, but he chooses to rely on his phone's navigational skills instead, since he wants Avery to believe he can find his way from memory. (On the fifth date, you are always looking for ways to prove the path to the sixth, seventh, and eighth.)

Avery is waiting by his window, so he is aware of the snow, too. It isn't so dense that his delight needs to skid and swerve into worry. No, as he watches the downward drift, he doesn't picture Ryan in any wreck, or even imagine Ryan forced to turn back home. Instead he feels that elemental wonder that comes from seeing the world so casually altered, the transfixing sensation of watching something so intricately patternless fall.

When Ryan's pickup appears within the snowfall, Avery's heart becomes the opposite of snowfall—that strange, wind-blown moment when you look and see the snow is actually drifting upward. Snowrise. When Avery sees Ryan pulling into his driveway, his heart is snowrise.

He is trying to guard this heart of his, but the guards are distracted. He is trying to cage his excitement, but he keeps leaving the door unlatched. He knows it is dangerous to like someone so much.

There is nervousness, too. Avery has control of his room, but he doesn't have control over the whole house. His mother likes to hang up family pictures, and as a result there are lots of photos of Avery as a kid, Avery before everything was known, Avery before everything was understood. His mother had been very clear about this: It would hurt more to erase the past. Better, she said, to come to peace with it. There was no reason to hide it, no reason to disown the child Avery had been. Avery thought it was much more complicated than this, but at the same time, his parents had been so cool with everything else that he didn't think it would be fair to tell them to take down all the photographs of the time before. In some of the photographs, Avery looks very happy. On some of those days, he was. On others, not as much. Only Avery has access to the feelings that lived underneath. Even when he was just a kid.

He certainly can't ask his parents to take down the photos now, just because Ryan is coming over. He knows it isn't worth it to try to curate his past, to try to present it to Ryan as if it had been otherwise. One of the most exciting and intimidating things about Ryan is the fact that Avery wants to tell him the truth. This is what they've recognized in each other. No pretending. They will talk to each other undisguised.

This makes Ryan anxious, too, but it's an anxiety he's willing to navigate, the same way he's willing to step into the snow and walk through the wind in order to get inside. He can see Avery in the window as he pulls into the driveway, can see his pink hair and the lamp right next to him, the way it beacons out on such a dimming day. Ryan once heard the phrase *Leave a light on for me* and thought it was one of the most romantic requests ever made. He liked the idea that when you fall in love with someone, the other person becomes your lighthouse keeper, even if it means staying up all night, even if it means staring out into the darkness until the darkness assumes the shape of your love and comes back to you.

Ryan turns off the truck and almost immediately the windshield is covered. He turns off the headlights and for a moment there is the sincere silence of an entirely natural world. Even though his lighthouse keeper waits, he sits for a few seconds and listens to the music of the snow, to the slight tintinnabulation of snowflakes conversing with glass. He opens the door and lets his sneaker sink into the sparse accumulation that covers the driveway. The cold immediately attaches itself to his ears, his fingers. He races up the steps, inaugural footprints marking his trail. When he gets to the door, it is already open. When he gets to the door, he finds Avery in a blue sweater, Avery smiling as if Ryan's arrival is the greatest gift a boy could ever want.

They stop and look at each other. A little more snow falls on Ryan's shoulder and dusts his hair. He doesn't notice. Not until he is inside and Avery is brushing it off, using it as an excuse for immediate touch, a welcome that starts at the top of Ryan's head and works its way to the side of his face and down his neck.

"I'm so glad you're here," Avery says.

"And I'm so glad to be here," Ryan answers.

Avery, having been inside the past couple of hours, has no idea how warm his house is, how it feels to Ryan as if cookies are being baked a few feet away. It is the kind of warmth you want to nestle into.

There are footsteps from another room, Avery's mother calling out, "Is he here?" Ryan stomps his shoes on the mat, takes off his coat, and hands it to Avery, who hangs it on a doorknob to dangle until it is dry enough for the closet. Avery's mother appears from her home office, welcoming Ryan and asking him about his drive. Ryan isn't used to this kind of chitchat from a parent—maybe his father would have given him an "Is the truck driving okay?" but he wouldn't have wanted to know anything beyond that. For Avery's mother, it seems like the chitchat is meant as an entryway into more conversations, more topics.

She asks Ryan to leave his sneakers by the door, but she makes it feel like a favor rather than a command. Ryan complies, then worries he is broadcasting the hole in the heel of his left sock. If Avery's mother notices, she doesn't say anything.

(Ryan's mother would have said something, and it wouldn't have been very nice.)

"Well, I won't get in your way," Avery's mother promises, getting in their way a little bit longer. "If you need anything, you know where I'll be. There should be muffins in the kitchen. I think we have blueberry, maybe some carrot—or that might be bran. I'm not sure how you feel about bran, Ryan. Or about raisins—I think those have rai—"

"We've got it, Mom," Avery interrupts. Ryan is amused to see him so exasperated by prolonged muffin talk.

Avery's mother laughs, holds up her hand in surrender.

"As I said, I'll be in my office if you need anything."

She shoots Avery one last look—*I love you even when you're rude to me in front of your friend*—and skedaddles.

When Avery's mother leaves the room, Ryan steps away from the door and takes up Avery's old position at the window. The snow is now blowing in gusts, clouds dissolving in the midst of a fight. The branches of the trees are beginning to bow and sway, as if beckoning the snow to fall even faster.

I'm lucky to have made it, Ryan thinks.

Avery walks up behind him, and for a moment doesn't know where to put his hands. To have Ryan so close after spending so much time imagining him close . . . Gently, he moves his arm under Ryan's arm, moves his hand across Ryan's chest. Then he presses his own chest against Ryan's back, peeking over Ryan's shoulder so they can look at the snow together.

Neither one of them says out loud how beautiful it is, but both of them think it is quite beautiful.

Avery feels Ryan tense for a second, then realizes why. Mrs. Parker from across the street is coming out of her house, as she has every twenty minutes for the past two hours, to spread salt on her path. It is the same motion she uses to scatter seed for birds in the summertime.

She is not looking up, but Ryan is tensing at the idea of her looking up. Seeing them. Taking this moment that is theirs and making it into something else in her head.

Avery knows she wouldn't care, might even find it sweet, to see the blue-haired boy and the pink-haired boy entwined like journal and clasp. But there is no way for Ryan to know that.

Ryan turns. Avery loosens his grip, to allow another hold to form. Now they are face to face, moving back into the hallway, blocked from the outside by the door.

"I've missed you," Ryan says.

Avery leans in and kisses him. Once, but lingeringly.

"I've missed you, too."

Ryan and Avery talk every day, and text nearly every hour

they're awake and allowed to have phones out. They chat for long spells each evening, a running commentary that often ripples into digression. But none of that can cure the missingness they've felt; if anything, it makes the missingness more acute. As Avery put it to Ryan late one night, long after they were supposed to have gone to sleep: *What we're doing right now is watermelon-flavored. When we're together, it's watermelon.* This made sense to Ryan then, and it makes even more sense to him now. Kissing Avery is watermelon. Having his arms around him is watermelon. Being able to see the look on his face as he talks is watermelon.

"What do you want to do?" Avery asks.

And Ryan thinks, *This. Watermelon.*

Here, in the fifth date, another precious inkling of a truth about love: That there is a point you reach when it doesn't really matter what you do, that the question of what to do becomes beside the point for long stretches. The answer reduces to the smallest, most important words:

You.

Here.

Us.

This.

All so easy to fit into the equally small word *Now,* and the slightly longer word *Love.*

But Ryan is sixteen. He doesn't realize that any of these small words are worthy answers, just as Avery at the same age doesn't know it's alright to not have a plan for what to do next.

Not knowing what the answer should be, Ryan replies, "It's your house. You lead the way."

Avery would love to stay right here, kissing Ryan for a few minutes more. But there is always the risk that his mother will remember another flavor of muffin in the kitchen, and will return to tell them about it.

"How about my bedroom?" he proposes. Then, blushing, he feels compelled to add, "Not because it has a bed, but because it's, uh, my room."

Ryan smiles. "Sounds good."

This is the geography of a house, at five in the afternoon on a fifth date:

In one room, a mother types. Every now and then, she stops to think about what she's typing, but her thoughts rarely stray farther than that. In the kitchen, the refrigerator and the clock have a barely audible conversation. The garage waits like a sleeping whale; when a father comes home in an hour, it will open its mouth with a bellow that everyone else in the house will notice. For its part, the family room gently offers some spilled lamplight to the growing night. The front hall is damp with footprints; a pair of sneakers waits by the door. In the hallway, two boys walk single file, both in socks, both looking at one another far more than they are looking at their steps or anything lining the walls. Ahead of them, a bedroom waits for the flick of a switch to bring it to life. Beyond that, there's another bedroom, currently resting.

In the bathroom, a faucet drips, as if trying to imitate the precipitation outside. A toilet seat has been left up. Three toothbrushes stand at attention; since they aren't speaking, we must assume they are listening to everything else that goes on in the house.

All of this is surrounded by snow. The roof is now covered. The truck in the driveway is as white as the driveway. Were you looking from above, you would have to look closely to see a house at all.

But you are not looking from above.

Ryan examines Avery's room with an affectionately curious eye. The posters on the wall belong to artists, not bands. The bookshelves have been arranged in stripes of color— blue then red then blue then red then green then red then green then yellow then green, and so on. The bed is in the corner, the room's single window at its head.

Ryan walks over there and looks out. In a few minutes it will be too dark to see the snow, but now it can still be traced and tracked. Avery joins him, and together they watch the snowflakes fall like punctuation marks shaken from a sentence.

Avery sits down on the floor, his back against the bed. Ryan follows, sitting right next to him so their legs touch and their arms overlap. It's weird, Avery thinks, how this works. When someone stares at you, you can feel so much like a body, with all your flaws obnoxiously blaring. But when someone is next to you, when someone is as much of a body to you as you are to them, it becomes more comfortable, more valuable. Feeling Ryan's skin and knowing that at the very same time Ryan is feeling his skin. Knowing they are different, but maybe the sensation of it is the same, just like breathing is the same, like a heartbeat is the same. Avery leans into that. Feels.

"So how was your day?" Ryan asks, and for the next few minutes they talk about school, about friends, about the snow first appearing in the sky. This is part of what they need, too—to be like everyone else, to have the time to lean like this and recount the time since they last spoke. There are no revelations here. The most exciting part of their day has been anticipating this, being excited about this very sharing.

"Is that a yearbook?" Ryan asks, looking at the bottom of Avery's bookshelf. He moves to pull it over.

"No!" Avery says. "No you don't!"

Ryan makes an exaggerated grab for it. Avery makes an exaggerated tackle. Conceding with a playful lack of resistance, Ryan stretches out on the floor. Avery pins him anyway.

This is where it can turn from playfulness. This is where heat can subsume warmth. But neither Ryan nor Avery wants that—not now, not yet, not this early in the date. So instead they keep it playful—Avery leaning down for a kiss, then pulling back right at the moment their lips should meet. Laughing. Then going down for a real kiss, Ryan arching up to meet it.

Avery loosens his grip. They kiss some more, conversationally. Ryan reaches out, as if he's about to mess with Avery's hair or trace the curve of his shoulder. But it's another fake-out—Ryan's arm extends just long enough to get to the yearbook, to take it from the shelf.

Avery groans, but doesn't fight it. Not even when Ryan sits up and starts to thumb through. It's last year's yearbook, and since Avery was a sophomore then, he didn't make much of an impression in its pages.

As Ryan thumbs through, Avery watches him do it, notices small things he hasn't noticed before—the places where Ryan's blue hair is starting to revert to bleach, the Little Dipper of birthmarks on his arm. Ryan asks a few questions about a few of the people in the photos, and Avery answers when he can—his school is too big for him to know everyone, and he isn't attitudinally inclined to know everyone, anyway. He has his small pod of friends and all the kids he's doing the school play with, and that's where he spends most of his time.

Ryan finally comes to the page where Avery's sophomore picture resides, part of the mosaic of stamp-sized malcontents forced by the class photographer into their frames. The photo is too small for Avery to really hate it, although the person in it already feels like a skin he's shed.

"Nice haircut," Ryan says, with no real meanness in the tease.

"I was experimenting!"

"With what?"

"Bad haircuts!"

It is a black-and-white photo (only upperclassmen got color), so you can't really see the pathetic orange that Avery had occasioned for photo day—it was something that looked like marmalade when he'd been aiming for jack-o'-lantern. Pink had soon followed.

"I used to wear mine down to my shoulders," Ryan confesses. "I was twelve or thirteen, and I thought it made me *tough*. Like, if I could have grown a beard then, I would've done that, too. I look back now and know it was camouflage—and not even good camouflage. My mother caught me tossing it over my shoulder one day, total super-model mimic, and asked me point-blank, 'Why are you doing that?' And I thought, *Oh, right.* The next time we went to the barber, she didn't have to say a thing. I told him to cut it off, and he called out to the rest of the guys in the barbershop for a round of applause."

"Do you miss it?" Avery asks.

Ryan snorts. "Not at all. I probably could have wrung the grease out and bottled it, it was getting so gross."

Avery instinctively itches his hair. Ryan notices and smiles.

"Sorry," Ryan continues. "I guess it's my way of saying we've all got bad haircuts in our past. Or bad lack-of-haircuts."

The garage opens its mouth at this point, filling the house with its call. Avery looks at the clock—it's a little early for his father to be home.

"They must've closed his office because of the snow," he

says to Ryan, acknowledging the noise. "It must be getting pretty bad out."

They leave the implications of this unsaid. If it is bad enough for Avery's dad to leave early, it probably means Ryan should be making an emergency exit. But Ryan decides he has no intention of doing that.

(It doesn't even occur to Avery that Ryan might have to leave early.)

"Boys!" Avery's mother calls out. "Half-hour warning for dinner!"

It wasn't Avery's plan for them to have dinner with his parents. He thought they'd go out, even if it was just Burger King. He stands up to look back out the window and sees that, yes, it's going to be an eating-in night. Their road is not on the priority list to be plowed, and by now it's hard to tell where the curb stops and the road begins. Ryan's truck is starting to look like an igloo.

It still doesn't occur to Avery that Ryan might have to leave early. Or has already lost his chance to leave early.

"A half hour," Ryan comes over and whispers in Avery's ear. "What can we do with a half hour?"

The answer?

His hands are on Avery's hips.

The answer?

Kisses. Variations of kisses. Repetitions of kisses. Learning each other through kisses.

The answer?

Clothes staying on, because there are parents walking in

the hall, because this isn't that, not yet. But just because clothes stay on, it doesn't mean there aren't bodies to be felt through fabric, skin to feel the pressure, feel the touch.

The answer?

It doesn't really matter what they do.

There is food in the pantry, food in the refrigerator, and even candles and matches waiting on the kitchen counter, just in case the power goes out. There is also the constant narration of the Weather Channel from the television in the family room, the entire storm looking like a single cloud marauding over a quarter of the country.

Ryan and Avery act as one another's mirrors, making sure all their clothing looks settled before heading to the kitchen. If Avery's parents notice anything is off, they don't say a word. Plus, Avery's mother is busy with dinner and Avery's father is busy with the weather. Since it is now dark out, the television is his window.

"There you are," Avery's mother says when Ryan and Avery walk into the room, as if she hadn't known where they were all along. "I think we need to have a talk. First off, I realized I didn't ask you if you have any allergies or food restrictions, Ryan."

"I'm good with whatever," Ryan replies. There are about a hundred foods he hates, but he figures this isn't what she's asking. His position here is untested enough that he'll eat anything she makes.

"Great. We're having chicken, potatoes, and broccoli—I figured that wouldn't be very controversial. The bigger issue is the snow. They're saying the highways are a complete mess, and the storm's not going to slow down until midnight at the earliest. So it's looking like you're going to have to spend the night here. There's no way I'm letting you drive home in this. I'd like to talk to your mother, if that's okay. Explain what's going on. I can't imagine there's going to be school tomorrow."

Avery tries unsuccessfully to suppress a yip of joy, afraid that if the universe knows how pleased he is by this turn of events, it will send a sudden heat wave. Then he realizes this is silly, and allows his mom to take some satisfaction in the way he buzzes and beams.

Ryan's spirits can't bounce quite as high as Avery's. He is sure that Avery's mother is right, and that there is no feasible, safe way for him to get home. He even knows his parents will concede that. But there will still be the matter of why he came here in the first place, why he hadn't turned back at the first glimmer of trouble. There won't be hell to pay so much as he'll get a bigger weekly allowance of hell.

"I can just call her," he tells Avery's mom. "Explain the situation."

"Trust me," comes the reply, "I'm a mother. She's going to want to talk to me."

Sure enough, after Ryan calls and tells his mother what's up, and that what was supposed to be a date (he doesn't use the word *date*) has turned into a sleepover (he goes nowhere near the word *sleepover*), she immediately asks to talk to Avery's mother. As if the blizzard is some moon landing he's shooting on a sound stage.

Ryan has no idea what, if anything, Avery has told his mom about Ryan's parents, but Avery's mom ups the cheer factor in her voice by at least three whorls when she says, "Hi there!" at the start of their conversation. Then there is a serious "Yes" and an empathetic "Oh, believe me, I understand." After that—Ryan has no idea, because Avery's mom walks out of the kitchen, and stays out of the kitchen for another five minutes.

"Clearly, they're arranging our marriage," Avery comments in the interim.

"If I weren't so terrified, I'd find that funny," Ryan replies.

Avery's father comes into the kitchen, plucks a grape from the refrigerator, and pops it into his mouth.

"Smells good," he says.

"We'll be sure to pass that on to Mom," Avery vows.

Avery's father looks around. "Oh. Where is she?"

"Talking to Ryan's mom. He's staying tonight."

"Good deal," Avery's father says. Then he turns to Ryan. "You don't mind sleeping in the backyard, do you? We've got a great sleeping bag somewhere in the basement. I think it's *insulated*."

"Dad. Not cool."

"I wasn't aiming for cool. I was aiming for *frigid*."

Avery's mother returns to the kitchen. Avery thinks she looks a little less carefree than before. Ryan thinks she looks like she's just talked to his mother.

"Well—that's all sorted out. Apparently, Ryan, your father wanted to drive over here to pick you up—but I convinced your mother that would be a bad idea. I don't think they understood how far away we live. But no matter—they're now on board. I promised to take care of you, so please, no knife juggling or tying each other up." (She does not mean this as a sexual reference. Ryan and Avery totally hear it as a sexual reference.)

"And," she continues, "I also promised that you'll stay in the guest room. Which in this house means the couch. The good news is that it opens up."

Avery knows better than to challenge this decision, but is already strategizing ways around it. The idea of sharing sleep with Ryan is undeniably appealing.

Ryan wonders if he should call his parents back, apologize. What would make it better?

Nothing, his instincts inform him. *Just be happy you're not there. Be happy you're here.*

Avery touches him on the back and he startles. He can't appreciate Avery's affection as much with Avery's parents watching. It feels . . . wrong. Not bad—just something that has to be worked up to.

Sensing this, Avery puts his hand down. His mom, meanwhile, curses loudly and makes a lunge for the oven, sighing with relief when no smoke billows out as she opens it.

"Dinner," she says, "will soon be served."

* * *

During dinner, Ryan observes the way that family short-hand can be used not for accusation but for humor. There are things they are saying that are perfectly understandable on their own—*Where's the avocado?*—but don't make much sense for an outsider within the context of the conversation.

During dinner, Avery observes how shy Ryan becomes, how reactive. Avery is keenly aware of how ridiculous his family is, and he makes sure to fill Ryan in whenever what they are saying makes no sense. ("There was this deeply unfortunate period when I was eight when I wanted avocado on everything. Since avocados are not cheap, and are not something you just pick up at 7-Eleven, this was a royal pain for Mom and Dad. They'd give me a steak and I'd say, 'Where's the avocado?' Or spaghetti. Or, I don't know, a hot dog.")

During dinner, Avery's mother also observes how shy Ryan becomes, although she has much less to compare it to.

During dinner, Avery's father tries to wrap his mind around the fact that Avery has brought a boyfriend home for them to meet. It feels like a big step, but since Avery isn't acting like it's a big step, his father tries to keep his pride to himself.

Outside, it continues to snow.

When dinner is over, Ryan stands to clear the table. Everyone else tells him he doesn't have to, that he's the guest. But he refuses their refusal, unable to explain to them that he feels he has to contribute in some way. Avery and his parents back down, working Ryan into their routine of clearing and scraping and rinsing and drying. There are some hiccups (a spoon down the sink, a prolonged search for the Saran Wrap's tongue), but for the most part, Ryan works in well. And in this way, he stops feeling like such a guest. In this way, he starts to feel like he belongs in this kitchen, with these people. They talk to each other instead of watching TV as they do the dishes. He answers questions when he is asked, but doesn't have any questions he feels comfortable asking in return.

This changes when it goes back to being him and Avery, back to them alone. Avery's mother and father beat their retreat—even though it isn't even eight o'clock, they say they're going to turn in. Probably watch a movie. Go to sleep early. Avery's father jokes that he'll be waking them up at dawn to help dig out the driveway. Ryan is ready to say that's alright with him—it only seems fair to reciprocate the hospitality—but Avery, sensing this voluntary spirit, says, loudly, "No, I don't think that's going to happen."

Ryan would never talk to his father like that.

Avery's father laughs.

"Alright, alright," Avery's mother says, shooing him out of the room. Then she turns to Avery and says, "I've put out towels for Ryan in the bathroom and sheets for the sofa in the family room—I mean, *guest room*." Then she gets more thoughtful, and looks at them both in turn. "I'm right to trust you two, correct? Keep it PG. Maybe PG-13. You're just getting to know each other and—"

"We know!" Avery is mortified. "PG-13!"

(For his part, Ryan wants to sink through the floor.)

"Okay," Avery's mother says. "We have an understanding." She looks squarely at Ryan, who somehow manages to meet her eye. "Here's the thing—I promised your mother that you would sleep in the guest room. So you have to sleep in the guest room." Then she turns to Avery. "I did not, however, make any promises about where *you* would sleep. Because I trust you both to . . . take it slow."

"Mom! We get it!"

Avery's mother smiles. "Good. And if you go outside, for heaven's sake, wear boots."

They do not go outside at first. Instead they go to the family room, as if that's what is expected of them. They sit on the couch and watch the Weather Channel on mute, face to face with the satellites' rendering of the storm. Avery picks up the remote control and is about to ask Ryan what he wants to watch . . . but Ryan is already watching something: a photograph of Avery and his family at Disneyland, the summer before third grade. Avery is wearing Mickey Mouse ears and his expression is, frankly, goofy. He has no idea who took the photo, who allowed their molecular family to retain its formation—Avery the middle smile, bookended by his parents'.

"It's so corny," he says now. "I begged them to take it down, but they like to taunt me."

22

"I like it," Ryan says quietly. "It looks like you had fun."

We learn each other by listening, and in this moment, Avery remembers that Ryan's time at Disneyland wasn't nearly as fun. He learns that the things that might be embarrassing to Avery might not be embarrassing to Ryan. He learns that while he doesn't have to be careful with Ryan, he does have to try to avoid being careless.

"It was fun," he admits. "I kept correcting people—they wanted me to be Minnie and I was like, no, do you see any bow on this head? I'm *Mickey*."

Ryan reaches for his hand. Holds it.

"But you're so much *cuter* than Mickey."

Avery laughs. "Oh, thanks!"

The photograph no longer has their attention. Now it's their hands, their fingers. The epicenter of their calm, the point of most connection.

Each in his own way experiences a small shock of surprise within the comfort of their pleasure. When you have to fight for your identity and win your identity, there is always a part of you that thinks there has to be a trade-off, that by stepping away from the norm you have been sentenced, you risk stepping away from happiness as well. You feel you will have to fight harder for someone to love you. You feel you will have to bear the risk of more loneliness in order to be who you need to be.

And yet.

Much more often than not, with that small shock of surprise, the fight will come loose, and the risk will fall aside like a broken cocoon, and you will find yourself completely unalone, not only seen by someone else, but felt. This was part of what you were trying to get to, and now it is here.

Avery closes his eyes and leans into Ryan. Ryan closes his eyes and leans into Avery. For a few minutes, they let that be their lives. From the parents' bedroom, there is the indistinct sound of some TV show. Outside, there are the fairy footsteps of snow. Avery can feel Ryan breathing. Ryan's eyes are closed, but in his mind, he is seeing them on the couch, is imagining what it looks like with Avery's head on his shoulder.

Then: a squeeze on Ryan's hand. Avery sitting up. Ryan opens his eyes, turns to him, and sees him smiling.

"Outside," Avery says. "We need to go outside."

There is no way Avery's old boots will fit Ryan, so Ryan borrows Avery's father's. (Avery swears it's okay.) They bundle one another as best they can—Avery wrapping the scarf around Ryan so fervently that his neck is temporarily mummified; Ryan insisting on zipping Avery up, on putting the hat on his head. Just so his hands can linger on Avery's cheeks. Just so it can lead to a kiss.

All the paths—even the driveway—have disappeared with the hours. When Avery and Ryan step outside, it is into a crystalline silence, a white darkness. The snow still falls, but almost as an afterthought, a gentle patter.

Avery takes Ryan's mitten in his own mitten and leads him into the yard. Ryan thinks for a moment of the neighbor across the street, of any neighbor . . . but then he chooses to put those thoughts aside. He focuses on the way his boots sink into the surface with every step. He focuses on the frosty filaments that land on his cheek. He focuses on mittens, and Avery, and the depth of the quiet around them. This is a world without cars, a world without any alarms set for the next morning.

Avery lets go. He can't help himself—the snow is just too perfect to be ignored. Ryan doesn't understand until too late what he's doing. By the time Avery has formed the snowball, Ryan is only just reaching for his own scoop of ammunition. Avery takes aim. Fires.

Bull's-eye.

Ryan retaliates, but Avery dodges, then fires again and hits. Ryan assembles a snow boulder and moves closer to pounce. Avery tries to wrangle away, but is only half successful. More salvos are lobbed. More footsteps cover the yard.

Finally, Ryan can't take it any longer, and tackles Avery to the ground. Their coats are so thick, it's almost like a pillow fight, only with the boys acting as the pillows. It's a soft landing, a soft tackle. Avery tries to wriggle out of Ryan's grip, and then he stops trying. He lies there in the snow and Ryan lies there next to him, and then they are kissing again, snowflake eyelashes and cold-flush cheeks.

Ryan rolls onto his back and they both face the sky, watching the snowflakes fall. Like stargazing, only the stars come when they are called. Ryan's head is next to Avery's head, his hip next to Avery's hip. Avery puts his legs together, in the shape of one leg. And Ryan, knowing what Avery is doing, does the same. His left mitten finds Avery's right mitten and they hold. Then, on the count of three, they extend their other arms, lift their way to wings. A single snow angel, larger than either of them could be on their own.

"This is not what I thought I'd be doing right now," Ryan says. On a regular night, he probably would have been driving back at this hour.

"I know," Avery whispers.

Ryan can feel the damp cold seeping into his jeans. He can tell his nose is unpleased and ready to run. The crack between the back of his hat and the back of his coat is allowing an unkind chill to set in at the back of his neck, despite the scarf. But still, he has no desire to move.

Avery blinks away the snow that gathers around his eyes. He listens hard and can't hear anything but snow language (faint), tree language (fainter), and the tiny rustle of Ryan's jacket against his.

"We are the only people in the world," he says.

"We are," Ryan agrees.

They move their legs. They pull in their wings. They turn in to each other. And as they do, they lightly alter the surface of the ground, the shape of the world. They don't realize this, not in these terms. But they feel it nonetheless.

Strands of pink hair peek out from underneath Avery's hat. Damp pieces of blue hair cling to the side of Ryan's face, curving around his right eye. Ryan wants to kiss Avery again, but his nose is now too runny. Avery is happy to listen to the quiet, to look at this boy in front of him.

They hold there.

Snow absorbs into their jeans. Snow gathers on their coats and their hats. Ryan wipes his nose with his mitten, then wipes his mitten off in the snow.

"If I'm not mistaken," Avery says, "I think this is how people die of hypothermia."

He sounds exactly like his mother. He does not notice this. Ryan does, in a good way.

"Time to return to the real world," Ryan says.

"No," Avery corrects. "This is the real world, too."

Is it? Ryan asks himself, not entirely free from doubt.

"It is," he answers aloud.

Avery stands up, then extends a mitten to help Ryan up. Ryan doesn't really need the boost, but takes it anyway.

He also uses it as a decoy to take Avery's attention away from the snowball he's formed in his other hand.

Coming in from the snow: At no other time does home seem so much like hearth. Avery and Ryan don't appreciate how wet and bedraggled they are until the door is closed and they are shucking off their coats and slicking off their boots. Their shirts are fine—maybe a little sweaty—but their jeans and socks are soaked through.

"Let's get those pants off you," Avery purrs, and they

both laugh, because neither of them aspires to turn this particular moment into porn.

It's not that Avery isn't curious. It's not that he hasn't scrutinized every bare moment of skin that Ryan has ever shown.

It's not that Ryan isn't tempted. He is so far away from his parents, so far away from any restriction. But he is also wearing an embarrassingly shoddy pair of briefs. And it is so quiet that he feels if he undid his fly, the sound of the zipper would ricochet throughout the house and cause Avery's parents to come running.

"I'll be right back," Avery says. He runs to the small laundry room off the garage, and is relieved to find the dryer has been run, not yet emptied. He pulls out a pair of his father's sweatpants and a dry pair of his own jeans. Quickly, he changes into this new pair of jeans, then empties out the dryer and puts the old pair inside, along with his socks. Then, barefoot, he returns to Ryan, offering the sweatpants and pointing him in the direction of the bathroom, where his dry towel awaits. Now it's Ryan's turn to say, "I'll be right back," before he tiptoes off to change.

They aren't separated for longer than five minutes, but each of them feels the separation, feels the other one in another part of the house, waiting. In the bathroom, after bunching up the ankles of the sweats so they won't drag on the floor, Ryan looks at his watch and is amazed to see it's ten-thirty. But he can't figure out if he's amazed that it's so early or already so late. They seem to be the same thing in the snowbound night.

When Ryan returns to the family room, he finds Avery has transformed the sofa into a bed, and is besheeting it. For a second he stands in the doorway and watches as Avery throws his body over the bed to tamp down the fourth corner of the fitted sheet. Without a word, Ryan puts his wet clothes on the floor and goes over to help.

"Here," he says.

Avery unfolds the top sheet and throws half of it over to Ryan. The truth is, he never, ever makes his bed if he can get away with not making it—but since this is where Ryan will be sleeping, he feels he should make it right. So there they are, smoothing the surface, making parallel movements to tuck it in, make it even.

Next, the blanket. The same teamwork of two.

Pillows are put in place, and the job is done. Avery looks across the bed at Ryan and wants to crawl right over, pull Ryan down, mess up everything they've just made.

But Ryan doesn't catch the signal. He feels bad about his wet clothes sitting on the carpet. So he moves and picks them up again, asks Avery where they should go.

"I got it," Avery tells him.

"No, no, it's fine—just tell me where they go."

"In the dryer. Here."

Avery walks Ryan to the laundry room and opens the dryer for him, as if he's its doorman. Ryan bows his thanks and throws his jeans and socks on top of Avery's. With the press of a few buttons, they begin to tumble.

"So what now?" Avery asks, hoping the answer will be a return to the bed they've created.

"I want to see more of your room," Ryan replies. His way of saying *I want to know your room*, which is another way of saying *I want to know you*.

"Okay." If there is any disappointment in Avery's voice, Ryan doesn't hear it.

Once they're in the room, Avery expects Ryan to sit down, stay awhile. But instead he remains standing, surveying.

"What's the most embarrassing thing that you're proud of here?" Ryan asks. As soon as he says it, he doesn't think he's made any sense. But Avery knows what he means.

"Over here," he says. He walks over to his bookshelf, where a pink plush unicorn is guarding the collected works of Beverly Cleary. "This is Gloria. And she was, without question, my best friend for a very long time. We were never apart for long. She used to be much brighter, but she's mellowed. I guess we both have. My parents did not know what to make of my deep affection for her. They thought I could aim higher in the best friend department. There was no way for them to understand that I'd made her into the part of me that I needed to hear . . . even if it was in unicorn form. But, hey, my parents had to unlearn a lot of things. Which is just another way of saying they had to learn a lot of things. We all did. We all still do. You do. I do. We're all really new at this."

Ryan walks over to Avery, stands right in front of him.

"I'm definitely new at this," he says. He isn't talking about what Avery is talking about. Instead he is saying that all those things can be unlearned and learned, but the really hard part, the really awkward and scary and wonderful part, is being in a room with someone you like and trying to find the right things to say, the right things to do with your body, the clearest signal to send to say that this means a lot, that this really means a lot.

Avery raises the unicorn so its horn touches Ryan's nose. Ryan laughs.

"She approves," Avery assures him.

We find someone to love, and in finding that person, we find our own capability to love them.

Most of the time—no, all of the time—we have no idea what we are capable of.

Two boys kissing in a room.

One boy pausing to tell the story of the time he brought a unicorn to school.

The other boy talking about his own brush with unicorns, this one on a folder he had to keep hidden under his bed. When his parents found it, he told them it belonged to a girl from school, that she had used it to give him her part of a joint assignment. Which was true, but not the reason he'd kept it long after the assignment was done.

Both boys talking about unicorns and parents and erasers shaped like stars. Both boys debating whether there was really anything guilty about guilty pleasures. Both boys taking pleasure in deciding there was not.

Everyone here has forgotten about laundry, about bedtime, about snow.

Midnight is just another minute, when you're not looking at the clock.

It is Avery who yawns first, and the moment he starts, something is set off in Ryan, and he yawns, too.

They are leaning against Avery's bed when this happens, but they know this is not the bed where they will end up. They promised. Plus, the bed in the family room is bigger.

Avery's mother has put out a new toothbrush for Ryan, from her dentist-visit stash. This means Ryan and Avery can stand side by side at the bathroom sink, brushing and spitting together. This is a first for both of them, and they share the intimacy of it, the significance of such a quotidian joy. It's no big deal, and that's why it's a big deal.

They do not talk about the sleeping arrangement; they simply go to the bed and arrange themselves for sleep. Ryan wasn't sure this would happen; Avery wasn't sure Ryan would want it. Their uncertainty shows, but so does their want, their almost existential want. They lie beside each other, but it isn't like it was in the snow. There are layers between them, but the layers are thin. They lean in and kiss, and the longer they kiss, the more feverish it becomes. Kissing with their lips, yes, but also kissing with their hands, their skin, their whispers and their heat. Ryan reaches around Avery, pulls his body close, and Avery reaches around Ryan's back and pulls his body close, too, and together they feel like they are fusing, feel like they are both two and one. No clothes need to be shed. No lines have to be crossed. This is everything, this closeness. This sensation of one another. This sense that touch can generate such feeling.

Then the slowdown. The lighter touches. The lying there and breathing. Wondering how the heartbeat can spread through so much of the body. Feeling the heat subside, but not entirely.

The drifting of voices and the approach of sleep. Avery watching Ryan fight it, blinking out and blinking back, and then coming unmoored again. Avery wishes him a goodnight. Ryan smiles, cuddles in. Wishes him a goodnight back. Then falls—the gentlest kind of fall.

Avery cannot slip into sleep as easily. Avery needs to think about this as it's happening. Avery needs to understand it in order to enjoy it. So he watches Ryan through the blue-black darkness, watches as his chest rises and subsides, extraordinary machine. *How did this happen?* Avery asks himself. *How is this possible?* Because this is a room he knows well. His parents are asleep down the hall, allowing this. The snow keeps falling outside, the sole reason Ryan is still here. All of it. This. You watch this person you are just getting to know, this person you want to tie possible futures onto, and suddenly the world is no longer a conspiracy of forces against you. There are good conspiracies, too; there are forces that will help you, that want you to find this remarkable form of personal peace, this four-letter universe of a word.

In Avery's head, this all translates into *I really like you* and *I want this to work* and *I don't believe this* and *I want to believe this* and *This is real. This is real. This is real.*

There is no way to fall asleep to such thoughts. You have to wait for them to slow. You have to wait for them to cool.

While you do, you watch the person across from you. And somehow, you watch yourself, too, and gasp at how everything seems to fit.

There is no way of knowing this, and no way of proving this, and there will certainly be no way to remember this, but the moment Avery falls asleep, the snowfall stops.

Just before dawn, Ryan hears tanks scraping through the streets. His first instinct is to think the alien invasion has begun . . . but then he hears the sound some more and realizes it isn't tanks, it's a snowplow.

Go away, he thinks. *Stop doing that.*

Later, Ryan is the first to wake for real. Disoriented by the house, by the room, by the bed—but then grounded by the pink hair just a few inches from his eyes, the soft truth of the sleeping body at his side. And not just at his side—sometime in the night, Avery's arm reached for Ryan's arm and stayed there, once again overlapping.

The room is lit only by the sunshine filtering in from outside. Ryan stands up and walks to the window, bends back the shade and looks at the blanketed landscape. Icicles, some the length of swords, dangle from the edge of the roof.

"Is it still snowing?" Avery asks from behind him.

"No," Ryan answers, turning. Watching as Avery slowly sits up, impulsively stretches—those early-morning infant movements, when we see if everything is still working, and if we remember how it all works. Even though Avery's hair is a pink nest and his eyes are scrunched up and his cheek bears the imprint of a pillowcase's seam, in this light, this pale morning filter, Ryan feels such a remarkable attraction toward him—desire, yes, but also a profound fondness, a deep cherishing.

"Let's build a snow dragon," Avery mumbles, eyes closing.

Ryan doesn't think he's heard this right. "What?" he asks—gently, just in case Avery is going back to sleep.

"A snow dragon," Avery repeats more emphatically, eyes

still closed. "Surely they have snow dragons where you come from?"

"Nope," Ryan confesses.

"Well then." Avery opens his eyes, sits up. "I guess I'll have to show you."

They don't bother changing out of their sleep clothes. Instead they go back to the dryer and Ryan pulls his jeans on over the sweats. Socks return to feet. Boots return to socks. Mittens return to hands.

It is so bright outside, and no longer quiet—the morning is scored by the sound of dripping, the sound of shovels being used a few houses over. If he looks closely, Avery can see shallow commemorations of last night's footprints. Even the snow angel remains as a shadow of its former self—still there, but partly lifted.

The boys gather up some snow, but never scoop so deep that the grass will begin to show, spoiling the illusion of white. What starts as a mound slowly becomes a shape. What seems at first a shape evolves into a body. And from this body, a neck is grown, a head. Wings on the ground. A tail. A bystander might not be able to decipher it. But when Avery's mother looks out the window, she turns to her husband and says, "Oh, look, they're building a snow dragon!"

We all know that nothing built with snow will last.

But we all remember what it's like to have snow in your hands, to make something soft less soft so you can build with it. We all remember the sensation of being outside, of making a shape, of building.

So some part of it must last.

Later, Ryan will find the texts from his father, telling him the roads are fine now, so he should come home. And after Ryan replies by turning off his phone, Avery's mother will receive a call from his mother, saying just about the same thing. Later, Ryan, Avery, and Avery's parents will take turns with their two shovels, digging out Ryan's truck, making a path for him to leave. But not before lunch. Not before a last round of kissing in Avery's bedroom. Not before photographs are taken with their creation.

As they build the snow dragon, they talk, but not about the snow dragon. Avery doesn't tell Ryan what shapes to make; Ryan doesn't make suggestions on the scale pattern they trace with their bare fingers into the dragon's skin. It doesn't matter that Avery has done this before. It doesn't matter than Ryan hasn't. The end result is nothing like what it would have been if Avery had built it alone, or if Ryan had. You will never be able to entirely tell who did what. Whatever results is unique to the two of them.

It is, they will say later, the first thing they built together. It is the first of many things that will be entirely theirs.

Grounded

(the sixth date)

Ryan is grounded. When he gets home after his snowbound overnight with Avery, he receives a nearly unprecedented tongue-lashing from his parents, the end result being that he is not to leave the house for anything but school or his job for an unspecified time—or, rather, the specified time of *until you learn your lesson.* As soon as he gets home each day, he has to deposit his car keys on the kitchen counter. One of his parents also calls the house fifteen minutes after his school day or work shift ends, to make sure he is there.

This pisses Ryan off for a number of reasons. He is unsure what lesson he is supposed to be learning—to be sure to drive in hazardous, snow-blind conditions? To never put his mother in a situation like the one where she had to justify her irrationality to Avery's mother over the phone? Or maybe he is supposed to learn that there is no place for a boy in his life until he escapes to college.

Then there is the matter of the car keys. His parents did

not contribute a single cent to the purchase of his pickup truck. He has always been fine with this, because it means the truck is entirely his. His parents have no claim to the keys. But they are claiming them anyway, landlording it over him.

His parents are aware of how far away Avery lives; they know it's not a quick trip for him to sneak over there after school. Still, Ryan's father can't help but mention the cameras they now have on the front door and the garage, which can be monitored on both parents' phones. The house has become his parents' accomplice.

If there's any loophole, it is that he still has his phone. Maybe his parents know such a confiscation would be the straw that causes the camel to attack. Maybe they understand that he'll comply with his confinement as long as they leave a window open. Or maybe his father has secretly turned Ryan's phone into a tracking device; Ryan wouldn't put it past him.

Avery's first reaction to the grounding is much worse than Ryan's, for the simple reason that Ryan needed to react in front of his parents, while Avery merely has to react over the phone to Ryan.

"It's not fair," Avery keeps saying. "It's just not fair."

Ryan admires the way Avery holds the concept of fairness in such high esteem, as if it's nature's default instead of its grail. How has Ryan found a pink-haired boy with faith in the universe doing the right thing?

Ryan finds himself reassuring Avery, "It'll be fine. I promise. We'll figure something out."

"Okay," Avery says. "I just wish . . ."

"What?"

"I just wish it was still yesterday. I wish you were still here."

"Me too."

Ryan knows he can't lose hold of this fact: It was worth it. Even if he's grounded. Even if he and Avery have to be apart a little longer than expected. It was worth it, to spend a night in his arms. It will be worth it, to reach another night where that can happen again.

Being grounded would be a pleasure if it also meant he got to stay home from school. But that isn't how it works. The day after he gets home, the day after he's grounded, the roads are plowed, the furnaces are reignited, and school is open again.

He texted his best friend, Alicia, to tell her what happened. She is waiting at his locker first thing in the morning with a sympathetic look and a chocolate croissant she picked up at the Kindling Bakery, the only spot in town worth a stop on the way to school.

Ryan is glad that Alicia has met Avery. It makes her sympathy feel more genuine.

"You look even worse than usual," she observes. This is the way they say good morning.

"You look like you've been stuck here all your life," he replies, taking the croissant gratefully and breaking off a piece.

Alicia sighs. "You at least got to enjoy your snow day. I babysat."

"Where was your dad?"

"Out shoveling bullshit."

Now it's Ryan's turn to let out a sympathetic *damn.*

Alicia shrugs it off, doesn't want to talk about it anymore.

"Tell me more about your time with your boyfriend."

Ryan tells her about sleeping over at Avery's house, about how nice his parents were. He can tell she's happy for him, and then sad for him when he gets to the part about being grounded. He registers all this, but the whole time, he also feels he's answering a question under false pretenses. Because didn't Alicia just ask about his boyfriend? Is Avery really his boyfriend?

This is uncharted territory for Ryan; he knew it existed on other people's maps, but this is the first time he's wandered out of the confines of his ordinary plot to discover it waiting.

The whole day, it's all he can think about. Can you be boyfriends if you haven't had the conversation about being boyfriends? Is it too soon to even think about using that word? Is there a certain number of dates you have to ace before you can raise the question? Five dates is too soon, right?

But . . . what about how it feels? Because when he's with Avery, when he's there beside him, it feels like boyfriends.

Or at least it does to him. How does Avery feel?

It's not like Ryan can text and ask.

Hey, just wondering . . . are we boyfriends?

Was just talking to Alicia and she called you my boyfriend. Cool to agree?

41

When you talk about me, what word do you use? Maybe one that starts with b, *ends with* d?

He can't do it. And so he gets stuck in a rut carved by wondering back and forth.

The only time he peers out of that rut is sixth period, when he has Mr. Castor's American history class. This isn't because history is his favorite—Ryan doesn't really have a favorite subject, since they're all pretty much tied for last place. But Mr. Castor is the only teacher he cares about, the only teacher who's bothered to connect with him on a human level. A lot of other history teachers focus on dates and places, but Mr. Castor likes to talk a lot about things like how the word *depression* has three meanings—economic, emotional, and physical. He says they all go hand in hand, and a lot of the time, Ryan knows he's caught in all three at once. He's stuck here because he's dependent on his parents to support him. This makes him sad a lot of the time, being surrounded by people who mostly don't understand him. And physically it feels like there is a dent in the earth, that his life now is something he'll have to climb out of if he wants to get somewhere else, somewhere better.

He's never said any of this to Mr. Castor. But when they talk, Ryan has the strange feeling that it's an unspoken thing they share. Mr. Castor always treats him like he'll leave someday, like he'll get out of here. When Ryan dyed his hair blue, a few of his teachers were disdainful (the word *dramatic* was used a lot) and others pretended to ignore it. But Mr. Castor approved. The day after Ryan did it, when he walked into class, Mr. Castor went out of his way to say how good it looked. Ryan was embarrassed that other kids might have heard this compliment, but he was also pleased to receive it.

Now Mr. Castor switches to talking about the WPA, and while Ryan isn't exactly taking notes, he *is* paying attention. He knows it isn't the point of what is being said, but he has this daydream about being hired with Avery to make a mural together, just the two of them, in some quiet town neither of them has ever been to before. In his mind, the mural is in a big church that has been converted into a queer youth center—it's a daydream, so why not? He isn't much of an artist, but he starts to sketch out a little of what it could look like. At one point, Mr. Castor walks past, sees what he's doing, and smiles. Any other teacher, Ryan is sure, would yell at him, tell him to put his daydreams away.

Ryan wants to tell Avery about all of this. He wonders again if this makes them boyfriends, the fact that Avery is now the person he wants to tell all his stories to, as soon as they earn their words.

When school finally ends, Alicia tries to convince him that it won't be breaking the rules if she comes over to keep him company, but Ryan is pretty sure that such companionship won't go over well with his parents, since it will interfere with the intended isolation and misery.

This is reinforced when he gets home and receives the check-in call.

"You're home?" his father asks—a remarkable question, considering Ryan has just answered the landline.

A thousand sarcastic answers fill Ryan's mind, but somehow a simple "Yes, I'm home" makes it through.

"Good. You are not to leave the house again, nor are you allowed to have anyone over. Is that understood?"

"Yes."

"Your mother should be home at the usual time. She will expect the house to be clean."

"Understood."

"Excuse me?"

Perhaps some sarcasm has crept into his voice. He erases it when he replies, "I said I understand."

"Good."

His father hangs up, and Ryan goes to his room to call Avery.

They have all this technology to bring them closer, especially video calling. There is a certain intimacy in being able to see one another as they talk, but there is also a disconnect within the connection. Ryan can view Avery on the screen, can hear his voice and his laughter, but the whole time, he can't shake the knowledge that he is sitting alone in an empty bedroom.

They talk more about the unfairness of the situation, although Avery points out that because he has play practice most days after school, they wouldn't have been likely to see each other until the weekend anyway. Avery is in a classroom near the auditorium, hiding away as the director blocks a scene he isn't in. Ryan is on his bed, the phone propped up against a pillow so he won't have to hold it the whole time. For a half hour, they share the details of their days.

"I wish you were here," Ryan says, both because he means it and because (*admit it*) he hopes Avery will say it back.

"And I wish you were here," Avery replies. "Or that we were both somewhere else. The same somewhere else."

Ryan wants to ask if that makes them boyfriends. But he feels silly asking. It's too much like he's setting a trap.

Avery looks at something off-screen, then takes a breath. "Okay," he says on the exhale, "I gotta go. Call you later?"

"Yes, please," Ryan says.

"Try to stay out of trouble."

"It'll be easy to do, if you're not here."

The call ends. Ryan knows he should start his homework.

Instead he closes his eyes and takes a nap. The world is just too much.

His mother's voice wakes him.

"What are you doing?"

His parents are clearly testing him with these questions.

"I guess I fell asleep?"

"Being grounded doesn't mean you get to sleep all you want, Ryan."

"I'm sorry. I didn't mean to."

His mother actually tsks her tongue. Then she spots the phone on his bed.

"I'll take that," she dictates, holding her hand out. "You can get it back tomorrow morning before school."

"Come on," Ryan says before he can stop himself.

"Now."

He powers off the phone before he hands it over. The last thing he wants is for his parents to see any texts that come in.

His mother says, "Do some homework before dinner."

"Okay."

Ryan gets up and opens his laptop. Satisfied, his mother leaves the room.

The first thing he does is message Avery to tell him not to bother calling.

The next week is awful.

There is only a small window when Ryan and Avery can actually talk—when Avery is free from play practice, before Ryan's mom gets home. These check-ins are something, but they aren't enough. All Ryan and Avery can do is catch up on the things they're creating without each other. They can't create anything new together.

Ryan is grateful when he has to work at the grocery store, because there he can talk to people, even if they aren't Avery.

The weekend is the worst. Ryan's parents don't give his phone back on Saturday morning, and they hide his keys. He goes to watch TV, but his father turns it off, saying there isn't going to be any TV, not while he's grounded. The same thing happens when he tries to watch something on You-Tube; they don't take away his laptop, but they say he has to keep his bedroom door open at all times, so they can make sure he is doing "valid work." But the thing is, he only has so much homework to do. He's finished by Saturday afternoon. Ordinarily, his father would make him do yard work, but the snow is still on the ground, and the garage is too cold for them to spend the time needed to straighten it up. So Ryan has nothing to do. If he tries to nap, his parents wake him. They tell him to read a book.

Being with Avery is starting to feel like something his mind invented as a coping mechanism. How can memory do anything besides approximate what it felt like to have his neck kissed, to feel Avery's warmth beside him, to feel the same warmth from a smile? And how could he fully trust an approximation to be true?

Then the nightmare thoughts make their visits. Avery is so great—wouldn't it make sense for other boys to be interested in him, too? Other boys who aren't grounded, who aren't stuck like Ryan is. Maybe someone at play practice. Another actor, or a cute boy on the crew. It wouldn't even be disloyal for Avery to go for it, would it? It's not like he and Ryan are boyfriends. It isn't like they've said they're going to stop seeing other people.

On Sunday morning it snows again, and what was once magical is now muted, melancholy. No one warned him that the intensity of sharing could lead to the desolation of its absence. The uncharted territory is starting to disappear from the map.

By Sunday night, Ryan is getting desperate. While his parents are safely watching football in the den, he risks sending messages on his laptop. He unleashes his full despair on Alicia while trying to keep it managed for Avery. Avery is constantly asking him if he knows when it will be over, and Ryan wishes he had the right answer to give.

I hate this, Avery types.

Don't give up on me, Ryan types back.

When Avery replies, *I won't,* Ryan tries to believe it.

Alicia wants to turn the tables, to go all *Home Alone* on Ryan's parents so they can see what it's like to be held captive in their house. Ryan thinks this is an inadvisable course of action. Running away also doesn't feel sustainable—since Alicia's father is no better than Ryan's parents, it's not like she can take Ryan in.

He wishes he could ask Avery to visit him at work, but he knows he'll get yelled at if he tries to take more than a ten-minute break. ("That toilet paper won't stack itself!")

He thinks about saying he needs to go over to a classmate's house to do a group project—but then his parents will want to see the project.

Late into Sunday night, he keeps himself awake, trying to think of another way.

Right before he falls asleep, he wonders if maybe he's found one. When he wakes up, it's still there. It's a long shot, but as he grows more and more certain that whatever he has with Avery is in peril, he figures any shot is worth taking.

Mr. Castor looks surprised to see Ryan waiting at his office door so early on Monday morning.

He looks even more surprised when Ryan asks, "Do you think you could give me a fake detention?"

Ryan has never been in a teacher's office like this. He has never asked for a favor from a teacher or anyone else at school.

Mr. Castor ushers him into the office and closes the door. He puts his coffee down on his desk, clears some papers off a chair, and motions for Ryan to sit.

Awkwardly, Ryan does so. The hallway was empty, but already he feels like everyone saw him come in here to ask for help.

Mr. Castor doesn't answer right away. He doesn't even ask what "fake detention" means. Instead he asks, "What's going on, Ryan?"

Ryan is sure Mr. Castor has to know that he's gay; all his teachers seem to know. But Ryan has always stubbornly refused to say it to any of them, to invite them into that part of himself.

Now, though, Ryan finds himself telling Mr. Castor about Avery, about how Avery drove all the way to Kindling to go to a dance that very few kids from Kindling attended.

He tells Mr. Castor about the snow day, about how amazing it was . . . and then he tells him about coming home after, what a comedown that was, followed by his parents' uncompromising and apparently unending punishment.

"So you thought . . ."

"I thought that if you emailed them and said I had detention, then Avery could come here and I could see him and save everything from falling apart."

It sounds so foolish when he says it out loud. Far too much to ask. If Mr. Castor isn't going to laugh at him, somehow the walls of the school will.

After taking a sip of his coffee and thinking about it for a second, Mr. Castor says, "Do you realize there's a flaw in your plan?"

"I'm sorry," Ryan says. "I never should have asked you—"

"No," Mr. Castor interrupts. "It's not that. It's that if I were your parents and I got a notice saying that you had earned a detention, I would *increase* your punishment, not ignore it. You might get your afternoon with Avery, but it might be months before you get another chance."

It's so obvious. If Mr. Castor wasn't sitting right there, Ryan would punch himself in the face. For real.

Mr. Castor goes on. "Detention is not the answer, Ryan. Forensics, however, might be."

Ryan doesn't follow. "Forensics?"

"Speech and debate tournaments."

Ryan still doesn't get it. "I don't do that," he says.

Mr. Castor leads him gently. "I think it might be time for you to start. We meet on Thursdays after school. You might even have to go to a tournament this Thursday."

"But I don't—oh. *Oh.*"

Mr. Castor smiles and lifts his coffee cup in a toast.

"Welcome to the team, Ryan."

Thursday is the one day Avery doesn't have to be at play practice and Ryan doesn't have to be at work. There is no way Mr. Castor could have known this. It just happens to be the case.

Ryan's parents do not fully subscribe to his sudden interest in performative oration. But the email that Mr. Castor sent them appears to be legitimate, requesting Ryan's presence in a match over an hour away. Ryan explains that a bad flu has knocked a number of the ordinary members out of contention, causing Mr. Castor to pull deep from the bench.

"But you don't like speaking," Ryan's mother says, confounded.

"He does, however, like to argue," Ryan's father counters, satisfied with his own observation.

Permission is granted.

* * *

Ryan messages Avery later that night to tell him the news.

Mercifully, Avery is still free on Thursday.

They make plans to meet somewhere halfway between their towns. Their sixth date.

Ryan believes Avery is genuinely excited to meet again. But still, the electronic distance is there, the experience of words without voice, smiles without face. Ryan finds himself having to visualize the trail: *My thoughts turn into words; the words go from my mind to my fingertips; my fingers touch the keys and the letters appear on the screen and split off into waves; the waves travel through my room to the wi-fi; they are converted into a different kind of wave that pulses through a network of wires that runs from my room to his; when the words get to his room, they leap from the wires, back into the air; his computer catches them and relays them to his eyes; his eyes take them in, and send them to his brain, where they go back from words into thoughts.* In this way, he can imagine them still connected. In this way, the speed of words can overcome the pain of distance.

Three days. He only has to hang on for three more days.

He wants to see his Aunt Caitlyn, who's met Avery and liked Avery and will understand Ryan's desire to be with Avery. She is the one person in his life who will be able to explain that the closer you get to a person, the more you leave behind with them when you have to be apart; the feeling of reunion that comes when you are back together is not only a reunion with the person you love, but also a reunion with the part of yourself you left behind. If the love is worth its weight, then the part you've missed is one of your better, kinder, happier parts. Which is why you feel better, kinder, and happier when you're together again.

Maybe this is why Ryan's parents have told him he can't go see her. They know Aunt Caitlyn will be sympathetic—in their mind, too sympathetic. He is allowed to call her exactly once, on Tuesday evening, because on Wednesday nights he often goes over to her house to watch a show they both like featuring drag queens and crime fighting. This Wednesday, she'll have to record it for them to watch whenever his sentence is over.

"I'm so sorry," Aunt Caitlin says when he calls to cancel.

"It's okay," Ryan tells her. There isn't much else he can say; he's on the kitchen phone, and his parents are sitting right there.

"You holding up?"

"Yup."

Aunt Caitlin sighs. "I swear, if this lasts much longer, I'll spring you myself."

Ryan wants nothing more than that.

His mother coughs, motions that it's time to hang up. This isn't supposed to be a social call.

"I gotta go," he tells his aunt.

"The water is wide, but your boat will come," she assures him. "And I have a feeling it will hold another passenger."

Ryan smiles, but not so much that his parents will see it. He hides most of it with the receiver as he says his goodbye.

Wednesday night doesn't feel like a night at all—it feels like a *night before*. He wants to get some sleep, but every time he comes close, excitement sings in his ear or anxiety peels open his eyes. He shifts positions, but fear is there to make his back ache, and when he shifts again, the intensity of his longing steals the covers away. When he pulls them back, the risk of it all makes him overheat.

I'm not wrong to want this, he keeps repeating to himself.

His heartbeat isn't sure it agrees.

At breakfast the next morning, his parents ask about his truck.

"I assume you'll be taking a bus to the tournament," his father says. "So you'll just leave your truck in the high school parking lot."

"Mmm hm," Ryan answers, cereal in his mouth.

But why is his father asking? To test him about how a forensic team travels? Or are his parents going to drive by the high school parking lot while he's away?

He's been planning to take his truck to meet Avery. Now he feels he can't. Just in case.

Once again, he is waiting for Mr. Castor when he arrives at his office before the morning bell.

"Is there a bus?" Ryan asks his teacher. "If there is, I think I need to come."

Mr. Castor looks amused. "Is this your way of officially joining the team?"

"I guess it is," Ryan says. "As long as I can sneak away."

Neither Ryan nor Avery has ever been to Bluff Lake, where the tournament is being held. It's actually closer to Avery than Kindling, but still more than halfway.

I did some research, Avery texts Ryan over lunch. *There's a donut shop.*

Before he boards the bus, Ryan lets Alicia know what he's doing.

"You realize I could have just driven you, right?" she points out.

But Ryan doesn't want her to have to be his waiting chauffeur. He knows she'd be willing. But he also wants this relationship with Avery to be something that doesn't depend on everyone else. He wants to do at least part of it himself.

He tries to explain this to Alicia. She, in turn, tries to understand.

* * *

Ryan has no idea if he knows anyone on the forensics team. It's not something he's ever paid any attention to.

They're taking a bus like all the other buses in front of the school; Ryan would have been confused if Mr. Castor hadn't been standing by the correct bus's door.

"Remember," Mr. Castor says when he walks over, "if anyone asks, you're coming for a trial run, to see how it works before starting next week."

Ryan nods. "Got it."

"And then you start next week."

Ryan nods again and gets on the bus.

There aren't that many kids inside, and most of the faces are familiar. These are the honors track kids, and a lot of them are what Alicia would call "not bad." (As in: "Callie's a bitch, but Rebecca's not bad.") With a slight heart pound, he sees that Kim Davis is on the bus; her mom is friendly with his mom, and it is entirely possible that this bus ride could come up in their conversation at some point. Base, covered.

Ryan sees that Ben Samuels has taken a seat a little farther back than the rest of the team, but still a few rows from the actual end of the bus. Ryan takes the seat across from him.

Ben looks up from his phone for a second and asks, "Are you on the right bus?" It isn't sarcastic. He genuinely thinks Ryan has walked onto the wrong bus.

Ryan repeats the explanation that Mr. Castor provided him.

"Oh. Okay," Ben Samuels says. Then he goes back to his phone, and Ryan is invisible again.

It doesn't even occur to Ryan to wish there were someone

on the bus he could turn to and say, *Hey, I'm here because I'm heading on a sixth date with this boy who may or may not be my boyfriend.* These are his classmates, but they know him about as well as a random group of people on a bus would. And they are even less curious than strangers on a bus.

When they get to the school where the tournament is being held, Mr. Castor receives a sheet that informs them which forensic categories are in which room. He tells the other students where to go, and tells Ryan in front of everyone else to stay with him to watch the extemporaneous competition. Their team disperses, and when they are out of view, Mr. Castor asks Ryan to come with him for one round. Then he can have an hour outside, returning with plenty of time before the bus heads back.

Ryan has no idea what extemporaneous speaking is, and even after he and Mr. Castor watch the first two contestants, he isn't that much more clued in. Basically, it looks like the judges spring a topic on you and you have about a minute to figure out what to say about it. The boy and girl at the front of the room seem into it, but it comes across to Ryan as the worst pop quiz ever.

After sitting through the girl ranting about the Electoral College and the boy talking about the merits of democratic socialism, Ryan is starting to feel like he's being punished. Mr. Castor looks at him, releases a snort of laughter, and says, "Okay, you can go. Just remember—one hour. And make sure your phone is on, because I'll call you if anything changes."

Ryan doesn't have to be told twice. He jumps out of his seat, out of the room, out of the school. He checks his messages—nothing from Avery. He assumes this means Avery is still driving.

He summons his maps app and makes his way to the donut shop.

Driving into Bluff Lake, he could see it was just like anywhere else, with big-box stores perched among stripped-out strip malls, lonely gas stations, and overbright fast-food establishments. The downtown area also looks a lot like anywhere else, with a few shops and far fewer people. The two clothing stores display the kind of sweaters and pants your great-aunt would give you for Christmas and you'd never wear. The shoe store is very proud that it has some Crocs in stock. The pizza place is called Giuseppe's, but it's unclear whether there is really a Giuseppe or if someone just thought that's what a pizza place should be called. There isn't a Starbucks in sight, though there was one on the highway, drive-through.

In this context, the donut place is an exclamation point. The glass cases can't contain all the frosting and sprinkles— versions of them dance across the brightly colored walls as well. The music coming from the speakers is also super sweet, and the tables are much more excitably busy than anywhere else Ryan has seen in town. He imagines the availability of coffee has something to do with this, because while a few customers have donuts in front of them, almost all of them have coffee at hand.

Ryan can see some people look at him when he comes in—he can't tell whether it's because he's a stranger or because he has blue hair. (It's both.) The idea of sitting at the table without coffee or a donut, waiting for Avery, feels weird, so he buys a large coffee and holds out on the donut, to justify taking up the space before getting to the good part with Avery.

Once he sits down, he checks his phone again. Still no word. The traitorous chamber of his proverbial heart is already pumping out the panic that Avery isn't coming, that Ryan is going to be stood up. It gets so bad that Ryan ventures a *You near?* text. The phone tells him it's received—but that's all it tells him.

The uncharted territory is starting to dim in the low light of his thoughts. He is staying still, but the horizon is receding.

He is so focused on his phone, on waiting for those three dots of response, that he doesn't even see Avery until Avery is at the table.

"This seat taken?" Avery asks. Ryan looks up and there he is, with his pink hair and mischievous grin.

What is it like to see Avery again? It's like life has suddenly elevated to a higher level, and the present is a much better place than it was a second ago.

Ryan is smiling now, too, but it isn't enough. He gets out of his seat and knows he has to walk the delicate path between *not enough* and *too much*. As is often the case with that path, the answer is to put his arms around Avery, to pull him close, to linger in each other's arms a beat or two longer than friends would, to send the message that even though they aren't going to kiss in front of all these strangers, this hug is a kiss in its way.

"I've missed you," they both say at the same time, pulling apart so Avery can take off his coat and put it on the back of his chair.

Then Avery says, "Donuts."

And Ryan agrees, "Donuts."

Some of the options at the counter sound divine and others feel unholy. Avery says he doesn't see anything wrong with putting bacon on a donut; Ryan, who is fine with bacon in most other instances, says he's going to stick to raspberry, and maybe one topped with Fruity Pebbles.

They order two donuts each, and instead of coffee, Avery gets a glass of milk. Then they weave through the tables and sit back down at their own.

If life elevates to a higher level when your maybe-boyfriend steps into the room, there is also the dip that comes shortly after, when life threatens to drop back down to the mundane world you've been elevated from. Ryan looks at Avery across the table and doesn't think there is anything he can say that will be worthy of these first minutes back together. He can't just ask about the drive. He can't bring up that they only have an hour. He can't say how much he missed Avery, because he's already said that. He can't blurt out the contents of his heart, because they haven't sorted themselves into a sharable display. So in the middle of his happiness, there is a strong pinch of despair.

Avery shifts his chair forward so their knees are touching. He presses, and Ryan presses back.

That is all it takes to dispel the despair.

Contact.

"Thank you for coming all this way," Ryan says.

"Thank you for joining forensics in order to be with me," Avery replies. "Plus, you drove longer for our last date. And have since been imprisoned for it."

Ryan makes a show of looking out the window. "I want another storm to come," he says, moving his hand across the table so their pinkies can flirt. "I want us to be stranded here."

"We could live for weeks on donuts alone," Avery says. "I'm on board. Bring on the snow."

This is the vocabulary of the sixth date, all these different ways of saying *I like you, you know?*

Ryan tries to make his donuts last, but it's like each bite has a subliminal message planted within it, insisting *You must take another bite right now this moment.* Both donuts are gone within two minutes.

Avery has been slowing himself down with milk, but can only last about a minute longer.

This isn't the time to talk about play practice or parents or how their school days have gone. No, not when they only have an hour together—forty-two minutes, actually, since it's timed from when Ryan had left Mr. Castor, not from when Avery arrived. Yet another unfairness, c/o the universe.

"Do you want to walk around?" Avery asks.

Ryan says sure.

Since neither of them has been to Bluff Lake before, they have no idea where to go. Ryan resists the urge to give a running commentary of how he's feeling, which would sound something like *I am so glad you're here I really hope you are too I hope we can keep doing this do you?*

Also, he wants to kiss Avery again. Because that always feels the most real.

Avery gestures to a dollar store named Dollar Store.

"Want to buy some dollars?" he asks.

"How much do they cost?" Ryan asks back.

I like you, you know?

It doesn't take long for the stores to give way to offices—law offices, tax offices, dentists.

"There," Avery says, tilting his head to indicate a parking lot behind one of the tax offices. There aren't any cars.

"Here?" Ryan asks.

Avery takes his hand. Pulls him around a corner so they're out of view of the street. Smiles again, and keeps holding Ryan's hand as he leans in for a kiss.

It doesn't feel like last time, which hadn't felt like the time before that. It's still early enough that each kiss contains the revival of all the earlier kisses . . . and then brings its own twist, its own reason for being. Kissing is always a confirmation, and there are times when this confirmation is needed more than others. Right now Ryan needs it badly. Confirmation of intention, of desire. Of feelings shared, of dreams being true.

"Oh, Ryan," Avery says when they stop for breath. It is all there in the way he says Ryan's name—confirmation of the confirmation.

"Oh, *Avery*," Ryan says back, drawing the name out so he can fit as much affection as possible within it.

They kiss and hold and move their hands under one another's coats. For a few minutes, they fall out of the timekeeper's domain, only to be brought back when Ryan's phone vibrates against both of their thighs.

Avery pulls away, though not without another kiss. Ryan sees he has a message from Mr. Castor, telling him to start heading back. Ryan shows it to Avery, and Avery says, "I'll come with you. I'll just pretend I'm from one of the other schools."

"You don't have to do that," Ryan tells him.

Avery smiles. "I figure if I come see your imaginary forensics match, then you'll have to come see my actual school play at least once—maybe twice."

A plan.

A future plan.

This is what it takes for Ryan to finally see it clearly: Avery's *I like you, you know?*

Now he feels comfortable making his own visible, without anything else written on top of it.

"I wouldn't miss your play for anything," he says. Then,

even though the door hasn't been opened perfectly, he decides it's opened enough to add, "And, if possible, I'd really love to be the boyfriend waiting for you with flowers after the show."

Ryan has never waited with flowers for anything or anyone. At first he has no idea where this idea has come from. Then he realizes it must have come from Avery, from what Avery has introduced into his thoughts.

Avery pulls him close again, gives him another kiss. "I guess that means I'm about to be the boyfriend cheering from the sidelines at a forensics competition. Except that you're not competing. And I don't think cheering is allowed."

Ryan laughs. "Yeah, I don't think so."

When the laugh is over, he sees that Avery is looking at him—*really* looking at him, that intense concentration that comes when you're reading a book, only directed at another person.

"What?" Ryan asks.

The book is still open, still being read, as Avery asks, "We're going to do this, aren't we?"

There is no *how* in this question. No *what*, no *why*, no *where*, no *when*. This is what lies underneath all of those. The foundation from which all the other questions will be built.

Ryan takes Avery's hand again, squeezes it. "Yes," he says quietly. "I think we're going to do this."

Avery, who is always such lightness. Avery, who brings

the music into the room. Avery, who Ryan thinks is so much better at this than he is—this same Avery balances precariously on the verge of tears.

"I'm sorry," he says, wiping at his eyes. "I'm really sorry. It's just that—we were joking about it, about flowers and debate and everything. But I need you to know this is not a joke to me. Not at all. It's a really big deal, and I need to know it means a lot to you, too, because I haven't done this before, not like this, and I think I need you to know that. You need to know that I have been thinking about it constantly, ever since you left my house, and it scares me to want something so much. I don't think you have any idea how much I think about you, Ryan. I don't think you have any idea how afraid I am, because I've been trying so hard to avoid showing it to you. But here it is, right in front of you, and I guess what I'm saying is that if we're really going to be boyfriends, you need to know that I'm scared, and you also need to know I'm scared because I like you so much. You might not want a boyfriend like that. And if that's the case, I'll be sad and disappointed, but I'll understand. I just think it's fair to tell you all this. I have to. You have to see how bad I am at this, right?"

If before Avery looked like he was lost in reading Ryan, Ryan now looks like someone who has come to the part of the book he wasn't expecting, and instead of being lost in it, he looks around the room at people who aren't there, to say, *Can you believe this is happening?*

He wants to laugh, it's so ridiculous.

"I'm even worse than you are!" he swears to Avery. "I promise! Everything you just said? Well, triple it. Quadruple it. That's me. I have no idea what I'm doing, but at the same time I know I'm doing the right thing, being with you. Does that make sense? I hope it makes sense. Because you—you are the most sense I've felt in a long, long time. Maybe ever. I have no idea what it's like to be a boyfriend. I have no idea what it's like to have a boyfriend. But what I do know is that I want to learn what both of those things are like with you."

Avery shakes his head, then says, "Get over here." They kiss again, hold tight.

"What a pair we are," Avery says into Ryan's ear.

"I guess we deserve each other," Ryan tells Avery's neck.

Avery nestles in and kisses his cheek. "I guess we do."

The phone vibrates again. Ryan texts Mr. Castor to say he's on his way. Then he takes Avery's hand, and they step out of the space they've made their own.

"Which way is the school?" Avery asks.

"That way, I think."

"You think?" Avery moves for his phone. "Here, I'll look it up."

But Ryan stops him. "No," he says. "We'll find it."

And so they set out, still holding hands.

* * *

The moment arrives. You aren't simply walking through un-charted territory anymore. No, you realize it's more than that.

You've started to build a home here.

And you're not building it on your own.

Opening Night at the Drive-In

(the fourth date)

Queerness is, among other things, driving two hours to see a movie just because it features characters whose lives may loosely resemble yours.

For Ryan, the drive is actually closer to three hours. He's picking up Avery for their fourth date, and then they're heading to the closest college town, since college towns tend to be the county seats of queerness in America's less-than-queer regions. The cab of his pickup has become a nest of blankets, since it's not going to be an ordinary shared-popcorn, shared-armrest kind of movie night. No, tonight will be a drive-in affair, the one-night-only kickoff of a local film festival. A few weeks ago, Ryan might have come across the listing and stored it where all his other lost opportunities are kept. Sure, there are a few friends he could've dragged, had he been willing to owe them one, but he wouldn't have felt comfortable asking. It wouldn't have been like it was when he asked Avery: an enthusiastic response to a hopeful invitation, a knowledge that they are excited about the movie for similar, queer reasons. Having someone eager to see the movie with him is just as remarkable to Ryan as having the movie within driving distance tonight.

A fourth date might be early for love, but it's right on time for gratitude.

How lucky and how dangerous, to be thankful to someone before he even gets into the truck.

Avery spends too much time deciding what to wear. Not just because he wants to look good for Ryan, but also because he's going to be a sixteen-year-old in a space populated by queer college kids. He feels like he'll be auditioning for the role of his future self.

It's a beginner's mistake, to think queerness has a dress code. Queerness is coding-optional. Avery hasn't figured this out yet, but he's close.

Because it's sure to be a cold night at the drive-in, Avery layers up. It relieves some pressure on his T-shirt (Tegan and Sara, predictable yet personal) to know there will be a striped sweater over it.

Ryan texts that he's five minutes away. Avery takes one last look in the mirror and heads downstairs. His parents have made it clear they want to meet Ryan, but Avery hasn't relayed this to Ryan yet. Instead he's bought some time by telling his parents Ryan will come inside on the way home. There isn't any way to do it now, if they want to make it to the movie on time.

Avery's parents give him some popcorn money before he leaves and don't say anything besides *have a good time.* They know he'll be embarrassed if they wish him luck. They are happy he's going with a boy to a drive-in, and in this way, they are old-fashioned and new-fashioned at the same time, the two combining to become something that might be called *good-fashioned.*

Meaning: They've let their son fashion himself while keeping a safety net beneath him. They are doing the best they can.

Ryan and Avery both smile when Avery slides into the passenger seat, because at this point, physical presence is the most reliable evidence for everything that's been playing out in their heads. It hasn't been long since they last saw each other, rowing on the river. But in the intervening days, both boys have doubted that things could really be going this well. Avery is the dream that Ryan is having, just as Ryan is the dream that Avery is having. Now that they are together, they get to share the dream. And what is more astonishing than a shared dream?

Two hours in a truck is a long time for two boys who haven't yet found the comfort of a togethering silence. Avery is a better master of solo silence, so his barometer doesn't measure a lack of conversation as acutely as Ryan's. Fortuitously, their destination lends itself easily as a topic of conversation. The movie they are seeing, *You and Me,* is the first nonbinary love story to reach movie screens in their part of the country. (The title comes from the idea that in a relationship, the only binary should be you/me . . . and even that becomes a bit of a blur.) Ryan and Avery have been poring over interviews with the young writer-director, whose unabashed desire to make the love story that they most wanted to see in the world is itself a love story, as far as Ryan and Avery are concerned—a love story between the writer-director and the audience they want to reach, a love story between the writer-director and their younger self, who felt the absence of a movie like *You and Me,* and a love story between the forces of creativity and necessity. The writer-director has created something bigger than themself that still manages to represent themself, which is something that Avery and Ryan both aspire to, even if they have no idea how to get there right now.

They talk about this, and talk about the times they've seen themselves on the screen, knowing that the tragedies are important, but not the entirety of how they want themselves to be mapped onto the world. They'd rather step into *Moonlight,* into *Booksmart,* into the wish fulfillment of *Love, Simon.* There aren't enough stories like theirs. Which, on the one hand, makes their lives and their love feel more original. But it would still be nice to see how other people deal with the things they have to deal with and navigate the feelings they find themselves feeling.

That's what they're hoping for tonight.

Especially Avery. Because Hollywood's still put many

more jelly beans in Ryan's (cis, white) jar than in his. He knows there are plenty of filmmakers out there like him. But he's also keenly aware of how little power they've been granted to tell their stories.

"I want the trans superheroes," Avery requests with a sigh.

"I want the gay spies," Ryan says. "There have to be gay secret agents. I mean, duh."

"And animation!"

"Yeah—we get a male frog that, like, bats its eyelashes at another male frog for a nanosecond, and they call that progress."

It isn't fair, especially because it pretends to be fair. Ryan and Avery feel that so deeply, it's part of who they are.

They start talking about other movies—mostly what they feel are queer-adjacent movies, like anime or musicals. (Avery adds another item to his wish list: "I want a queer *Hamilton*." Ryan knows better than to admit the full depth to which he's never gotten into *Hamilton*. But he does wonder aloud if a queer *Hamilton* would win him over. And/or a gender-bent version. Let Janelle Monáe play Hamilton and Lizzo play Burr. That, he'd watch in a second.)

For two hours it goes like this. They share what they love and what they want that isn't there, and in doing so, they bring themselves a few steps closer to understanding each other, which is just another way of saying they bring themselves a few steps closer to falling in love. They don't have to agree on everything, but they find themselves agreeing enough that it matters, in ways both unexpected and delighting. (Ten minutes spent recounting a *SpongeBob SquarePants* episode; five minutes disclosing their *Avatar: The Last Airbender* elements; fifteen minutes singing along to Ariana, including her cover of Whitney Houston's "I Have Nothing," which contains notes neither boy can attain, but they reach for them anyway and crack up when they miss.)

It's only when they hit the outskirts of the college town that the focus must turn to the far more mundane task of direction. They are led down the all-American alley that loops all major and minor cities—BurgerKingExxonStarbucks SubwayWalmart in excelsis—until they see the punctuation of a marquee, rainbow-lit even though it's a far cry from June. There's a long line of cars waiting to make it inside, so Ryan and Avery content themselves by watching the Morse code of brake lights spelling out a welcome until it's their turn.

The ticket-taker looks like she was born in the booth, and plans to die there in the very near future. She doesn't cheer at the sight of a blue-haired boy and a pink-haired boy sharing a pickup, nor does she scowl. The only thing she considers is their cash, and the only change she requires comes in coins.

Avery has never been to a drive-in before. Ryan has, but never as a driver. He follows the car in front of him and hopes whoever's inside is making good choices. The theater itself is a parking lot organized with poles at the front of each space, the screen looming above like a gracious overlord. They end up about seven rows from the front, and Ryan reverses into the spot so the back of the pickup faces forward. The air has reduced itself to dusk, and the people spilling out of the cars react to it like neon. As soon as Ryan turns off the ignition, he and Avery hear a concord of laughter and happy anticipation, the merrymakers merrymaking as snacks are shared and viewing positions are staked out.

As Avery fumbles for his phone and wallet, Ryan steps around the pickup and opens the door for him. He offers Avery a hand down, even though Avery doesn't really need it, and then, in a movement that feels as essentially human as putting one foot in front of the other, they hold hands as they make their way to get popcorn. The handholding is not just because it's a safe space—if you are defining a space by its safety level, there is still a certain amount of fear involved in the measurement. This opening night at the drive-in is a joyous space, a holiday from the world. For the first time in their lives, Ryan and Avery are using a queer default in an adult crowd. That alone is joyous, and more than a little surreal. If there are any straight people around, they're doing their best to blend in, and as a result Ryan and Avery feel a collective kinship toward everyone they see, a feeling of having something in common that isn't very common at all.

Which isn't to say that Ryan and Avery are seeing the same people in the exact same way. Ryan is still playing the guessing game in his head, reaching for the words to spell out each person's identity. Avery, meanwhile, is trying to dismantle that part of his mind, to see everyone with the termlessness he feels each of them deserves, at least until they themselves ask to be seen a particular way.

From the glances Ryan and Avery are getting, Avery understands that people aren't looking at them and thinking *queer* or *gay* or *trans;* no, they're looking at the two boys holding hands and thinking *young.* Even though the bystanders are mostly college students, Ryan and Avery represent what they once had, or never did. Most of the glances are accompanied by smiles; only occasionally do people turn away.

Avery notices how he and Ryan are among the only solo couples around. Most of the other queerfolk are here in groups, setting up lawn chairs behind their cars as if it's a cookout or a family reunion. Avery has had a couple of queer friends over the years, but never in the same constellation. It's reassuring to him to know that such a sky is only a two-hour drive away from his home. He feels silly for thinking it, but it's almost like the spaces he's found online have come to life for the first time in a physical place. Which is also strangely reassuring.

Ryan looks out into the crowd with a little less confidence. It feels like every queer person from a hundred miles around is here, so he's started to wonder if he's going to run into Isaiah, the one boy on the face of the earth who he'd legitimately be able to call an ex. Of course, the primary reason they stopped seeing each other was because Isaiah said he felt pretty sure he was straight, but Ryan has monitored

Isaiah's social media for long enough afterward to know that Isaiah's actions don't always anchor to this particular conviction. When he and Ryan were seeing each other, Isaiah would never have been caught dead watching a movie like *You and Me,* not even in private. But that was a year ago, and Ryan can't help but wonder if the year has brought Isaiah closer to being the sort of person who would let himself be here.

Avery notices Ryan scoping the crowd and asks, "See anyone you know?"

Ryan slips his mind back to the boy he's brought and answers, "Nope. I saw one girl who I think might have gone to my school—she was a senior when I was a freshman and was the first person I ever saw with a pink-triangle nose ring. But I'm not even sure it's her."

They get in the popcorn line just as there's an announcement that the movie will begin in ten minutes. The trio in front of them is arguing over whether popcorn at movie theaters is the most site-specific food in American culture.

"What about hot dogs at ballparks?" one friend challenges.

"Not even close. Hot dogs are eaten in plenty of other places. But I would guess that over ninety percent of the popcorn eaten in America is eaten at movie theaters, or in front of movies at home. No other foodstuff comes close."

Ryan smirks at Avery. *No other foodstuff comes close.* If Avery is excited about plunging into collegiate queerdom, Ryan is more skeptical; to him, college appears to be as full of poses as high school. They're just different poses. Or maybe the same poses with a wider vocabulary. Ryan can't tell. He's also pretty sure that being skeptical of poses is a pose in itself, so it's not as if he's setting himself apart. Skepticism is just how his nervousness manifests itself.

They get to the front of the line without having discussed what they want. After they caucus, Ryan orders a large bucket of bottered popcorn and two not-even-close-to-calorically-compensating Diet Cokes.

As the concession stand worker (their age, forlorn) scoops the popcorn from its glass cage, Avery asks Ryan, "Did you say *bottered* popcorn?"

Ryan smiles. "Yeah. That's what my dad calls it. Because it's not, y'know, butter. *Battered* popcorn sounds abusive and/or deep-fried. *Bettered* popcorn just isn't true. And *bittered* popcorn isn't what the taste buds want to experience."

"So *bottered* it is."

"Yup. *Bottered* it is."

Avery gestures to the concession stand worker, who is cursing at the soda dispenser. "They don't look particularly bottered by your order."

"Wow. You went there."

There's a brief skirmish when Ryan takes his wallet out before Avery can do the same. The popcorn is handed over, and Avery exclaims, "Ooh . . . it's hot *and* bottered!"

Ryan groans.

"You started it," Avery points out.

"But how to end it?" Ryan ponders.

"With kisses," Avery says. "Always with kisses."

"Awwwww," a college kid with mascara to spare says from behind them.

Even though it's well into twilight, Ryan can see Avery's endearing self-consciousness. Were he not carrying a big bucket of popcorn, he'd take Avery's hand back in his and parade to the truck. *Let the world see us,* he feels, and feels it so strongly, so naturally, that he doesn't even realize he's never felt it before.

An announcement that the movie will begin in five minutes is greeted with a cheer. As Avery makes sure their popcorn and sodas don't fall to the ground, Ryan retrieves the blankets he's brought and fashions a cocoon in the back of the pickup. Avery hands over the concessions, then climbs in beside him. Their legs are covered, swaddled. Ryan raises his arm so Avery can lean in.

This is new. Closeness. Warmth. The blurring of bodily borders. It's never a perfect fit. There are always limbs that might go numb. Hair in the mouth. An unsureness of where to put one's breath. Sweat that comes with the warmth. Especially in places that don't usually sweat, like fingers. But the discomfort, the condensation, the awkwardness of appendages—these are all slight compared to the greater laws of togetherness. While Ryan and Avery are conscious of their smaller, graceless movements, they are conscious of them without truly feeling them. What they feel instead is the communion that occurs when the orbiting ends and they find themselves as the center, the convergence of not just their bodies, but their lives.

It is not that everyone else at the drive-in disappears; they simply become less important. It is not that the night isn't a little too cold and the back of the truck isn't four pillows short of being plush; it's simply that the accommodations are beside the point.

While the Diet Cokes will each remain in their respective corners of the flatbed, the bucket of popcorn is pulled into the cocoon, spanning both boys' laps. The welcome reel announces itself onto the screen, a parade of happy hot dogs shaking their buns, spritely sodas twirling their straws, and cavalries of ice cream cups thrusting plastic spoons aloft like proper majorettes. It's the same opening that Ryan's and Avery's parents or even their grandparents might have seen on their own drive-in dates, so uncool it's become cool again.

Someone three cars over accidentally leans against a horn, and in response four other cars honk along. Avery laughs, while Ryan is glad he wasn't the person who leaned on the horn in the first place.

The movie begins, and there is another cheer, followed in a matter of seconds by complete silence. All that can be heard is the dialogue and the score, traveling across the air from the speakers hooked to the parking poles.

When I found you, I wasn't even sure I was me, the voice-over begins as one of the main characters runs into a hospital, asking for help for their frail grandmother. The young nurse is kind and professional, and about the same age as the grandchild. Once the grandmother is taken care of, the nurse and the grandchild keep talking.

I was afraid that how you saw me would never compare to how I saw you.

The grandmother is fine. She hadn't eaten, felt faint. Before the grandchild leaves the hospital, they ask the nurse if the conversation the two of them have started can continue. That's how the grandchild says it, that they want the conversation to continue. The nurse appreciates the way this is said, and the conversation continues. The next day, the two of them meet for coffee. The nurse is still in their uniform. The grandchild, who wants to be a photographer but works at the admissions desk of an unpopular museum, has worn a tie, thinking it will make a good impression. It is awkward at first, but then the two of them realize it's only awkward because they want so much for something good to happen. They talk about this . . . and since they talk about it, something good happens.

There is a reason the word you *is longer than the word* me. *I will always feel that* you *contain more to know, more to learn.*

There are no gender origin stories. They do not draw the outlines of their histories and then erase these outlines in order to demonstrate the current shapes of their lives. They approach each other in the present tense.

Ryan looks over to Avery, who is paying rapt attention. While Ryan is still reveling in the warmth of their cocoon, Avery has ventured out of it to step into the story. Ryan does not know Avery well enough to understand what the story means to him as he watches, but he can tell the connections between Avery and this story are not threads but veins. He is careful not to interrupt. Some boys would jostle, would try to make it about themselves, since it's a fourth date and on a fourth date you always want to interrupt the programming with your own advertisements. But Ryan lets that go. Ryan lets Avery be somewhere else.

Parts of you begin to define me. Parts of me begin to define you. We do not ask for this. It is the direction we grow when we're together.

The nurse meets the photographer's family; the photographer's mother is welcoming, the father curt. The photographer meets the nurse's best friend, and enjoys her company greatly until it's discovered that she and the nurse were once a couple. The photographer starts to feel uncomfortable around the best friend. The nurse thinks the photographer is overreacting. The photographer thinks the nurse is uncaring. They spiral.

Once I have begun to define myself in terms of you, it hurts to discover that you are not as you've been defined for me. The great test is how we handle this adjustment.

The photographer's grandmother dies. Not from the earlier fainting spell. Something else. On the way home from the funeral, the nurse and the photographer take a detour into the woods. They need to walk in the dense shade. They want to talk about time. They need to be together with only the trees watching.

Ryan needs to pee. He thought he could wait, and he wasn't going to leave Avery in the middle of the funeral, but now that it's over he whispers, "I'll be right back." Avery nods, understands. When Ryan crawls out of the cocoon, Avery leaves space for his return.

Just as Ryan felt the intensity of the communal joy before, now he marvels at the communal silence. Everywhere he turns, he sees how the audience has fallen into the story, how they are reacting to it as if it were part of their own thoughts. It is the shared dream again, only this dream has been made visible.

Ryan is the only person entering the gender-free bathroom. He prefers that phrase or *all-gender* to the hideous phrase *gender-neutral*, which makes it sound like the genders are at war with each other, and this bathroom is the demilitarized zone.

The graffiti in his stall is not, alas, gender-free, or even gender-neutral, but Ryan appreciates that someone with a different-colored pen has trapped every slur or provocation within a speech bubble, and then has drawn a ridiculous cross-eyed pug to be the speaker. It contains the hate while still acknowledging it exists.

When Ryan emerges from the stall, he finds someone standing in front of one of the two sinks, staring at the mirror as if it's going to say something back. As Ryan gets closer, he realizes it's the worker from behind the counter, who so miserably passed him a bucket of popcorn a short time ago, now taking the kind of deep breath that's usually a side effect of tears. As Ryan nears to use the second sink, the worker's shoulders get tense.

Normally, Ryan wouldn't say anything. He might even

(heaven forbid) leave the bathroom without washing his hands. Not out of a lack of empathy, but out of the fear that anything he says will only make it worse for the person who is feeling the actual pain. It strikes Ryan that if Avery were here, he would most certainly ask what was wrong. Avery is clearly that kind of person—that *better* kind of person. So Ryan asks himself what words Avery would offer to a teenager crying at the sink beside him. When he gets the answer, he acts it out.

"Is there anything I can do to help?" he asks gently.

A shake of the head. "No. I'm sorry for being such a mess."

"These days, you should only apologize if you're *not* a mess."

The concession worker lets out a staccato *hmpf* at that. As Ryan begins to wash his hands, he's told, "It's just that my ex is here. With some of his friends, who never really liked me. I sorta knew they'd want to see this movie, so I should've been prepared. And they didn't even come in for popcorn or anything. But I saw them and it hurt me much more than I was expecting it to."

Ryan, who has no idea what this is like, nonetheless says, "God, I know what that's like. But you get through it, right?"

A look into the mirror. "Yeah, I get through it."

"If you give me his license plate number, I can go slash his tires." (This is not, Ryan acknowledges, what Avery would say.)

"Not necessary. But I appreciate the offer."

Ryan has finished washing his hands. He turns off the tap and looks around for something to dry them on.

A laugh. "We haven't had paper towels since Tuesday. Your best bet would be to grab some napkins on your way back to your car."

Now that Ryan has done what he needed to do, he realizes how close he is to the end of the conversation. The concession worker seems to be a little better than before . . . but who knows what will happen when Ryan leaves?

"Good luck, then" is all he can think to say.

This gets a smile. "Yeah, good luck to you, too."

Ryan stops off for napkins, because after the suggestion it seems even more wrong to dry his hands on his pants. Then, as he walks back to the truck, he looks at all the couples and friend groups again, lit by the world on the screen. They pay no attention to him, and because of this, he feels like a spirit walking among them. *Good luck,* he thinks to one couple curled together in a hatchback. *Good luck,* he thinks to four friends on a blanket. *Good luck,* he wishes a group of seven in a Toyota that should only fit five.

Then he is back to his own truck, to the other half of the couple he is forming. To wish Avery good luck feels selfish, because Ryan is hoping that Avery's good luck will naturally curve toward his own. But then, as he's sliding back under the blankets, he thinks it anyway. *Good luck.* Avery breaks from the movie for a second to welcome him back, to resume their warmth. Then the story on the screen takes over again.

I lost myself. But it was you I needed to find.

After a brief time apart, the photographer goes to see the nurse, to apologize for the confusion they've felt. The nurse does not like how the photographer jumped away as soon as fear hit. It is clear the photographer is afraid again. But they do not run. Instead, together, they name the confusion. They try to transform the unknown into the known.

Ryan is not surprised. Nothing he has read about the movie has led him to believe that this is a movie about a couple that doesn't end up together. But Avery . . . Avery is quietly crying, is holding Ryan's hand and squeezing it, as if he needs Ryan's grounding to get through this storm.

We reach the point when I cannot define me without you. When I'm asked who I am, no answer is complete without a mention of you.

The nurse and the photographer are in a nightclub, ecstatically dancing among their people. As they dance, the drive-in is bathed in pinks and purples and glitterball flashes. A few people jump up from their perches and begin to sway and jangle along. Ryan plays a few notes with his fingers onto Avery's arm.

Then the scene switches, and now the photographer and the nurse are walking down a near-empty street after their night in the club. It's not a pretty part of town. They are a burst of color in the shadows. The camera pulls back, watches them from a distance as they continue to dance and kiss in the middle of the street, where anyone out at three in the morning can see.

Ryan starts to tense. Avery grips his hand tighter. They think they know what's coming. Queerness, at this point in time, still means that you wait for tragedy to emerge from any dark corner, that you are sure that hate will inevitably be part of the narrative, that things have to get worse before they get better.

But the photographer and the nurse continue to dance down the street. The camera rushes to catch up with them, to be there for a kiss that lasts and lasts and lasts. A kiss that ends in a smile and the continuation of a song. The dark corners have been empty all along. The only story here is the story of their love and how it came to be.

Avery lets out a breath he didn't even know he was holding. Ryan hugs him tighter. They both laugh at what they'd been expecting. They recognize each other in this laughter, in the way their breathing has become steady again. This time the smile comes before the kiss. But the kiss is there, as easy to find as the breathing.

I am still learning about you. Which makes sense, since I am still learning about me.

The movie doesn't end with them dancing in the street. Instead it flashes forward ten years. The photographer and the nurse are asleep in bed, slightly entwined and slightly free. The camera holds on them for a full minute so you can really see them, so you can get a palpable sense of the comfort of their mornings together. Then they wake up. First the photographer, then the nurse. The photographer stretches, turns. The nurse's eyes open. They look at each other, and the way they do, you can tell how much they love each other, how well they love each other. They've made it. They've won.

Now it's Ryan who tears up. The tenderness of the moment catches him by surprise. It is an illustration of something he's never tried to picture. It is not something he can relate to, but it's something he wants to relate to so badly that it's breathtaking.

Avery sees this play across Ryan's face, a utopia made of people waking up to each other for a decade and still feeling whole. Avery feels it strongly, too. It's far too much to contemplate on a fourth date, far too presumptuous to attempt to frame what they've found in these terms. But to feel it's possible . . . that is a resonant chord, a view that's become a vista. Avery squeezes Ryan's hand again. This time to be the grounding. This time because it's a stirring rather than a storm.

As the credits roll, Avery is astounded by how unalone he feels. He has just kept the company of two characters who are older than him, but still somehow like him. He has kept the company of this boy by his side, who is just as moved by what he's seen in the reflection. And he has kept the company of the rest of the audience, some of whom are singing or sighing themselves back into their cars, while others linger as the names unfurl across the screen.

Like most people, Avery has always seen the credits as an afterthought, a coda. But now he sees this list as something else, as an accurate representation of how many people it takes to create a simple love story.

He thinks: Here's to all the people who've made the sets, sewn the costumes, provided the lighting and the popcorn and the words already written in his and Ryan's hearts. Here's to the separate crew who did all these things for the two girls a few feet away dancing over the end music, lit now by the headlights of departing cars.

"This was such a good idea," Ryan says, looking around, too. He's forgotten the idea was his.

Avery thanks him, because he's forgotten, too.

They move their cocoon back into the cab. Once the screen goes dark, they can appreciate the stars that have been watching all along from their seats in the sky. Most cars' windows are still rolled down, so Ryan and Avery can hear an hour's worth of songs playing all at once as a slow line trails to the exit. Hip-hop and pop and folk and jazz and country all sharing the queerness of the evening. When Ryan turns the ignition, he looks over at Avery, and Avery has a flash of the first time they saw each other, in an equally queer crowd, much messier and more nervous than this one. He wonders how he can have only met Ryan such a short time ago. He wonders how this can only be their fourth date.

But since it's a fourth date, he doesn't wonder this out loud.

It's later than they thought it would be. Which means they'll be home later than they said they'd be. Queerness means being worried that it will take only the slightest movement on your parents' part to pull the plug. Or maybe that's not exclusive to queerness. But queerness makes you believe it is, that your actions carry a unique set of repercussions.

They talk a little about the movie, but neither of them can fully articulate what it means to them yet. Nor are they ready to consider the balance of their own *you* and *me*. It still feels too theoretical, even though it's theory that's been applied from the very start.

Eventually the conversation ebbs into the rhythm of the highway. Ryan needs to pay attention to the road, and after a spell of particular concentration, he looks over and sees Avery has fallen asleep.

Ordinarily, this would worry Ryan. They don't have much time together, and now they're letting sand fall out of the hourglass. But instead of worrying, Ryan reassures himself. They have plenty of time. They're going to make plenty of time.

At this point, Ryan could watch Avery sleep for hours. Because maybe this is what turns threads into veins, knowing something so quiet could have such consequence for your heart.

Avery is apologetic when he wakes up, but Ryan tells him it's fine. They talk a little about the week ahead, and as they near Avery's house, the clock draws close to midnight. Avery doesn't tell Ryan about how his parents want to meet him, about how he promised to bring Ryan in after the movie. It's too late for that, and Avery doesn't want to switch this night into anything other than what it already is. Because he knows his parents will undoubtedly be up, he has Ryan pull over a few blocks before his own block, so they can kiss and enjoy themselves without having to worry if anyone's at a window.

Queerness is stolen moments and stolen victories. It is stolen time and stolen glances. It is the thrill of the theft, for sure, but also the knowledge deep in your heart that none of this stealing is wrong. It is, in fact, the most honest thing you can do.

When Ryan pulls up to Avery's house, they make plans for Ryan's return. He'll come back here, and this time he'll stay for the day.

It's only taken them four dates to learn: Parting is much easier when you've plotted the return.

There will be no end credits. Not tonight. Just a brief transition. The kind that can make a week pass in a few seconds, and seem like not much time at all.

Practice

(the seventh date)

Three weeks and three days after he was abruptly grounded, Ryan is just as abruptly ungrounded. No reason is given for this timing. Ryan suspects his parents have simply gotten tired of enforcing their own rules.

When he calls Avery to tell him the news, Avery is busy with play practice. But later, when they have time to talk, Avery says, "We need to celebrate."

They plan a date for Saturday night. This, they feel, is what boyfriends do when they've earned their freedom.

Avery doesn't understand how he's supposed to fit his life into the time he's being given to live it. Forgoing sleep would be the natural solution, but his eyelids think otherwise. Whoever scheduled the school play for the end of exam week is clearly a monster who feeds off the stress of youth. And what's worse, Avery wants to do well in the play *and* ace the exams. That takes more time.

Then there's Ryan. Patient, eager Ryan. Way-too-far-away Ryan. Avery is thrilled to have a boyfriend . . . but instinctively knows relationships are like plants: You need to water them in order for them to grow, especially at the start. And the hitch is that you can't water them with water. You have to water them with time.

Avery is not ecstatic about this metaphor. It's only a short leap from here to imagining your relationship as the plant in *Little Shop of Horrors,* insatiably demanding "FEED ME! FEEEEEEEED ME!" That's not what he and Ryan are about. It will never be what they're about. It's just a thought.

The awful thing is that the couple Avery is closest to, his friends Aurora and Dusty, totally have a *Little Shop of Horrors* relationship. It devours all their time and most of their attention. When Avery's with them, he's not a third wheel—he's a spare tire waiting in the trunk. Neither of them knows about Ryan, because finding out about Ryan would require them to talk about something other than themselves, and they've proven to be almost humorously incapable of that since ninth grade.

Avery's friends in the play are a little more attuned to what's going on, and not just because Avery's had to explain why he disappears with his phone every now and then. When you get to the seventh date, it starts to matter who you've told and who you haven't, because it's crossed the line from something that might happen to something that's actually happening. Especially now that they're using the b-word—part of having a boyfriend should be feeling able to tell people you have a boyfriend. That's not a reason to do it; Avery didn't say yes to Ryan in order to have bragging rights. It's just become a part of the story of his life, so he wants to be able to share it with the people who include him in their own stories.

The most curious member of the production is Pope, who is the kind of teenager who can be cast as a gossipy octogenarian society matron without any discernible change of personality required. On the first day of rehearsal, Avery received his share of *I'm trying to figure you out* glances from kids who didn't really know him; Pope was the only one to come up and say hello. Within five minutes, Avery knew Pope was a first-year, nonbinary, and went by their last name, in no small part (they said) because they were an only child and didn't have to worry about a sibling who'd want to do the same. Pope thought it was hysterical to have the last name they did. "Someone in my family had pretty twisted aspirations" was how they explained it. "Someday I'm going to get a gaudy ring just to make people kiss it."

Pope had been at the dance when Avery had first met Ryan, and even though Pope didn't have anything to do with the match, they still took some credit for it. "You wouldn't have been there if I hadn't gone, too," they insist now. "So therefore you wouldn't have met Ryan if it hadn't been for me." Avery doesn't want to put his relationship's origin story through this particular butterfly effect, but he can't resist the pride and investment Pope feels in seeing it all work out. There are times when Avery sneaks off to a classroom to talk to Ryan and he swears that Pope is guarding the door, to make sure the lovebirds have a chance to trill without anyone else hearing their song.

Pope pretends to be a cynic about love, but asks wide-eyed questions that betray their true belief in love as a perpetual engine of happiness. Talking to them, Avery sometimes wonders if he's the opposite, an open optimist who harbors a fierce cautionary voice, who meets love reluctantly rather than gratefully. Not that he's thinking of Ryan in terms of love right now. He's thinking in terms of like, in terms of boyfriend. Not the same thing.

It's not accurate to say Pope is more excited about Avery's Saturday-night date than Avery is, but Pope is certainly louder about it. As soon as rehearsal is over on Thursday, Pope besieges Avery with questions—*Where are you guys going? What are you going to wear? Do you think there will be more than kissing?* And, unrelated, *Can I get a ride home?*

Avery can never deny Pope a ride home. They live pretty close to each other, and Avery remembers all too well what it was like to be a ninth grader, exposed to high school opportunities without the transportation to match.

As it happens, Ryan calls as they're walking to the car. Avery answers and makes it quick, telling Ryan he'll call back when he's home. Pope and Avery are both in the car by the time goodbyes are exchanged.

Pope doesn't say a word until the car is out of the parking lot. Slumped in the passenger seat, they check out the contents of the glove compartment. Then, finding nothing interesting there, they close it and say to Avery, "I hope I didn't interrupt anything."

Avery gives Pope a quick sideways turn of the head. "Not at all. Ryan and I will talk later."

"But, like, if I weren't here, you'd probably be talking right now."

"I mean, probably. On speaker. Because I'm driving."

"Oh my God." Pope sits up straighter and actually palms their forehead. "I'm totally interrupting some sex talk!"

Avery laughs. "I think we'd be having how-was-your-day talk for the drive home."

"Ohhhh. So the sex talk comes *later*."

At first Avery thinks Pope is joking. Then Pope goes on.

"C'mon . . . you're in a long-distance relationship. There's got to be a lot of sex talk. You know, *oral* sex—but, like, oral in the talking-out-loud sense, ha ha. Sexting, but with voices. Like he says, 'Hey, what're you wearing,' and you tell him, and he says, 'Ooh, that's so hot,' and—"

"Pope," Avery interrupts, exasperated. "I know what you mean."

"And . . . ?"

"*And* . . . it's none of your business."

Pope pouts. "You're no fun. If I were having sex, I'd tell you."

"I promise you, I wouldn't ask."

"Fine. You've got to hear this song. Where's the cord so I can plug in my phone?"

Pope isn't introducing Avery to a cool new artist. Instead they just want to blast some classic Miley Cyrus.

Meanwhile, Avery is wondering if it's weird that he and Ryan never have sex talk.

It's not that Avery doesn't think about sex. He does. But the truth is that when he thinks about sex, it's often to think about why he isn't thinking more about sex, or thinking the same things about sex that he's been led to believe everyone else in the world is thinking. Every seven seconds. Every. Seven. Seconds. Is he the only person in the world who questions that statistic, who thinks he wouldn't actually be able to function if he thought about sex that often? He knows he could type a few words into his phone's browser and witness pretty much any sex act there is to see. When he first started understanding who he was, it helped reaffirm his inclinations, to see which sections of the menu he was choosing from. But after a while, it wasn't exciting—he started to feel his reaction was as formulaic as the scenes he was watching. He felt porn was turning him into a robot, that something that should have felt intrinsically human was starting to feel detached from any human interaction. So he stopped.

He and his first boyfriend, Lyle, had messed around, and that had been great. There were times he completely lost himself while they were making out, and it was so different to lose yourself to another person instead of to a picture on your phone. He loved the mutual lostness, the mutual foundness of being with someone else, how you can be a blur one moment and then the other person does something and draws you into this vividly tactile sense of where you are, what you're doing, how your bodies feel. It's like that when he kisses Ryan, and when they make their bodies close. To Avery, that's the best part, to share such intimate proximity. To say that sex is the only thing that matters disregards the words of the sentence and focuses only on the exclamation mark at its end.

All of this has remained unsaid with Ryan. Avery assumes this is because they're in agreement. He doesn't feel the pull toward sex from Ryan, not like it was with Lyle, who would get jumpy about it, whiny even. Ryan seems to enjoy the pleasure of the moment, instead of spending most of his energy planning the next step of the pleasure. Avery really likes this about him. But now he's starting to wonder whether this is just his own wishful interpretation. What if their unsaid feelings don't actually match up? What if Ryan isn't bringing up sex because he has no desire to have sex with Avery?

No. Avery knows at heart this isn't it. And he also knows he's falling into the exclamation-mark traps of believing sex is the goal, the home run, the only way to get onto the scoreboard. It takes so much more work to avoid these traps than it does to give in to them. Where are the points given for *that*?

It even feels weird to say *I'm not ready*. Because that still sets sex up as the ultimate destination, the ultimate proof, the thing toward which all preparation leads.

Avery doesn't believe in that.

But he also realizes he doesn't know for sure if Ryan feels the same way.

That same Thursday, Alicia finds Ryan at his locker after school.

"You know you love me, right?" she starts.

Ryan doesn't stop putting his books away. He knows this is her version of *Don't get offended, but*. She doesn't really mean it as a disclaimer anymore; it's more like a signal, so he can at least have a moment to get ready for whatever's coming next.

"I do," he says. Because that's always his line.

"Good. Because, Ryan . . . only someone you love would be able to tell you that your hair needs a serious touch-up."

Ryan feels his body relax. This is not a serious problem. He's been aware of how his hair's been growing out, pushing the blue to the borders.

"Call your aunt," Alicia continues. "Now that you're al-lowed to go over there again. Otherwise, I might have to take matters into my own hands."

Ryan closes his locker and pretends to shudder away from her.

"My hair! My precious hair!" he calls out. Which is all he

needs to do to evoke the disastrous haircut Alicia gave him nearly two years ago. ("Was she drunk when she did this to you?" Aunt Caitlin had asked when she'd seen it. And Ryan had confessed that, no, Alicia's imprecisions could not be blamed on any intoxication other than that which comes from the power of wielding a scissors.)

Alicia laughs. Two football players passing in the hall give them a strange look, which only makes Ryan and Alicia side-eye each other and crack up further.

Ryan texts his aunt to make an "appointment" the next afternoon, then shows Alicia the phone to assure her he's done it.

"Good," Alicia says. "We want you looking suave for your big date on Saturday."

Ryan has no idea where Alicia has plucked this particular word from. *Suave.* He teases her about it, but then it comes back to him later on that night, when he's getting ready for bed. He pauses while he's putting on his pajamas, so when he looks in the mirror, he notes his messy, unevenly colored hair; the three o'clock shadow on his chin; his chest with maybe a dozen hairs on it; his not-quite-abs-not-quite-belly; his pajama bottoms hanging on his hips. He doesn't feel suave at all. He doesn't feel ugly, either. He just feels like maybe he's not attractive enough. For what, he's not sure.

He isn't thinking of Avery, not when he's looking in the mirror. This is good; it means he isn't worried about how Avery sees him. Avery isn't the one he's trying to impress.

Ryan pulls away from the mirror, throws on an old

T-shirt, and takes his phone with him into bed. He and Avery text for a while, choosing a town roughly halfway between them for their Saturday-night date. It takes a ridiculously long time to pick a restaurant, considering there are only about six options. When they're done, Avery texts Ryan, *Are you in your pajamas?*

Yeah, Ryan texts back. *U?*

Yup. I bet you look cute in yours.

Thanks. Ryan smiles, thinking about sleeping over at Avery's house, seeing him ready for bed. *You too.*

The three dots of an incoming response hang around for a bit. Then Avery's next text appears: *Can I see?*

Ryan hasn't turned out the lights yet, so he types back, *Sure.* He takes a picture of himself in the old T-shirt and the flannel bottoms. He keeps his messed-up hair in the frame.

Looks comfy, Avery replies.

Ryan reaches over and turns out the light.

Very comfy, he types.

The three dots take their time again. Ryan's expecting a long paragraph to appear. But for over a minute, nothing does. And then there's a single line:

They look really good on you, followed by a winking emoji.

Ryan chuckles. *U think we should wear pajamas on our date?*

This time, Avery's response is quick. *Haha. Maybe.*

I can't wait, Ryan tells Avery.

* * *

Even though he could replay the conversation by reading it on his phone, Avery replays it in his head instead, after he and Ryan have gone back and forth saying goodnight and sweet dreams. If he replays it in his head, he can include all the stupid things he typed out and then deleted—*What are you wearing under those pajamas?* and *Do you want to see MY pajamas?* and *I wish I was inside those pajamas.* Trying to find a way to test if one thing could lead to another, even though there isn't another spot he necessarily wants to arrive at. It's Pope in his head, saying how every long-distance relationship has to have sex talk. He, Avery, doesn't particularly want to have it. And Ryan doesn't seem to want it, either. But shouldn't two boyfriends lying in their own beds, texting last thing at night, want to get their pajamas off? Isn't that how it's supposed to go?

Sweet dreams, Ryan wished him. But something sour has gotten into the night, keeping Avery awake, trying to figure out its source.

It would take intense torture techniques to force Ryan to tell his parents he's going out on a date with Avery on Saturday night, but Aunt Caitlin gets the story out of him within two minutes.

When he shows up at her door after school on Friday, he tells her hi and she responds by pulling him into a hug, a real hug. Inside this hug are the hours she wasn't allowed to see him, all the words she wanted to say to her sister in protest, all the words she held back because she knew they could lead to something irreparable. And when Ryan hugs her back, he is telling her how glad he is to be here, how he will never hold his parents' actions against her, how he wishes this hug with her was what home was like, this welcome. The past weeks are in this hug, and the past sixteen years are in this hug. Which is why, when it's over, nothing more needs to be said, except, "Come in, come in."

Caitlin has set everything they need on her kitchen table: scissors, towels, dye, wide plastic bowl, brush, and comb. One of the kitchen chairs has its back to the table, facing the sink.

Ryan sits down, and as soon as Caitlin asks him how things are going, he finds himself talking about Avery, updating her about their last clandestine meeting and the plans for Saturday night. She's brushing out his hair, taking in its current shape before determining the shape it needs to be.

"We're boyfriends now," Ryan tells her. Then he confesses, "But I'm not really sure what that means."

Caitlin smiles, takes a towel from the table, and wraps it loosely around Ryan's neck, tucked over his collar.

"What do you want it to mean?" she asks.

"I don't know. I guess I want it to mean we're both serious about wanting to be together. That each time we see each other, we're less like strangers, and that if it keeps going, we won't be strangers at all."

Caitlin is glad she's standing behind Ryan, glad he can't see his words rise like flower buds in her heart. She has never heard him say anything like this, has always hoped he'd feel this way for someone.

"That's wonderful," she says to him.

"It's scary!" Ryan replies, laughing.

Caitlin puts her hand on his shoulder. "Oh, I know. The jitters are one of the less fortunate side effects of falling for someone. I like to think they're there to keep you careful. Or maybe they make so much noise just so you appreciate it when they stop."

"Do they stop?"

"They *transform*. Now hold still."

She takes up the scissors and starts to trim. She doesn't need to ask Ryan what kind of cut he wants. She knows.

Ryan sits in the chair and feels his aunt's fingers pull and pick at different tufts, then the dry-grass snip of the scissors.

"I'm not sure how much advice you want from your straight old aunt, who's never managed to put a ring on it . . . but the best advice I can give is to always be respectful. At the start, it's easy to fall into the trap of wanting to be impressive. But most people aren't looking for impressive—they're looking for respectful, someone who listens as well as they speak, someone who wants to understand the things they don't understand, rather than assuming they know how it is from the start. Also, you have to be a good kisser. But don't worry—bad kissers don't make it to the seventh date. Not if Avery has any sense."

Ryan can feel himself blush. Caitlin's giving him an opening here, if he wants to talk about kissing or anything else. And the truth is, he'd love to talk about it to someone, to make sure he's not messing that part up, and that it makes sense that making out with Avery is so much better than making out with Isaiah was, because even though it was hot with Isaiah, there was always the nagging hitch of its meaninglessness. With Avery, it's so much more meaningful, and that's one of the things that's scary and wonderful. He'd love to talk to someone about that. But he also doesn't want to be the guy who talks to his aunt about kissing boys. So he keeps his mouth shut; his blush is the only public statement he'll make on the matter.

Caitlin doesn't expect him to talk to her about it, even though she wishes he would. She's sure any sex lecture her brother-in-law had with his son would have dodged like birds and stung like bees. The only way she can think to counteract this is to make sure Ryan knows about the heart part, that whatever he does should come from a place of affection, not need or obligation. *Respectful* is the best word she can find for it, but she also feels she's emphasizing the bare minimum, not the full rush of it.

She has the radio playing, and when a Fleetwood Mac song comes on, Ryan starts to sing along quietly. Caitlin keeps cutting his hair, but inside she's marveling at the moment. This is what she wants to convey to her nephew, the way that people are at their most vivid when they're completely unguarded, and that's what love brings—the ability to be unguarded around someone else, and to treasure how unguarded they are in return. But she knows this is not the time to tell him that. She files it away for later, for when he's not as open and needs to be.

Ryan barely realizes he's singing. The music is just another part of the comfort of the room. By the time Caitlin has finished the cut and is washing all the loose hairs out in the sink, preparing him for the bleach and the dye, he is feeling a serene blankness, so peaceful that all his thoughts can take a rest, all his worries lulled into hibernation.

It's only when he's upright in the chair, waiting for the dye to set, that the conversation resumes. He tells her more about being grounded, about what it's like to text with Avery late at night, what it's like to have someone to wish goodnight. She tells him about her first serious high school boyfriend, Sam, and how each of them would always try to be the last voice the other heard before sleep, to the point that if her mom came into the room to ask her something after she'd already said goodnight to Sam, she'd have to call him back, to hear his goodnight again. There was even this one night—Caitlin can still remember staring up at the glow-in-the-dark constellations on her ceiling, feeling sleep pushing the phone from her ear. And Sam, instead of saying goodnight, said, "I'll see you in my dreams." Then he fell asleep—Caitlin could hear it right there on the phone, the shift of his breathing. Instead of hanging up, she fell asleep that way, too. And in the morning, she woke up and the connection had held. She said "Good morning" into the phone, and she could hear the smile in Sam's voice when he said "Good morning" back.

She tells Ryan all this, and he says it's an awesome story. She doesn't tell him she has no idea where Sam is now, or even if he saw her in his dreams that night, because there must have been a part of her, back then, that was afraid to ruin everything by asking.

Miles away, play practice isn't going well.

Play practice is always hard on Friday afternoons—the thing you look forward to on weekdays becomes the thing standing in the way of your weekend. Avery knows this. He also knows there's only so much you can do with a play like *Don't Forget Your Shoes!*—a comedy that, if he's being generous, was much funnier when it was written in 1936 than it is today. He once overheard Mr. Horslen, the drama teacher, tell Ms. Paskins, another English teacher, that the reason they were performing it was because the playwright had never bothered to renew the copyright, so it was free, and thus one of the most produced plays in American high schools. To the students, Mr. Horslen said that performing *Don't Forget Your Shoes!* was a way to "demonstrate old tropes while at the same time questioning them." From what Avery could tell, this meant that Liz Macy could play the spinster aunt as a proud lesbian without Mr. Horslen or anyone else getting upset.

Today they are rehearsing a scene in which Pope, playing an easily flustered matron named Lavinia Stranglehold, is insisting that there is a ghost in her attic, and her great-nephew Lucius LeFevre is trying to prevent her from going up there to discover his secret fiancée, Betty Lou Templepot. Avery, playing Lucius's brother Laurent (who also thinks that Betty Lou is his fiancée), and Liz, playing the lesbian aunt, are waiting in the wings; once a commotion is made, they will storm in to see what the commotion is all about.

The problem, as it has been throughout rehearsals, is that Dennis Travers, who is playing Lucius LeFevre, has yet to comprehend that the play is a dated comedy. He is a senior, currently applying to colleges, and he seems to think that universities send recruiters to high school plays in the same way they're sent to football games. So, it follows, if he wants to be taken seriously as an actor, he must take Lucius LeFevre very seriously. What are Lucius's motivations? What did he eat for lunch? Has he ever really gotten over his parents' death? (Mr. Horslen tried to point out that nowhere in *Don't Forget Your Shoes!* does it say that Lucius's parents are dead; he is merely visiting his great-aunt, not living there. In response, Dennis merely set his jaw, looked Mr. Horslen in the eye, and said, "Look . . . *I just know*.")

Pope's understandable vamping as Lavinia and Dennis's naturalistic rage as Lucius are making for quite a dog-day afternoon.

Clocking the scene from stage right, Liz sighs and tells Avery, "I think we're going to be here for a while."

Normally, Avery might suggest they run some lines, but at this point the performances are only a week away, and the lines are as embedded in his recall as they ever will be.

"Got any big weekend plans?" he asks.

"Honestly? There's a lot of farmwork that needs to be done, so my brothers and I will probably be fixing fences. Very glamorous. How about you?"

"I have a date on Saturday."

"Well, that sounds like more fun than my plans. I invited Hannah to come over and help, but I don't think traipsing through cow shit with me and my brothers is her idea of a romantic time."

"Yeah, that's not what Ryan and I have planned, either."

They talk a little more about what he and Ryan *do* have planned, all while Mr. Horslen is trying to tell Dennis not to deliver the line "But, Auntie, what if it's the ghost of one of your ex-husbands? There are so very many!" in a "manner similar to Hamlet's."

Avery and Liz aren't friends, but they're not not-friends, either. They have the basic queer bond, which is often enough to inspire confidences.

After Liz has spoken approvingly of Avery's Saturday-night restaurant choice, he feels bold enough to ask, "Do you think it's strange to get to a seventh date without ever talking about sex?"

Without a moment's pause, Liz answers, "No."

"Not even a little?"

"Not even a little."

"If I am to be the host to a ghost, the most I can propose is to offer it some roast!" Pope/Lavinia calls from the stage. This means their cue is near.

"Do you want to be having sex?" Liz asks, her voice so neutral that she might as well be asking Avery if he wants some pretzels.

"No. Not really."

"And has Ryan said anything about wanting to have sex?"

"No."

"People who want to have sex don't tend to be particularly subtle about it. That's been my experience, and from what I've read, I think it's a universal truth."

"But, Aunt Lavinia!" Dennis calls, with all the anguish of a thousand Parisian grad students. "Don't go up there! It's such an imposition!" For some reason, he puts the accent on the second syllable, so it comes out "im-PAHS-ition." He's been doing this for weeks. Nobody wants to tell him to correct it, since it's the only humor he brings to the scene.

Avery and Liz move into place, ready to step onstage after the next line.

"Don't worry about it," Liz whispers. "The first dates are all practice. You're allowed to stumble and search to get to the way it's supposed to be."

"What are those . . . voices?" Dennis intones.

"It's only us!" Avery calls, stepping forward.

Ryan and Avery don't get to talk much that night. The reality of exam week is kicking in for Avery, and Ryan, whose exams are a different week, understands. They both wish they were in the same classes, in the same place.

Ryan swears to Avery that at least *some* studying would get done. But maybe not a lot.

Saturday arrives. Avery makes sure his studying is conspicuous, so his parents don't give him any grief when it's time for him to take off for dinner. He and Ryan talked about dressing up for the date, since it's a Saturday night and all, so he's got on a jacket and tie. (The jacket is forest green; the tie, Fanta orange.)

There's some traffic, but Avery still gets there first. They've chosen a Greek place called Parthenon, mostly because there's a dish on the menu described as "flaming cheese."

The waitress is a woman with witch-black hair and magenta earrings. Seeing Avery's tie, she asks, "Special occasion?"

"A date," he replies.

"First date?"

"Seventh."

She smiles. "Still counting them and still dressing up, eh? Bodes well."

The time for the date arrives and passes. Avery checks his phone. After ten minutes of checking, he sees the waitress giving him pitying looks. He texts Ryan to make sure he's okay. Ryan answers by walking in the door.

He's not wearing a jacket or a tie, just a button-down shirt.

There's also something different about his hair. Avery can't figure it out at first. Then he realizes: bluer.

"I'm so sorry," Ryan says as he sits down. "It was a total shit show. My parents didn't want me to come. I told them that being ungrounded wasn't a conditional thing, and that once they told me I wasn't grounded, that meant I could make plans. I won't give you all the details, but basically it ended with me shouting something like 'You don't know me at all!' and then driving away. It's so stupid."

"It's okay. I haven't been here long," Avery assures him.

"It's not okay. But thanks for saying it is." Ryan reaches into his back pocket and pulls something out. A wrapped-up gift? No, a rolled-up tie.

"I swear, I was going to wear this," Ryan says. "I tried putting it on, like, five different times at five different stoplights. I'm just not very good at it."

As if to prove his point, he tries to loop it around and make it take a proper shape. It ends up looking like two hands of a clock frozen at four-forty.

"Goddammit," Ryan says, and Avery can see where this is going. The fluster will only accelerate, feed on itself. So instead of sitting there watching Ryan curse and try again, he stands up and says, "Here, let me." He walks behind Ryan, puts his hands on his shoulders, squeezing a greeting, then leans over and undoes the clock hands. He's never done this before on anyone else, so he pretends it's his body, his tie. He lets the head of the tie dangle lower than the tail, then begins its sinuous dance, around, around. Then he lifts it to Ryan's neck, feels how Ryan holds his breath, smells Ryan's shampoo. The dance pulls in, becomes a knot. Gently, Avery guides the tie along Ryan's buttons. Then he tightens the grip.

There.

He folds Ryan's collar back over. Taps him on the shoulder again, all done.

Ryan remembers to breathe.

Avery thinks about reaching out to touch Ryan's hair, but it looks so inky, he feels his fingers may come away blue if they make contact. He sits back down and admires his handiwork. Ryan thanks him, and Avery waves the thanks away.

"You look nice," Avery says.

"You look spectacular," Ryan says.

The waitress, who's been watching it all with a smile, waits for a pause before bringing the menus.

Once they've ordered, Avery and Ryan talk about everything they've seen, everyone they've talked to, everything they've done over the past few days. The temperature of their attentions has been consistently high enough that the need for explanation has begun to boil away. Avery doesn't need to tell Ryan who Pope is, or why Dennis is such a menace. Ryan doesn't need to conjure Aunt Caitlin's house because Avery's been there; he knows not only what it looks like, but also how it feels. They tell some hair-dye disaster stories—

for a blue-haired boy and a pink-haired boy, it's funny they haven't had this conversation before. Ryan has always been blue. Avery has tried orange, purple, fire-engine red, but after he landed on pink, he didn't feel the need for further experimentation. At least not for now.

They are so caught within their conversation that they are both startled by a sudden explosion to the side of their shoulders. The waitress is lit with campfire glee as she lowers the flaming cheese onto their table. The smell of lighter fluid flourishes, then dissolves into a smoky lemon breeze. The Halloumi sizzles appreciatively.

Avery and Ryan both stare.

Once the waitress leaves, Ryan confesses, "I have no idea how to eat this."

And Avery confesses, "Neither do I."

These are confessions that the waitress has anticipated, so she returns with more bread for the table. She knows it's often easier to accompany the cheese, the first time.

The cheese tastes of char and citrus on the surface, then a chewy tang underneath.

Ryan loves it. Avery is simply relieved they weren't asked to eat it while it was still on fire, which is how he thought "flaming cheese" might be consumed.

Ryan turns the conversation back to the play. "I can't wait to see it," he says.

This is something he's said before, but this time it's not theoretical. Ryan asks which performance he should aim for; the Saturday matinee's a no-go because of work, but

Friday and Saturday nights are possible, and/or the Sunday matinee.

It's Avery's impulse to say, *You really don't have to.* Because it's not a great play. His role is hardly a lead. It's a long way to drive.

But the thing is: He wants Ryan to see it, and he knows Ryan genuinely wants to be there after hearing about it for weeks. It makes Avery's heart skip a beat to realize Ryan is so plugged into Avery's story he gets electricity from it, too. Ryan wants to see Pope as Lavinia Stranglehold. He wants to see how Dennis is ruining the play. He wants to see Avery step far out of his comfort zone, tasked with making strangers laugh at lines written before his grandparents were born.

"Come Friday," Avery says. "Even if it'll make me more nervous."

"Me being there will make you more nervous?" Ryan asks.

"Yes," Avery answers without hesitation. Then he clarifies, "That's a compliment, you know."

Ryan smiles. "I know now."

That smile. God, that smile. Avery feels he has to restrain himself from leaping over the once-flaming cheese to kiss that smile.

Oblivious, Ryan keeps eating. Between bites he says, "I'm not entirely convinced this is cheese. It feels more like an alien substance. Maybe something a manga character would eat. Or astronaut cheese. Only you wouldn't want an open flame on a space station, I believe."

He's saying anything that comes to his head, and Avery wonders how he could unlock someone else so fully, in such a short amount of time.

Can we really talk about anything? he wonders. Which immediately makes him think about sex. Not the actual act. Those images don't flash to him. But he remembers his conversation with Liz at the side of the stage. Ryan is now looking up Halloumi on his phone, reporting that it's made from a mixture of goat's and sheep's milk, with a texture often described as *squeaky*. As he does this, he does not appear to be a boy overly concerned with sex.

But Avery has to admit to himself once again: He's not sure.

"The word *Halloumi* is trademarked by the government of Cyprus to prevent other countries from claiming it for their own cheese. Isn't that wild? Switzerland must be like, damn, we should have thought about doing that!"

"Yeah. Totally."

Now that talking about sex (not sex talk) is on Avery's mind, he knows it's not going to leave unless he brings it up. He doesn't know how to approach the subject, so he grasps at whatever route in he can see, and makes up a conversation that never happened in order to steer in that direction.

"So," he says, "speaking of weird things . . . my friend Pope was talking to me the other day, and they were talking about how everyone says people think about sex every seven seconds, and we were both like, that can't possibly be true. Maybe as an average—like, someone thinks about sex for an hour straight and then doesn't for the next six hours. But every seven seconds seems a little extreme, don't you think?"

"I don't think that statistic is *science,*" Ryan responds. "It's like some third grader's older brother told him it happened every seven seconds, and that third grader told all the other third graders, and from there it spread to the whole world."

"I know!" Avery says, trying to figure out how to continue to lead the conversation where he wants it to go. "It's like everyone thinks sex is the point. But it's not the point, is it?"

"Only if you want to make a baby," Ryan says, forking more Halloumi into his mouth and chewing, chewing, chewing.

"I know, I know. But besides that. You know?"

Ryan looks a little confused. "I mean . . . yeah. I know. But even if it's not the point, it's still nice, right?"

"Of course!" Avery replies. "But not, like, right away."

Ryan's hand shoots up to his mouth and he looks at Avery for a second before lowering it and saying, "Oh God. You didn't think we were going to have sex *tonight,* did you?"

Avery feels his face flush. "No! Not at all!"

"Okay. Whew."

"Don't act so *relieved*!" Avery blurts out, even though he himself is very relieved.

Now Ryan looks panicked. "Oh shit. I don't mean that I don't want to have sex with you. Just not, like, tonight, in the backseat of a car in some parking lot. Jesus. No."

It's all so ridiculous, Avery starts laughing. And once he starts laughing, he honestly cannot stop. Even as Ryan is asking, "What? *What?*" he is crying with laughter, Ryan staring until Avery laughs out, "I don't want to have sex with you tonight, either!" and Ryan should be laughing, too, but mostly he looks confused.

"I'm sorry. I'm so sorry," Avery says once he gets his full voice back. "I just got it into my head that because it's the seventh date, there's a certain place we should be. Like, there's all this pressure for sex to be The Big Moment. But I don't want it to be The Big Moment. I want us to have a thousand different kinds of big moments. And I definitely want some of them to involve kissing and making out because whenever I'm near you, there's absolutely a part of my body that wants to be completely all over yours, this irresistible pull, like gravity . . . only hotter. But because we never talk about sex, I didn't know what you were expecting. Am I making any sense?"

Ryan puts his head in his hands, shakes it back and forth a few times, then peekaboos his palms into parentheses.

"You're making sense," he says. "But possibly there were other ways to have his conversation."

"You're not mad? Or disappointed?"

Ryan puts his hands down, makes sure no one else is within earshot, and says, "Avery. I didn't come here for a quickie. Or even a slowie, if that's a thing. That whole hot gravity thing you're talking about? I feel it, too. But it's about being with you, about being together. And to me, being together is this—talking and laughing and wanting to make out and having completely embarrassing conversations in public. Do I think we'll have sex? Yeah. Eventually. But *eventually* is a really wide range of time. And as for sex being the point? Honestly, it never even occurred to me to think that. In the list of things I was looking forward to tonight, I don't think it even hit the page."

Avery is still flushed, but now his shoulders are relaxed.

"But there *will* be making out?" he asks.

Ryan extends his legs so they touch Avery's, pulling them a little toward him.

"Oh yes, there will be making out. I swear by the dying embers of the flaming cheese."

It's the least romantic image imaginable. And at the same time, Avery can't imagine anything more wonderful.

They talk, they joke, they eat. Their legs stay largely intertwined. The waitress brings them a free dessert. When they ask her why, she says it's because they both dressed up.

"It's a sign of respect to wear those ties," she says. "I appreciate it."

It's only when Ryan and Avery start talking about next weekend, about whether Ryan will be able to stay over after the play, that Ryan remembers that his parents exist. He remembers the fight he had with them before he came here. He imagines what he'll be going back to.

But only for a few seconds. He doesn't want them anywhere near this date.

In the parking lot, they kiss between their cars. They both taste like honey and walnuts and vanilla ice cream.

They kiss with their lips and their hands. They can't help but keep their ears attuned for any sudden noises . . . but no sudden noises arrive. Their kisses intensify time, and also erase it.

Toward the end, Avery pulls back and apologizes for the awkward conversation before.

"No, it's good," Ryan says. "We have to have those conversations, about what we want. All the small conversations are practice for the big ones."

Avery likes that Ryan has made the sex conversation a small one.

A party of six loudly leaves the restaurant, and Ryan and Avery take this as their signal to call it a night. At home, dinner takes about a half hour. Tonight, it's been two hours and counting. That feels major to each of them.

After they kiss out one more goodbye, Ryan says, "Lord knows what my parents will think. I left without a tie and now I'm coming back wearing one. That can only mean trouble."

He grins at Avery then, and holds the grin until they each get in their cars and drive away.

Both feel this particular practice has gone well.

The Abandoned Course

(the third date)

The last thing Ryan wants is for Avery to meet his parents. Half the problem is solved because his dad is out of the house. But his mom is the bigger problem, because while his father will happily ignore whatever's in front of his face, his mom will ask questions.

Ryan's head is still spinning from meeting Avery, and while he suspects what the answers to a lot of his own questions might be, he doesn't feel like he can rely on any of them yet.

Not letting his parents into it is an act of self-preservation. Meaning: He is preserving the part of his self that he actually likes, because that seems to be the part that Avery likes, too.

His parents don't bring out that part of him.

He knows he can't just disappear from his house, so he's told his mom that he and Alicia are doing something. The problem is that his mom knows what Alicia's car looks like, so when Avery arrives, she'll know something's up.

Ryan understands he could have asked Avery to pick

him up somewhere else . . . but then Avery might have been the one with questions. And Ryan's not ready to bring everything down by answering those questions yet.

About ten minutes before Avery's supposed to get there, Ryan says goodbye to his mom and walks out the front door. Instead of waiting on the front walk, which is visible from at least four different rooms, he puts himself on the other side of the front hedges. It's not complete camouflage, but it's good enough.

His heart lifts a little when he sees Avery turn onto his street. Avery hasn't even had time to shift to park before Ryan has the door handle in his hand. He jumps in and says, "Let's go."

But Avery doesn't go. Instead he says he has to go.

"Could I go inside for a sec?" he asks. "I have to pee."

Ryan knows it's impossible for Avery to enter the house and get to the bathroom without his mother in some way intervening. Her maternal trip wire is too taut.

He feels there's no way to say, *I want today to be perfect, and if you pee in my house, the odds are too strong that it'll spiral into something far from perfect.* So instead he tells Avery, "We'll find someplace else. I promise, it won't be long."

Avery isn't comfortable enough with Ryan yet to say, *Are you serious? I have to pee.* He also doesn't want to explain that it's much easier for him to use a private bathroom than a public one. Especially in a town like Kindling.

121

So he starts the car and pulls into the street, as instructed. He waits for some explanation about why he can't go inside Ryan's house, but none is forthcoming. He can't help but wonder if Ryan is embarrassed by him, then tries to bury that thought.

"I have a plan," Ryan says. "Are you up for a plan?"

Avery nods.

Ryan seems encouraged by this response. "Okay," he says. "I've got this."

Avery follows Ryan's directions to a McDonald's.

"That work?" Ryan asks.

Avery can't say he's exactly enthusiastic about peeing in a McDonald's in a small town he doesn't know. But it's definitely better than nothing at this point.

Avery pulls into the parking lot. "You hungry?" he asks Ryan.

"Not yet. Not unless you're hungry. I just figured you could pee here."

Again, Avery doesn't want to explain. So he gets out of the car, heads inside. He doesn't make eye contact with anyone, but at the same time he feels unspecified eyes on him as he goes over to the men's room. People behind the counter glaring because he hasn't bought anything. People at tables staring because they know his destination and have some questions about that. Nobody has to be watching for Avery to feel watched. He is almost used to it, but will never truly get used to it, this feeling that he might be confronted at any moment by assholes. Because assholes are everywhere, and they fundamentally don't understand who Avery is.

He is relieved that it's a one-stall bathroom, that he can lock the door and have privacy. He is also embarrassed by his relief, uncomfortable with the fact that he's so uncomfortable. Ryan remains oblivious in the car. Avery envies that, and is also annoyed by it.

On the way out, the eyes are still there, the extra self-consciousness. Avery won't let it change his actions, not anymore. But he can't deny it's there.

When Avery returns to the car, he finds Ryan busy texting. He barely looks up when Avery gets in.

Avery half expects Ryan to say that something's come up, that the date is being canceled, even though this would contradict everything Avery's felt and thought about Ryan so far. They don't really know each other enough for any impressions to feel like truth.

From that half expectation, he's half surprised when Ryan smiles and explains, "Everyone wants to meet you."

This fills Avery with another kind of anxiety.

"Everyone?" he asks.

Now the change in Ryan is more pronounced—whatever edge was there when Avery got into the car has smoothed. He seems much more excited as he says, "I may have told one or two or seven of my friends about you. I mean, some of them saw us dancing the other night. I had to keep them updated."

Avery starts the car and asks, "Where to?"

"Do you want to meet some of my friends?"

The answer is yes, and the answer is no. The answer is that Avery wants to see more of Ryan's life, for sure. And the answer is that he likes it only being the two of them for now.

"Maybe later?" he offers.

Ryan takes this in stride. "Oh, definitely later. I just need to know whether to put them on standby or not. But we've got hours of us-time before that."

Avery likes the sound of this. But he still feels uneasy. Not because Ryan's making him feel wrong. He's just uneasy because nothing is easy.

Don't overthink this, he tells himself. *Live it instead.*

Ryan is so happy he's not driving. He doesn't need to look at the road. He can look at Avery instead.

It's like being on drugs, the desire he has to take everything in, to stop and ask himself, *Can you believe that you're here with this really cool boy, and you have a whole day to yourselves?*

These are not thoughts he usually has.

It's making him smile. He must look like a total dope. Which only makes him smile more. And he is not a smiler by nature. He comes from a long line of nonsmilers.

"What?" Avery asks, part confounded and part annoyed.

Oops. Ryan sees how the whole staring-smiling thing might be a little weird from the outside. "I'm sorry," he says.

Then he tries to explain. "I don't usually like people. So when I do, part of me is really amused and the other part refuses to believe it's happening."

"Oh," Avery replies. "In that case, feel free to keep staring. I was worried my shirt was inside out or something."

Ryan momentarily forgets he's giving directions, and they miss a turn. He decides if he doesn't mention it, Avery won't notice. He tells him to make a left now. Then, eventually, another left.

"What are we doing?" Avery asks.

Ryan has also forgotten he hasn't told Avery the plan. Now he says, "I figured we'd start with pancakes. Do you want pancakes?"

"It's hard to imagine a scenario where someone would say no to pancakes. I'm guessing that's our destination?"

"Yup."

The Pancake Century Diner is like a flamingo sitting in a row of hens, the most colorful thing this stretch of interstate has to offer. Avery parks, and as the two of them walk past the diner's locally legendary sign, he says, "I don't understand why they have to do that—put eyes and mouths on food you're about to eat."

"You know, in all these years, I've never thought of Mr. Hot Stack as a sentient being," Ryan admits.

"He has a name?! And a gender?!"

"And no doubt a family he's supporting by appearing on this sign."

Ryan is hoping Mr. Hot Stack will be the only familiar

face he finds inside the diner. As they wait for the hostess, he does a quick scan and is relieved to find it free of classmates or anyone else school-adjacent.

"All clear?" Avery asks once they're seated.

Ryan likes how much this boy notices. "All clear. Just habit, I guess."

"How many people are in your high school?"

"About four hundred. Yours?"

"Eighty."

Ryan shakes his head. There would be no way to be invisible with only eighty people in the whole school. "You must stick out," he says. "I mean, with the pink hair and all."

Avery shoots him a look. "I bet you blend right in."

"Trying to blend in would be like being put through a blender. I abstain."

Avery finds this funny. "What did you just say?"

"I said, 'I abstain.'"

"Is that what you say when all the popular kids try to get you to hang out with them? 'I'm sorry, but I abstain from blending in. There are just too many perks to being a wallflower.'"

Ryan leans in, as if he's sharing a secret. "Yup. That's precisely what I say. But do they stop? No. The popular kids keep bugging me. Calling. Texting. Showing up on my doorstep. Begging like dogs. I'm embarrassed for them."

"I know precisely how you feel."

To emphasize his point, Avery squeezes Ryan's hand. It's

such an openly lame excuse to touch him, and both of them smile in acknowledgment of this.

"Part of you is amused," Avery says. "And part of you can't believe this is happening."

Ryan is startled to have Avery give his words back to him in this way, perfectly understood. "And in the Pancake Century Diner, of all places," he observes.

With his free hand, Avery holds up the menu so it could be either him or Mr. Hot Stack replying. "Well," he says, "it *is* the Pancake Century, after all."

The waitress comes to take their order. Ryan thinks about pulling his hand away, but there's no indication that Avery's hand is going anywhere. And since they both like this awkward position, he keeps it there until the food arrives.

Avery knows it's a little silly for him to yell, "Ouch! Mrs. Hot Stack, what are they doing to meeeeee?!?" every time Ryan's knife cuts into a pancake. He does it at least two more times than he should.

One more time, Ryan thinks, *and I will definitely have to tell him to stop.*

"Okay," Avery says when the meal is done. "What's next?"

It's a natural enough question to ask at the end of a meal.

But it has the effect of shifting the weight of the day back onto Ryan's shoulders. He's not used to such responsibility. Of his friends, Ryan is not the one who usually decides what they're going to do. And with Isaiah, they rarely met up outside Isaiah's house. They never really had a date, not like this. They just did things. That felt different. There were times Ryan wanted it to be like this, but Isaiah never wanted that.

It's not like there are many places in Kindling where you can do something you can't do anywhere else. It's McDonald's McDonald's McDonald's. That's what most of the kids are like, too. They have McDonald's personalities. Ryan wants to reject that. He wants to scorn all the obvious paths that life offers teenagers here. It's not that he thinks he's better than everyone else. He just thinks that, unlike them, he'd be better somewhere else.

He directs Avery to Mr. Footer's, the old relic of a miniature golf course on the outskirts of town, a neighborhood where not even warehouses bother to exist. The mini-golf course has been closed for years now, and no one else has bought the land, so it sits in its abandoned state, nearly postapocalyptic in its decay. There's a lock on the gates, but the gates have undone themselves in places, making it easy to come and go. At night it's a breeding ground for misdeeds, but during the day it's graveyard quiet.

"Where exactly are you taking me?" Avery asks. Ryan has a flash of seeing the site through his eyes, and understands this might be a mistake. But he doesn't want to turn back now.

He tells Avery to park in front. "When I was a kid," he

explains, "this was the best place around. Like, if you were really good and did all your chores, Mom and Dad would take you here. You'd play all the mini-golf you could, and then there'd be ice cream and video games in the hut over there."

Avery takes it all in. "So what happened?"

Ryan shrugs. "One day it was here, and then the next day there was a sign saying it was over. It's sat here ever since."

But still, Ryan wants to say, *it's kind of the same. Like an old stuffed animal. Just because it's now a ragged version of itself, you don't stop loving it. You might not keep it with you like you used to, but you're still nostalgically happy to see it.*

"Do you come here often?" Avery asks. He makes it sound like a line from a dive bar.

"Only with special people," Ryan replies. It sounds sarcastic, but it's actually sincere.

"Oh, gee. I'm so flattered," Avery deadpans.

"Let's go," Ryan says. They leave the car and walk along the fence until Ryan finds a gap big enough to slide through. He pretends to be a gentleman holding a door open for Avery.

Inside, everything is broken. Toppled windmills, fetid moats, bottles left smashed and cans left crushed.

"Want to play?" Avery asks.

Ryan looks at the torn-up greens, the holes filled with cigarette butts.

"I'm not sure that'll work," he says. "There aren't any clubs anymore. Or golf balls."

Avery has what can only be called a mischievous gleam in his eye. "So?"

"So . . . it's hard to play mini-golf without those things."

"Use your imagination!" Avery walks to the base of the first green and puts down an invisible ball. "This is the most amazing mini-golf course ever created. For example, this hole is patrolled by live alligators. If they swallow your ball, it'll cost you three strokes. If they swallow *you,* it's five."

Avery takes an exaggerated swing with a nonexistent club, then makes a production of watching the ball soar into the air and drop to the green. "Comeoncomeoncomeon," he murmurs. Then he sighs. "Not a hole in one, but at least I dodged the gators. Your turn."

Ryan wants to kiss Avery on the spot, for sending their day on this diversion. But he doesn't want to interrupt the imaginary game, so walks over and puts down his own invisible ball. "I hope you don't mind that I took the pink one," he says.

"I don't mind at all."

Ryan swings at the ball. They both watch it rise and drop.

"Not bad," Avery says.

"At least I didn't hit a gator."

Ryan thinks Avery will stop then, will want to leave this desolate place. But he heads right over to his ball and makes the putt, then steps out of the way for Ryan to take his imaginary turn. Ryan follows his lead, but misses the shot. He gets the next one in.

Avery makes a gesture of gathering the golf balls from the hole, then walks to the next green.

"Your turn," he says. "What's the story?"

"Are you kidding? Do you mean to tell me you haven't heard of the Famous Fondue-icular Folly?"

"Wait!" Avery gasps. "You mean to tell me that's *here?*"

"Yes! You might not be able to see them with your very limited human sight, but this green is riddled with troughs of gooey chocolate. If a golf ball falls in, it will taste better, if you're into that kind of thing, but will also slow you down. Which is why we've switched our golf balls out for golf-ball-sized gobstoppers. They're not as aerodynamic, but they *are* easier to clean with your tongue."

"Excellent. I've only played with marshmallows, but gobstoppers should roll better."

Ryan lets Avery go first, go ahead. For a moment, it's like the greens are greens and the flags are aloft.

The thing is, at this point Ryan's used to it being wrecked. He's even *appreciated* how derelict it was, when he was feeling pretty derelict himself. In the past couple of years, there's been some catharsis in seeing his childhood so visibly trashed, as if there was some confirmation here about what growing up should feel like. He wasn't lying when he told Avery he'd only brought special people here—but he could just as easily have said he's never brought anyone here, not since it closed. This is also true. He's only come by himself, once he had his license and his truck and needed a destination other than his house. He's always been careful to make sure there weren't any other cars around, so he could experience the park in solitude, as if he were wandering around in the inside of his head. It makes him feel less alone, to feel his aloneness so powerfully. Mostly because it's a confirmation that this town is a place he needs to leave. It isn't him that's broken. He still lives, breathes, hopes. It's just that the landscape is dead around him.

These are teenage thoughts. Ryan knows that. And with Avery, a little of the old childhood wonder peeks through the clouds. Why experience a place like this as a clear-eyed adolescent when you can engage with it as a dream-eyed kid, seeing castles in every cloud, chocolate in every hiding place? Ryan plays along, and it's a relief to be playing for once. By the fifth hole they're not even golfing anymore; they're just describing all the things they don't really see. Avery erects the Taj Mahal on hole five, and Ryan presents the world's first antigravity mini-golf on hole six. At hole seven, they start walking hand in hand, surveyors of what's become a theme park of their own design. Instead of solemnly holding hands, mourning pose, they swing them back and forth, stretch their bodies away from each other and then pull back together. The sun isn't shining, but they think it is.

It is not as simple as Ryan looking at Avery and feeling they've known each other forever. In fact, it doesn't feel like that at all. Ryan feels like he is just getting to know Avery, and that getting to know Avery isn't going to be like getting to know anyone else he's ever gotten to know. Not if they can be like this.

There's a wishing well in the middle of the ninth hole. This is not imaginary—it is sitting there, largely intact from its glory days. Avery reaches into his pocket and pulls out a penny.

"No," Ryan finds himself saying. "Don't."

Avery shoots him a quizzical look. "Don't?"

"I've thrown pennies in that well all my life. Not a single wish has ever come true."

As a kid he wished for money or fame or toys or friends. More recent wishes have been for so many other things, all of them synonymous with love or escape.

He worries he's ruined it now, by suddenly being serious.

"Here," Avery says, offering his only penny. "Maybe you didn't do it right."

Avery takes the copper coin and moves it to Ryan's lips. Ryan holds there, not really knowing what's happening. Then Avery leans in and kisses him, kisses him so that they are both kissing the penny. When he pulls back, the penny falls, and Avery catches it in his palm.

"Now make a wish," he says.

And Ryan thinks, *I want to be happy.*

"Got it?" Avery asks.

Ryan nods, and Avery tosses the penny into the well. They both listen, but neither hears it land. Then Avery returns to him, comes closer again, and now they are kissing with nothing between them. Lips closed, then lips open. Hands empty, then hands entwined.

A minute or two of this, then Avery pulls back and says, "We're only half done!"

They walk, fingers still woven together, to the tenth hole.

"It's a cloud," Ryan says. "The whole thing is a cloud."

Avery is thinking, *This might be one of the best days of my life.* How fitting it is that they're golfing through clouds, because that's certainly where their heads must be. Avery likes that. His head feels free in the clouds.

"You're cirrusly good at this," he compliments Ryan, squeezing his hand.

"You're pretty cumulonimble yourself," Ryan replies, squeezing back. The fact that he stumbles while saying it makes it even more endearing.

The flow of the day feels so natural . . . so it's jarring when Ryan abruptly turns, looking to his right.

"What?" Avery asks. But even as he asks, he can hear people coming and looks to see four guys their age striding over. He tries to tell himself it's no big deal.

Then Ryan says, "Shit."

As the four of them get closer, Avery has some idea of where this is going. It's the sneering looks, the swagger, the almost aimless spite in their laughter. It's a particular brand of asshole, easily found in straight cis teenage boys traveling in packs.

"What's up, Ryan?" one of them taunts. "Who's your boyfriend?"

Ryan lets go of Avery's hand.

"What do you want, Skylar?" he says.

"We saw a car out front. What are you boys up to?"

Avery notices now that Skylar and one of the other guys are holding golf clubs. Skylar sees him looking and smiles. Then he spots a bottle on the ground and swings the club, knocking the bottle in Ryan and Avery's direction. Ryan doesn't flinch, but Avery does. All the clouds have left them now. They're too visible.

His instinct is to run, but since Ryan is staying put, he stays put. He understands it's easier to run from strangers. There's much less pride on the line.

Skylar lines up another bottle, and this time it smashes on impact, glass flying everywhere. The other guys find this hilarious.

Avery can feel himself shutting down, going into survival mode.

"What the fuck do you guys want?" Ryan spits out.

"So tough!" Skylar mocks. Then he throws his golf club at Ryan's face.

Or at least he makes it look like he's going to throw the golf club at Ryan's face. At the last possible moment, he holds on to it. But not before Ryan's lifted up his arm, cringed from the blow that doesn't come.

Avery can see Ryan's humiliation at falling for the fake-out. As the guys are laughing some more, Avery wants to walk over and put a comforting hand on Ryan's back, wants to tell him it's okay. But he can't do that, because he's not sure what kind of reaction that will get, and also he's not sure if it really is okay.

"Did we interrupt you guys making out?" Skylar says with a playful disgust. "Did we miss the show?" He's close now, too close. He takes the golf club and uses it to push Avery toward Ryan. "Don't let us stop you. Let's see what you've got."

Avery feels the guys' eyes on him and has no idea what they see.

"Come on!" one of the guys calls out. "Do it!"

Skylar starts to poke Ryan with the golf club, making rude kissing noises. Ryan grabs at the club, tries to pull it out of Skylar's hands. He expects Skylar to pull back, but Skylar surprises Ryan by pushing instead. Ryan's caught off-balance and falls back on his ass, knocking into Avery. Then Skylar takes back the club, easily shifting it out of Ryan's hand.

Everyone is staring at Ryan on the ground, even Avery. The other guys are loving it, shellacking on the insults. But Skylar stays quiet. He lets his satisfaction speak for him. No matter what Ryan does now, Skylar's already won.

"You need to get a new boyfriend," he tells Avery. "This one's damaged."

"Fuck you," Avery says. It feels lame to say it. Stupid. There has to be something better for him to say, but that's all he's got.

"No," Skylar says. "Fuck *you.*"

Ryan is getting up now. Skylar steps back and putts a piece of glass so it hits Ryan's sneaker.

Survival mode is on full volume now. Fuck pride. Fuck justice. Just get the hell out of there.

"Let's go," Avery says.

"What, so soon?" Skylar taunts. "That wasn't much of a show!"

Avery tries to read the expression in Ryan's eyes, but he can't. He has no idea what Ryan is thinking right now, what he's going to do next. It's like none of the rest of them are there—it's just Ryan and Skylar, facing off.

"I want to go," Avery says. Let them blame him. Let him be seen as the weak one, if that will get them out of here.

"Okay," Ryan says. It's directed at Avery, but he still doesn't take his eyes off Skylar. "It was great to see you guys."

"Yeah, great to see you, too," Skylar replies.

Ryan and Avery start to walk away. The guys respond by knocking more cans and bottles in their direction. Ryan doesn't break into a run. He just keeps walking, and Avery keeps pace. Glass and aluminum are hitting them, flying around them. The guys are whooping with joy. They follow for a short distance, then finally, at the sixth hole, let them go.

Avery starts walking faster. Ryan keeps up.

As soon as they are out of range, safely crawling back through the opening in the gate, the cork pops on all the words Avery has been keeping inside. "That was scary," he says. "But we're fine. We're totally fine. Those guys are ass-holes. The important thing is that we're okay. Let's just for-get about it, because there's no use in worrying about it now. We're okay, right?"

"I'm really sorry," Ryan says, "but I think I need us to be quiet for a second."

He tries to say it gently, tries to make it clear that it's nothing personal against Avery, but Avery can't help but feel a little rebuked.

Skylar's parked his car so it's blocking Avery's. And it's a truck, so it's not like Avery can ram his way out. Instead Avery has to do a twenty-point turn and run over a sidewalk to make an escape. The whole time, Ryan seethes.

"It's all right," Avery says.

"No, it's not," Ryan snaps.

Avery finishes the maneuvering and gets them out of the parking lot.

"What's next?" he asks.

Ryan knows he needs to extricate himself from what just happened, needs to step outside of it and return to the day that he and Avery were having. But the rage he's feeling is volcanic. If Avery weren't here, he'd be going back there with a golf club of his own. He'd wait until they weren't looking, and then he'd beat the hell out of them. Or at least that's what he wants to tell himself. These scenarios are much clearer when they're not actually happening.

"Ryan?"

Ryan hasn't heard Avery's question, and doesn't realize that Avery needs to know where they're going. He looks at his watch and realizes he told Alicia they'd drop by in about fifteen minutes.

"Make a left," he says.

He knows he should explain more to Avery, tell him who those guys were. But how can he explain when he can't understand it himself? He and Skylar used to play Little League together. They never had a single fight. But it's like one day half the guys in his grade decided it was fun to pick on Ryan. He wasn't even out then. Didn't even have blue hair. He just didn't want to be a part of their group, and that made him the group's enemy. But never like this. Never like what just happened. That wasn't taunting. That was an actual attack.

Avery wants it to be okay, wants to pretend it didn't happen. Ryan wants that, too. He's already nostalgic for the way they were fifteen minutes ago. But what just happened with Skylar is too big to let go.

Alicia senses something's off as soon as Ryan and Avery sit down at their table at the Kindling Café. Ryan introduces Avery first, then Alicia, Dez, Flora, and Miles . . . but he doesn't seem nearly as excited in person about having them all together as he was when he was texting. Alicia remembers Avery from the dance, but it's not like they got to talk or anything—as soon as he and Ryan connected, everyone else turned into extras in the scene.

This was supposed to be the chance for them to get to know each other. But Ryan isn't smiling . . . he's scowling. At first Alicia assumes it's because the date hasn't gone well, and Avery hasn't measured up to what Ryan had hoped he would be. But she knows if this were the case, Ryan wouldn't have brought him by at all. Also, there is a hope in Avery's eyes as he meets Ryan's friends. Avery wants this to work.

Alicia sends Ryan to the counter for coffee, because coffee deprivation can be a serious cause of surly moods. He asks Avery what he'd like, which is a good sign, but then insists Avery not join him, which is a mixed signal. Once Ryan's away from the table, Alicia asks Avery what they've done today, and he mentions pancakes and that abandoned mini-golf course, which wouldn't have been in Alicia's top twenty in terms of places to take a date. Avery says it was "wild" and then asks the rest of them what their favorite spots in town are. None of them can think of anything besides the café they're sitting in, although Flora advocates for a playground at their old elementary school until Miles reminds her it was torn down as a health hazard a few months ago.

"What're you talking about?" Ryan asks when he gets back to the table.

"Just telling embarrassing stories about you," Alicia answers.

This snaps Ryan out of his funk. At least for a second.

"No fair! I leave for ten seconds . . ."

"They weren't really—" Avery begins, but Alicia shushes him.

"Like, did Ryan tell you about his obsession with Pink?"

"Whoa, you're going *there*," Dez says.

Avery gestures up to his hair. "There's nothing wrong with pink."

Alicia shakes her head. "I'm not talking the color. I'm talking the *singer*."

"C'mon," Ryan says. Flora starts to hum "Raise Your Glass."

"Not that there's anything wrong with the singer, either. I love her. But there's love and then there's . . . obsession. She'd already been having hit songs for, what, a decade, but Ryan acted like he'd *discovered* her."

Ryan turns to Avery. "We're talking about sixth grade here."

"And part of seventh," Alicia corrects. "You know how I know that?"

Ryan clearly doesn't. But Dez goes, "OH, shiiiiiiiit."

Alicia sees it hit Ryan. His nostrils flare in that way they do when he's mad he doesn't control the universe and the behavior of everyone around him.

"Enough," he says.

Alicia turns so she's facing Avery as much as possible and Ryan as little as possible. "Seventh grade. Auditions for the musical. To make it fun, the chorus teacher says we can use karaoke backing tracks from YouTube. We just can't sing anything with sex or drugs or cursing in it. They say that to us about twenty times."

"Alicia, he doesn't need to hear this."

Alicia holds up her hand. "I'm talking here. So, they make it so anyone who wants to sit in the audience can— almost like a talent show. And we all know Ryan's going to do a Pink song because his locker is full of pictures of her and his notebook has her lyrics written all over it, the whole deal. There's a reason you can't get tattoos in seventh grade, right? Anyway, he even tells me he didn't choose 'Blow Me (One Last Kiss)' because it drops a curse. So I'm guessing he'll do 'Raise Your Glass' or one of the ballads. But no. He goes up there and he sings . . ."

She leaves it open for Ryan to fill in. He doesn't fill it in. So she finishes:

". . . 'U and Ur Hand.'"

"He didn't know what it was about," Flora says.

"Maybe he thought it was an Addams Family reference," Miles adds generously. "We were auditioning for the Addams Family musical."

Avery laughs.

Ryan does not.

Fine, Alicia thinks, changing the topic to talk about the time before they could drive when Miles's mom hit a mailbox after Miles freaked out over the radio station she was playing in the presence of his friends. While other people take up the thread, Alicia sees there's still something between Avery and Ryan, in both senses—something they share, and also something getting in the way. She also notices that Flora and Miles are liking Avery, acting like Avery's been a part of their group for a while. Dez is acting like he's never seen a trans boy before, which is just stupid. Alicia makes a note to talk to him about that later.

But first, it's time to figure out what happened.

It doesn't take much prying. When there's a pause in the storytelling, Alicia asks Ryan point-blank, "What happened to you two before you got here?"

Ryan immediately looks at Avery, who says, "I only told them where we went." Then Ryan sighs and explains that while they were at the golf course, Skyler and three of his assolytes came by and gave them shit. Everyone at the table's immediately sympathetic, muttering an almost endless list of synonyms for the word *jerk* to describe Skylar's crew.

Alicia hopes this will calm Ryan down, but he's still clutching his coffee cup so tight she's surprised it doesn't cave in.

"I really should have done something," he says. "Smashed up his truck. Called the police to report them trespassing. I mean, I guess it's not too late."

Alicia has never been a fan of macho bullshit. In fact, she thinks that most of the world's problems can be traced directly to macho bullshit. And she does not like hearing her best friend layering his own macho bullshit onto Skylar's usual macho bullshit.

"What do you mean, 'it's not too late'?" she asks.

"I mean, it's not like I don't know where he lives."

Alicia nods, then says, "Ryan, I get that you're mad. But I think you need to take it down a notch."

"Easy for you to say. You weren't there. Right?" With this, he looks to Avery for confirmation.

"I think you guys are much better company," Avery says, in a way that lets Alicia know that he's been trying to lead Ryan out of machobullshitopolis, too.

Poor Avery, Alicia thinks. She wants to assure him that Ryan isn't usually like this; only his parents and assholes like Skylar can set him off in this way. It's not who he is at heart. It's who he is when pushed.

There's also no real way to unwind him when he gets this coiled. You have to wait for the tension to ease, for the tangle to undo itself with time. So instead of challenging Ryan more or calling him on his macho bullshit in front of everyone else, which would only bring on the subset of macho bullshit known as defensiveness, Alicia asks Avery about his pink hair and how long he's had it, and then asks more questions about life in Marigold. Ryan is still plotting in his mind; she can tell. And she wishes there was a way to pull him aside, to remind him what this day was supposed to be about.

But that window doesn't appear, and Dez is starting to get itchy to do something else. She can only hope that time has done its job, and that watching Avery getting along with his friends has tipped Ryan off to how he should be behaving.

"What are you going to do now?" she asks him once the conversation's hit an ebb.

"I'm not sure," Ryan says.

But she can see it, clearly. The coil. It's still there.

"Is there anything *you* want to do?" Ryan asks when they get to Avery's car.

I want a do-over, Avery thinks. *I want the last two hours back.*

"It's your town," he says.

The funny-not-ha-ha thing is that two hours ago, he was nervous about meeting Ryan's friends. But with the possible exception of Staring Dez, they were all pretty cool, and certainly welcoming.

It's Ryan who's the problem.

"Do you mind if we go back to Footer's? I just want to drive past, to see if they're still there."

Avery wants to say that, yes, he does mind. But what will that get him, really? He silently complies as Ryan tells him to turn left, to turn right.

There it is again. The abandoned mini-golf course.

The truck is gone.

Avery can't tell if Ryan is disappointed or relieved. Maybe both.

"I think I know where they might be," he says. He tells Avery to pull out and make a left.

Avery makes it through two green lights. When a red

light stops them at the third intersection and Ryan says to take another left, Avery decides he's neither going to give in nor give up. He's going to give Ryan one last chance.

Instead of turning left, Avery shifts to the right lane and makes a right turn, pulling over into the parking lot of a law office.

"What are you doing?" Ryan asks.

If this is going to work, Avery knows, he has to be able to tell the truth.

So he tells the truth.

"You're ruining it," he says. "You have to stop now before you ruin it completely."

"Ruining it?" Ryan says. When he starts the first word, Avery can see he genuinely doesn't understand what Avery means. But by the time he hits the question mark, he does. So before Avery can reply, he says, "Oh. Yeah."

"I want to get the day back," Avery tells him.

"I wasn't the one who took it away," Ryan flatly replies.

I know that, Avery could say. They could get into a whole conversation about right and wrong, about fairness and anger. But Avery doesn't owe Ryan that conversation. Not at this point. Not yet. No, Avery needs the coil to unwind itself. Because if it doesn't this time, he knows it won't for all the other times ahead.

So all he says is "Please." To Ryan. To the universe.

The word hangs in the air, as if it's been rung on a bell.

Ryan hears it. He takes it in. Then he knocks the back

of his head into the passenger seat's headrest. After a few knocks, he turns and looks Avery in the eye.

"I'm sorry," he says. "Truly, I'm sorry. I'm such a dick."

Better, Avery thinks.

"It's okay," he says. "We haven't passed the point of no return."

Ryan shakes his head. "Yeah, but I almost put us there, didn't I?" His phone buzzes in his pocket, and he takes it out. When he sees the screen, he laughs. He shows it to Avery—a text from Alicia.

You're fucking this up, boy. Don't be a dick.

"Guess she liked you," Ryan says.

"I liked her," Avery says. "All of them."

"Even Dez?"

"Eighty percent."

Ryan nods. "Sounds about right. And where did I stand, two minutes ago?"

"Forty percent? Thirty-seven?"

"So what should we do? I want to get back up into the nineties."

Avery doesn't know much of what there is to do in Kindling, but there is one place he's sure will be better than here.

"Let's go get your aunt's boat," he says. "I want to head back to the water."

* * *

Ryan texts his aunt, who tells him to take the boat whenever he wants. It's warm enough that the river isn't touched by ice, but cold enough that there isn't another boat in sight. Avery offers to paddle, but Ryan asks him if it's okay if he paddles solo. He's still wound up, and paddling will help. Avery says that's fine.

Even though the boat is the same and the river takes the same shape, gives the same path, it doesn't feel the same as it did yesterday. Way back then, it felt like they were journeying into something together. Now it feels like they've already experienced some of the journey.

"It just makes me so mad," Ryan says. "The fact that they can be like that, and nothing will happen to them."

"I know," Avery tells him. "It's not fair at all."

"But it doesn't have anything to do with us," Ryan surprises Avery by saying next. He sounds as if he's almost convinced himself it's true, and saying it out loud will help solidify the conviction. "Nothing they say has anything to do with us."

"And now look what's happened to them," Avery ventures.

Ryan's confused. "What do you mean?"

"We didn't warn them about the thirteenth hole."

Now Ryan smiles. "Oh yeah. The thirteenth hole."

"The sharks . . ."

"The bears . . ."

"The piranha fountain . . ."

"The pop-up chain saws . . ."

"And that trapdoor, when you fall into a pit with no food, no water, and 'U and Ur Hand' playing over and over and over for days until you repent your full asshole life."

"I'm glad we didn't warn them about the thirteenth hole."

"Me too."

"And, Avery?"

"Yes?"

"I'm sorry again. Anger's its own trap, and I walked right into it when I should have been focusing on you instead."

"I understand."

They're facing each other in the boat. Now Avery stretches out his legs so they touch Ryan's like they did back in the pancake diner. Ryan leaves the paddle in the bottom of the canoe and leans forward so their hands can entwine and their lips can touch.

I don't want to mess this up, Ryan thinks.

Avery thinks, *I'm glad I didn't leave.*

Ryan leans back and resumes his rowing. He rows now like someone with nothing to prove. There's no rush. No need to be anywhere but the midst. He rows like someone who's learned that the key to floating merrily, merrily is to proceed gently . . . gently . . .

Where Do You Think You're Going?

(the eighth date)

"Where do you think you're going?" Ryan's father asked as Ryan headed off to meet Avery for their date at the Greek restaurant. Ryan was turning the knob on the front door, ten seconds away from being gone.

"I'm going out," Ryan nonexplained.

"Get back in here," his father ordered.

Ryan let go of the doorknob, faced his parents. He felt stupid because he still had his tie in his hand.

"You said I wasn't grounded," he reminded them. "I made plans."

"What plans?" his mother asked. So this was going to be a tag-team effort.

Is that any of your business? he wanted to reply. But where would that get him?

Where would any answer get him?

He decided to say, "I'm driving to Hollis to have dinner with my boyfriend."

150

He knew he was plunging deep into the gray area here. He knew his parents would ground him if he lied. But maybe they wouldn't ground him for having a boyfriend.

"No," his father said.

"What do you mean, no? That I can't possibly have a boyfriend I'm meeting in Hollis?"

"I mean, no, you can't go."

Ryan was not going to abandon Avery, not for this reason.

Trying to stay as calm as possible, he said, "Okay, it's way too late for you to tell me that. When I was grounded, I followed those rules. When I was no longer grounded, I followed *those* rules. Which include me being able to go out on a Saturday night if I want."

Look at me, he wanted to say. *I am wearing a button-down shirt. I polished my shoes. I tried for ten minutes to tie a tie, and now I'm holding it so I can try again in the truck. If you really look, you'll see how much this means to me. You'll see how serious I am.*

But they didn't see. They refused to see. All they could wrap their minds around was the fact of him leaving, not the why.

"Not this time, Ryan," his mom decided. "Not tonight. We can talk about next weekend."

Ryan reached for the doorknob again.

"No," he told them. "I made a date, and I am keeping that date. Avery is going to be waiting for me. I have to go."

In response, his father deployed his most threatening voice. "Don't you dare walk out that door."

Ryan's response to that voice is always like an allergic reaction. Instant irritation. Immediate inflammation.

"Or what?" he taunted. "You'll make my life miserable? Well, guess what—you've already aced that one! You know me about as well as this door knows me. But you know what? I like the door more. Because watch—the door's going to let me leave."

He could sense his father about to jump forward. But Ryan was quicker than that. He was quicker as he got through the door and slammed it behind him. He was quicker as he got in his truck and sped out of the driveway. The radio was already primed to blast; he couldn't hear what, if anything, his parents were yelling after him.

He got in his truck and drove.

He told himself he'd go see Avery, and deal with the rest of it later.

When he got home, the door was bolted. He didn't have the key to unlock it.

He checked his texts. There was one from his mom, telling him to ring the bell.

So they *weren't* locking him out. They just wanted him to have to wake them up to get back in. They probably had their lecture waiting on index cards.

He considered sleeping in his truck. But he had work the next day. He needed sleep. He needed to shower.

What he didn't need was that lecture.

When they opened the door, he pushed right through. They weren't expecting that. He ran to his room, locked the door. His father pounded. They told him he was acting like a baby. Exact words: *like a baby*. But eventually they were the ones who wore themselves out.

Ryan knew they weren't going to knock down the door. He knew he was safe.

But he still slept with his car keys under his pillow and got out of there before they woke up.

Now he's at work, a slow Sunday morning at the grocery. Avery is texting to see how he's doing. He tells the truth, that he had to sneak out of his own house to avoid a blowup.

Your blowup or theirs? Avery asks.

Unclear, Ryan replies.

Luckily Ryan doesn't have checkout duty today, just stocking the shelves. He knows he's not supposed to look at his phone while he's doing this, but the Sunday manager doesn't really mind as long as the work gets done.

Hey, boy, Avery texts. *What U stockin'?*

Cans of tomato soup.

Mmmm. Savory.

Cups of Greek yogurt.

Stir it up, boy. STIR IT UP.

Boxes of Cheez-Its.

Rub off all over my fingers. ☺

There are ten- or fifteen-minute intervals between these

exchanges, but whenever Ryan switches an aisle and taps out an update, Avery has a response in seconds.

Shouldn't you be studying? Ryan asks before opening a box of cinnamon swirl loaves.

I am. The unpacking habits of the blue-haired grocery worker. This is AP-level stuff. (A&P-level?)

Seriously. It's okay if you need to go.

Going is the last thing I need, thankyouverymuch.

Strangely, this sentence hits Ryan sideways, not in the way it was meant. He imagines Avery in his bedroom, his parents bringing him snacks and cheering him on. Of course Avery has no need for going. Of course he's happy where he is.

This is the imbalance. Avery is making Ryan happy, but he's the only thing making Ryan happy. Avery has plenty of other things to make him happy.

Still, that's not a reason to stop the conversation.

Cinnamon swirl bread.

It doesn't take three seconds before Avery replies, *Slather me in cream cheese and roll me up.*

Ryan smiles, and also wishes he didn't have to feel so grateful for the smile.

He texts his mom to say he won't be home for dinner. She texts back to thank him for letting her know. He works late, then grabs some food at McDonald's. There aren't any texts from Avery because, Ryan's sure, he's having dinner with his parents.

The problem with McDonald's is that he's done with dinner in ten minutes. He thinks about going to see a movie or maybe dropping by Aunt Caitlin's. But he's also sleepy and doesn't want to be a zombie in school tomorrow.

So he heads home. The benefit is that his parents are eating in the kitchen when he comes in.

"I'm going to bed!" he yells as he rushes up the stairs.

He hears a chair pushed back from the table, then his mom saying, "Just let him go."

He locks the door again. Puts his car keys under his pillow. Sits in bed and tries to read.

His phone comes alive next to him. Avery, finally free.

The message, though, is the opposite of free.

It's going to be a crazy week, with exams and the play. I probably won't get to answer as quickly. But I know I'll be seeing you for the show Friday. I'll owe you a week's worth of affection. ☺

Ryan responds, *I understand.*

And he *does* understand. Even though it will make the week harder. He's definitely feeling withdrawal, but the saving grace is that he knows it's not from Avery withdrawing.

He tries to focus on his own schoolwork, his own friends. At lunch on Monday he tells everyone about the date and his parents' reaction. Alicia is angry on his behalf, and he knows she can relate to some extent. Dez, whose parents let him do whatever he wants as long as he gets good grades, is more fixated on the date than the parent trouble.

"Wow, it's like you're really serious with them. They're a them, right?"

"No," Ryan says. "Avery's he/him. I've told you this before."

Dez raises his hands. "Okay, okay! *Sorry.*"

Ryan knows this doesn't come close to what Avery has to deal with, but it's a glimpse. He has the urge to pour Dez's soup over his head.

"Why are you such an asshole?" Alicia says. "Seriously. What the fuck?"

Dez looks to Flora and Miles for help. None arrives.

"He's my boyfriend," Ryan says quietly. "Do you have a problem with that, Dez?"

"Not at all! I was just trying to be respectful."

Ryan doesn't want to eat anymore. Not here.

Alicia tries to smooth things over. "I think it has to be serious, if he got you to wear a tie. I don't think I've ever seen you wear a tie."

Miles, his mouth full of chocolate milk, shakes his head. Then, after swallowing, he says, "The seventh-grade assembly! When he had to give the speech!"

Jesus. Right back to The Bad Year. Only Alicia knows how truly bad a year that was.

Miles looks at him now. "You still remember that speech?"

"Nope," Ryan says. "Not even a little."

"Too bad," Miles says, picking up his chocolate milk. "I remember it being a good speech. Woulda loved to hear it again."

Even as he's having the conversation, Ryan wants to be telling Avery about it. Wants to be explaining what it means.

But no text could convey that.

Ryan works more hours after school than usual, because he's planning to take so much of the weekend off. It also helps him avoid his parents.

Tortilla chips, he texts Avery.

It takes four hours before he gets the reply:

They're nacho problem.

On Wednesday after his shift is done, he goes to see Aunt Caitlin. She looks tired from her own day at work. But she brightens up when she sees him.

"The hair looks good, if I do say so myself," she says. "How'd the date go?"

They sit down on the old lime-green couch and he tells her what happened with Avery (the good part), and then what happened with his parents (the bad part).

"Oh, Ryan," Caitlin says when he's done.

"Why are they so awful?" he asks her.

"They're not awful," she says. Before he can argue, she puts her hand up. "No—listen to me. I have friends who grew up with awful. Your parents are wrong a lot of the time, but they're not awful."

"But why are they like this?" Ryan asks. "You've met Avery—does he seem scary to you?"

Caitlin smiles. "No."

"So why won't they let me see him? What are they so afraid of?"

Caitlin's smile disappears. Carefully, she asks, "Do you really want me to answer that?"

"Of course I do."

"Okay. But hear me out, okay? I'm not saying they're in the right here. Do you understand that?"

"Yes."

"So I'm not trying to justify the way they are. But there are reasons."

"I'm all ears."

Caitlin pulls back a little. The edge in Ryan's tone is a warning. He's not going to understand because he won't want to understand. At the same time, he is sixteen years old. He should know this.

"They're scared, Ryan."

"Why? Because I'm gay?"

"No," Caitlin says. "Because it wasn't that long ago that you were hurting yourself."

* * *

There it is again. The Bad Year.

Caitlin goes on. "I know it was harder for you, and I know it was scarier for you. But it was still hard and scary for the rest of us."

Ryan pulls back in shock. "What are you talking about?"

"We knew, Ryan. I'm telling you we knew a lot more than you thought we knew."

Seventh grade. He knew he was gay, but had no intention of telling his parents. Only his friends. That wasn't the problem. The problem was that he got it in his head—from reality shows, from websites, from surreptitiously watched porn—what a gay body should look like. And he thought his thirteen-year-old body could become that, could withstand whatever needed to be done to it. He tried working out. Running in layers of clothing, so he'd sweat more. Eating protein shakes instead of food.

It didn't make him a sex god. It made him sick and exhausted.

His parents didn't notice. Or if they did notice, they chalked it up to "adolescence," a too-easy excuse for all kinds of things. Talking back. Closing off. Eating very little at dinner as a way of being "difficult."

One of his teachers noticed and sent him to the school nurse—Nurse Tiernan, the sweetest man to ever walk the earth. It took maybe five minutes for Nurse Tiernan to figure everything out. What Ryan was doing, and why.

"We come in all shapes and sizes," Nurse Tiernan told Ryan.

Ryan wasn't ready to accept the *we*. Or even the premise. Because if Nurse Tiernan was doing such a great job being gay, why was he stuck as a nurse in a middle school and not living his best gay life in some big gay city?

He didn't say this to Nurse Tiernan. But his resistance was still noted.

Nurse Tiernan brought in Ms. Simon, Ryan's guidance counselor.

Ryan thought he had leverage, so he applied it; he told them he'd get help, and work to get better . . . as long as nobody else knew about it. Especially not his parents.

They agreed. Nurse Tiernan had a friend who was a therapist and was willing to make a "house call" at the school. So once a week for six weeks, Ryan missed gym in order to talk to Dr. Lindsay. Ryan realized he had been experimenting with what he perceived as self-improvement without really committing to it. Now, with the therapist's help, he abandoned it completely. Dr. Lindsay helped him focus on the coming-out part (which he called "inviting in"). Eventually, Ryan was ready to invite Caitlin in. Then she helped him with his parents. They weren't nearly as happy about the invitation.

* * *

"The school let them know," Caitlin tells him now. "They had to. But everyone agreed that if going through the school was working best for you, we'd go along with it."

"So you're telling me that when I first told you I was gay . . . you already knew?"

"Yes. We also knew that you'd been hurting yourself, with the disordered eating and exercise. *And* we knew you'd gotten better. I understood that it was more of a wobble than a fall. But your parents—they felt you'd gone down a bad path while they hadn't been looking. And I think they're still worried that you're on that path, even though by now it's clear you're on a different path, the one you were meant to be on. Again, I'm not trying to make excuses for them. I'm just trying to explain to you why they might be scared. The unknown is always scary, and when your kid is involved, it's exponentially scarier."

More than anything, Ryan knows that Aunt Caitlin loves him. And it takes every ounce of this knowledge to keep him on the couch, to keep him from screaming, to keep him from sobbing. The story of his life for the past three years hasn't been the true story. He hasn't known the true story of his own life.

What he says next surprises even him.

"Why can't I just live here?" he asks, the scream and the sob combining into a plea. "Why can't I just live with you?"

Caitlin opens her arms for a hug, and he gives in to it.

"Your body is longer than this couch," she murmurs to him. "And I don't think you want to be the guy in high school who shares a bed with his old aunt."

"I wouldn't mind," he whispers, choked up.

"If it comes to that, then so be it," she says, holding tight. "But it shouldn't come to that."

They stay there for a while. Finally, it's Ryan who pulls back, who continues the conversation.

"I appreciate you telling me," he says.

"I promise, there's nothing else I'm hiding. No other big reveals."

"So my parents really are my parents? Not you?"

Caitlin snort-laughs. "'Fraid so."

Ryan turns serious again. "Please don't tell them you told me, okay? If I want them to know we had this conversation, I'll tell them."

Caitlin nods.

"Thank you. And, Caitlin?"

"Yes, Ryan?"

"You know I'd never hurt myself now. Right?"

"I do know that. But it's still good to hear it."

"I promise. That was a bad year but it already feels like another life. I mean, I only met Avery a few weeks ago and *that* feels like years."

"Good years?"

Ryan smiles. "Yeah, good years."

* * *

I am going to have so much to tell you, Ryan texts Avery as soon as he gets into the truck.

I can't wait, Avery immediately replies.

Once again, he makes it to his room before his parents can catch him. He really doesn't want to talk to them now.

There's knocking on his door. His father saying he's acting like a brat and better open up. His mother saying she made dessert and kept some for him. Doesn't he want some dessert?

"The bribery doesn't work if the threats come first," Ryan tells the door.

Then, two hours later, he makes a stupid mistake. He's too loud going to the bathroom, and can't lock his bedroom door from the outside. So his room is unguarded, and when he comes back in his pajamas, his father is waiting.

"We're going to talk, whether you like it or not," his father says. "This kind of behavior will not be tolerated in this home."

"Get out of my room," Ryan says, even though he knows it will only make things worse. Then he screams it, "GET OUT OF MY ROOM!"

He clears the doorway for his father. He points to it. Insists.

"I only want to talk," his father says.

"There's nothing to talk about. I'm fine. I'm totally fine. I just need you out of my room right now."

His mom appears in the hallway, asking what's going on.

"Tell him to get out of my room," Ryan appeals to her. "I want to go to sleep. Tell him to get out."

"Okay," she says. Then she turns to her husband. "Let's do this tomorrow. He needs sleep."

"Jesus Christ," Ryan's father says. Ryan half expects him to say, *Don't think you've gotten away with this!* like an archvillain in a comic book. Or maybe that's something the hero says to the archvillain.

The moment his dad is through the door, he closes and locks it. But he still wakes up at least a dozen times during the night, afraid it's come unlocked.

Even the keys beneath his pillow aren't a comfort.

One more day, Ryan texts Avery the next morning.

Three exams, one dress rehearsal, and one more day, Avery replies a few minutes later.

"I want to see Avery's play!" Alicia says when Ryan tells her his weekend plans.

"Too bad," he replies. "It's all sold out!"

"I'm serious," she says, hitting him on the arm.

"I know. And I appreciate that. But I want some alone time with him."

"You're just afraid his parents will like me more."

"And that," Ryan concedes. "Definitely that."

Oreos, he texts that afternoon, even though he knows Avery's probably in the middle of his dress rehearsal and won't have his phone out like in regular rehearsal.

Frozen pizzas.

Sparkling water.

"Ryan?"

Ryan looks up from his phone, and there's his mother, stalking him in aisle three.

"What are you doing here?" he asks. She doesn't have a cart or any groceries.

"I need to talk to you."

"Mom, I'm working."

She looks at the phone in his hand. "Really?"

He puts his phone in his pocket and starts taking the bottles of Pellegrino out of their boxes, lining them on the shelf so they face perfectly forward.

She doesn't take the hint. "This can't continue," she says. "You storming in every night, shutting yourself in your room. Your father wants to take the lock off your door, but I told him, no, that's not the way to handle this."

Ryan wants to say, *Yeah, why bother changing the lock when he'll only lie in wait for me to take a bathroom break?*

His mom keeps talking. "I know you're not a child, but you're behaving like a child. If you want to be given independence, you have to earn it. And this is not the way to earn it."

"Mom," Ryan says as calmly as he can, "the thing I'm

trying to earn right now is a paycheck, and they're not paying me to talk to you. Can you please go before my manager sees?"

His mother takes one of the Pellegrino bottles off the shelf and holds it by the neck. "I'll say I'm a customer, and that you've helped me."

"Mom, that's not my point."

"Ryan. I'm not leaving without a promise from you that this behavior will stop. We don't want to ground you again, but we will."

"Of course you will."

"What does that mean?"

Ryan stops stocking the shelves and looks at her hard. "Are you serious? What I mean is that you are incapable of understanding that the way to help me, the way to be a half-decent parent, isn't to confine me in the house but to actually let me do the completely nondestructive things I want to do outside of the house. You're acting like I'm going out and getting arrested. When what I'm really doing is . . . wait for it . . . going on dates with a boy I really like."

This is the most he's said to her in what feels like years. He's put it all out for her. And how does she respond?

"I'm not sure about this boy you're going on dates with, if this is the way you act."

Ryan shakes his head. "Seriously?"

"See it through my eyes, Ryan. Before you met this boy, you weren't disappearing. You weren't locking your door every night. You weren't angry all the time."

"First off, I *was* angry all the time. And second, these days I'm only angry around you. Not when I'm with him."

"I just don't know what kind of influence he is. That's what I'm saying."

Ryan wants to kick over the remaining boxes, or run his arm over the shelves to make all the bottles he's so carefully placed crash to the floor. But he wants to keep his job. He wants to be responsible.

He isn't going to say another word to her. Not a single word. But then she says, "What? Tell me." And he thinks, *Fine. Enough.*

"You think Caitlin is a bad influence. You think Alicia is a bad influence. And now you think Avery is a bad influence. Why is it that you think everyone who might possibly love me is a bad influence? What could that possibly mean?"

"*We* love you, Ryan."

Ryan pauses, then says, "I'm sure you think you do."

He doesn't mean it as a cut-down. He actually thinks he's been generous, conceding that in their own twisted way his parents think what they feel is love. But his mom looks for a second like she's lost her breath. The bottle in her hand almost comes loose. Then she recovers and puts it back on the shelf.

"You are to come home as soon as your shift is over," she tells him evenly. "You are going to sit down to dinner with your father and me. We are not going to indulge your sulky behavior anymore. And if you cannot bother to listen to us, you will be grounded again. You really don't have to do this, Ryan. Whatever this is."

Ryan realizes there are other people in the aisle, and they are looking at him strangely, critically. They're wondering who this jerk of an employee is, to make his mom tear up in the middle of the grocery store.

He doesn't care enough for it to really be called caring. He turns his back to all of them, returns to the shelves. He works hard until the end of his shift.

It's only then he allows himself to realize:

I can't go home.

He could go to Caitlin's. Or Alicia's. Or even Miles's, if he had to.

But the thing is, his parents would find him in those places.

And if they find him, his keys will end up in their possession, and he'll never be able to see Avery's play.

So he texts Avery and asks, *How do you feel about me coming a night early?*

He doesn't expect an immediate response.

He starts driving toward Avery anyway.

As he drives, he tries to lose himself in music and the road. He makes promises to himself that he won't let his parents get to him, and breaks these promises immediately with the same fervor with which he made them. He assures himself that Avery will be welcoming, that this isn't too much drama to be bringing to his door. Then he succumbs to doubt and makes the music louder.

He can't turn off his phone, because he wants to see if Avery responds. So he has to sit there as his phone rings, his mom calling. And as it rings again, and again. He sees she's left messages, but he doesn't listen to them. She texts him and he doesn't check those, either. He's driving. He can already hear himself telling her, *I was driving—you don't want me texting while I'm driving, do you?*

He doesn't check when he stops driving, either. He's about a half-hour short of Avery's town, and since Avery's clearly still rehearsing, Ryan goes to a Target, because he's going to need some clothes for tomorrow, and maybe the next day. Also, a toothbrush.

It's only as he's walking the Target aisles that Ryan truly feels like he's making some kind of break from home. Knowing he has enough money in his account to pay for these things. Knowing he's in control of his own time. His actions feel purely his own.

He finds three shirts he likes, and decides to buy all three. He almost changes into one of them once he's back in the truck, just for it to feel more like a new start.

When he gets to Marigold, it's after nine, and there's still no word from Avery. If Avery hadn't been telling him how much they've been needing rehearsal this week, Ryan might be a little more worried. Instead of driving to Avery's house, he heads to Avery's school. Since there aren't that many cars left in the parking lot, Avery's is easy to spot.

Ryan pulls in a few spaces over. He goes to text Avery to say *I'm here*, but then he hesitates. What if Avery saw his earlier text and didn't know what to do with it? What if now's a bad time for Ryan to be here, after all? Ryan's fears force him to leave some margin for this potential error. Odds are that Avery will look at his phone before he leaves the building. So if he tells Ryan it's not a good idea, Ryan will be out of the parking lot before Avery can notice him there.

That's the plan Ryan hopes he won't have to use.

It's nearly ten o'clock when people start exiting the building, heading to their cars.

Ryan's phone lights up.

I'm so sorry—I was in rehearsal, no phones allowed. Are you okay?

Ryan texts back, *I am.*

Were you serious about coming tonight? Is it too late?

It's not too late, Ryan replies. Then he decides to risk it and types, *I'm outside.*

Oh! I'll be in the parking lot in three minutes.

Great, Ryan types. But he's still worried that it isn't, in fact, great. An "Oh!" can be an expression of pleasure. But it can also be one of surprise.

Ryan himself goes *Oh!* when he sees Avery leaving the school with someone who looks like his grandmother. Ryan assumes it must be a teacher helping out with the costumes. Then they get closer and he sees that, no, it's just a kid dressed like an old lady.

Ryan steps out of his truck, and when they get to him, Avery says, "Ryan, you remember Pope—they were with me at the dance?"

"Of course," Ryan says, even though the costume is making Pope very hard to place. "Nice to see you, Pope."

"Ooh, likewise," Pope says. "Don't mind my current look. The dress isn't quite fitting the way I want it to, so I'm going to ask my parent to take in some seams before tomorrow's performance."

"I have to drive Pope home," Avery explains. "Want to follow behind, and then we can get to my house at the same time?"

"Sounds good." Ryan can't tell if Avery's happy to see him, and wonders if there are things he isn't saying because there's an audience.

"I'm happy to ride with Ryan," Pope volunteers. "Get to know him a little better."

Avery quickly intervenes. "That's all right, Mrs. Stranglehold. You can come with me."

"A pity," Pope sighs. But they go with Avery in the end.

* * *

It's as Ryan follows Avery's taillights that the doubts really begin to chime. Not just worries about whether Avery wants him here. No, the underlying worry, too: What if no one wants him? What if, wherever he goes, he'll always be an inconvenience?

When Avery drops Pope off, Ryan half expects them to waddle over in their old-lady clogs to tell him his timing is poor, his manners worse, his expectations atrocious. But instead, shoes off, they head straight for the front door. Not even a wave in Ryan's direction. It's like he isn't there.

By the time they get to Avery's house, Ryan is ready to turn around. Text Avery later to say he understands how foolish he was being.

As it happens, Avery texts him first.

Don't worry. My parents know you're coming. It's all good.

Ryan pulls his truck in behind Avery's car. Steps out and grabs his Target bag from the passenger seat.

"Well, this is a nice twist to the evening," Avery says, smiling. Then he pulls Ryan into a hug.

Ryan lets go of the bag, uses both hands to hug Avery back. He isn't intending to get all emotional, but Avery's

172

welcome sends a signal to his brain, a permission that it manages to understand. Because all of a sudden the emotions he's been keeping in are coming out, and he's actually gasping right there in Avery's arms, tearing up and gasping.

"It's okay," Avery says. "It's all okay. You're here now."

Avery's parents are waiting when they get inside. They are welcoming to Ryan, but they also seem much more confused than last time.

They've barely said their hellos—they're still in the front hallway—when Ryan starts to tell them what's happening. He feels he owes them an explanation. He feels they need to know he doesn't think he can just sleep over without some explanation. Avery needs to know this, too, that he wouldn't be crashing the night before Avery's exams without a reason. And also, in a lot of ways, the explanation is for himself, too. Like when you dump out the contents of your backpack, clear it all out and line everything up on the floor so you can see what you've stuffed inside and then decide what can be thrown out, what can be put away, and what should still be carried around.

He tells Avery's parents some of the things Avery already knows, like how he was grounded after his last visit on the snow day, like the fact that he wasn't even allowed to see his aunt, who's the one person in town who really cares about him. Then he tells them all the things he hasn't been telling Avery this week, not wanting to throw anything his way that would interfere with studying or rehearsing. The arguments with his parents. His mom's visit to the grocery store. Her threat.

"I know I shouldn't have run off," he tells them. "I know I should have tried to go there and make it right. But I felt there was no way that was going to happen, that I'd only get trapped there again and I'd miss Avery's play, which I've been looking forward to so, so much. My brain said, 'Go there, Ryan. Go there.'"

He stops then, because he doesn't know what comes next.

Avery hugs him again, tells him, "It's okay. Everything's okay." And it makes Ryan happy, because it's what he needs. And it makes Ryan sad, because it's not something that would ever be able to happen in front of his own parents.

"Why don't we go in the kitchen and sit down?" Avery's dad says. "It sounds like you didn't have dinner, Ryan, and I doubt Avery got much sustenance while rehearsing. How about I make you some grilled cheese sandwiches? Are you a Swiss guy, a cheddar guy, or an American guy, Ryan?"

"Dad!" Avery exclaims in mock outrage. "Such personal questions!"

"I haven't even gotten to the bread yet," Avery's dad replies. "That's when I *really* get to measure a person's character."

"Boys," Avery's mom says, intimating that now might not be the time. But Ryan is grateful to feel some of the heaviness around him lift.

"Cheddar cheese. Rye bread, if you have it. And orange juice, if it gets to that," he answers.

Everyone laughs.

As they sit at the table over grilled cheese sandwiches, Avery's parents don't ask Ryan too many more questions. Instead they ask Avery about the play, about the final rehearsal, about what time they should get to the show tomorrow. They don't ask Ryan about school tomorrow. They don't assume he's going to leave after he's done with his grilled cheese. At one point, as the plates are being cleared and a chain of yawns spreads from person to person, Avery's mom tells Ryan he needs to text his parents and let them know where he is.

I'm at Avery's, he texts. *I'm fine.*

Then he turns off his phone.

Ryan isn't surprised when Avery says, "I'll go get the sheets for the sofa. . . . I think it's probably best if we each sleep solo tonight." He would love nothing more than to hold and be held all night . . . but he knows that would be pushing it.

So he waits in the family room as Avery heads to the linen closet. Both of Avery's parents poke their heads in to wish Ryan a goodnight. They tell him they'll be leaving around the same time as Avery tomorrow, and Ryan should help himself to whatever's in the kitchen. They'll be back by five, and then they'll all get some dinner before the play.

"That's great," Ryan says. "Thank you."

Avery has his arms full of pillows, sheets, and towels when he sees his parents leave the doorway of the family room. The three of them meet about halfway down the hallway.

"The poor kid," Avery's dad says.

Then Avery's mom looks at Avery with a slight tilt to her head and tells him, "You know this is only a temporary solution, right? We can grant him asylum here for the weekend, but he'll need to go back home Sunday, after the cast party. He can't skip school altogether. Maybe there's someone else there he can stay with?"

"His aunt," Avery says. "Maybe."

"Okay. If you need our help in having that conversation, let us know. He's always welcome here, but . . ."

"No, I get it," Avery says. "I really appreciate you doing this."

"Make sure you get some sleep," Avery's dad says, patting him on the shoulder. "Big day tomorrow."

Although he's stayed here before, Ryan can't help the feeling that he doesn't really know the house at all . . . and that the house doesn't know him, either. He doesn't feel like a trespasser—he understands now that he's welcome. But he feels more like a visitor than a boyfriend. He wonders when it is that you cross that line, and stop being a guest in someone else's life.

When Avery returns, Ryan laughs because Avery's face is barely visible over the stack of pillows and sheets and towels he's holding.

"Here, let me help you," Ryan says, but Avery just tilts his arms like the back of a garbage truck and everything falls beside the couch.

"Ta-da!" Avery sings.

Ryan smiles . . . but then he shakes his head and says, "I'm sorry this isn't much of a date. My timing couldn't be worse."

"What, you don't consider having grilled cheese with my parents to be a date?"

"In some cultures, maybe? But not sure about ours."

"Hmmm." Avery makes a show of thinking. "I have an idea. Let me take you somewhere on a date."

Before Ryan can ask whether he'll need to put his shoes back on, Avery is removing the big cushions from the couch and standing them up to make an L on the floor, touching one of the couch's arms. Then he takes the blanket and drapes it over the U shape the cushions and the couch make. He pulls two pillows from the linen pile and scoots them into the enclosure he's made.

"What's that?" Ryan asks.

"It's my hiding place. Let's go."

Avery crawls in, and Ryan follows. The red-blanket ceiling

is too low to allow them to sit up, and Ryan's legs are a little too long to fit entirely inside. So they put the pillows under their heads and lie there like they're sharing a single bed. Avery stares up as the light breaks through the blanket in places, fabric starshine. Ryan is on his side, watching as Avery gazes.

"It's great," Ryan says. "Although maybe not the most subtle hiding place?"

"Oh," Avery says, "that's where the invisibility powder comes in. There's some right by your elbow."

"Of course." Ryan reaches over and throws some invisibility powder in the air. "Did I do that right?"

"Perfectly."

"And when you used the invisibility powder as a kid, your parents weren't able to find you?"

"Um . . . most of the time. It depended on why I was using the hiding place."

"I honestly can't imagine my parents going along with that. Respecting a hiding place."

"Mine are good that way. And in general," Avery says. "But there were still plenty of reasons for me to need a hiding place."

Ryan finds this hard to believe. "Like what?" he challenges.

Now Avery turns to him. "I mean, some stupid things. My parents were always telling me not to run through the halls, but there wasn't anything I loved more than sliding around in my socks, so I kept doing it—and, sure enough, one time I slammed into the wall hard enough to make the picture that was hanging there fall. The glass of the frame just exploded. I was probably seven or eight—I had no perspective whatsoever. I thought I'd be sent to jail. So I ran in here, built the hiding place, and waited."

"I imagine the invisibility powder didn't work well then?"

"It did for a time. I think my parents let me calm down a little before talking to me about what had happened. I was probably more upset than they were."

"So many things seem like the end of the world when they're not."

"Exactly. And even with the more serious things . . . I know I told you my parents were cool about the whole gender thing, and they were. But that doesn't mean there weren't moments when it was hard. I get it now—kids change their minds all the time about things, so when your kid says, 'I'm a boy and you need to help me get my body to match that,' there has to be uncertainty. They never expressed it to me outright, but my dad, especially, was always full of questions. Most of all, 'Are you sure?' And honestly, I was always pretty sure. Like, it was obvious to me. But I still needed to come here sometimes as they debated it, as they decided whether *my* choice was going to be *their* choice. Which didn't feel fair to me at all, that it had to be both. I mean, it all worked out. But I didn't always want to be present for the deliberations, because they only frustrated me or, worse, made me feel like it was possible they'd say no, and I'd be stuck."

"Again, I'd say you're lucky you have your parents and not mine," Ryan says.

"You never know. When I get my first tattoo, I think it's going to be this quote from Virginia Euwer Wolff's book *True Believer*—'We will rise to the occasion, which is life.' Maybe your parents would have risen to the occasion."

Ryan knows Avery wants him to agree here. And who knows? While they weren't thrilled about him being gay, they didn't try to stop it, either. But Ryan's still trying to figure out what to make of what Aunt Caitlin told him. Was his parents' silence a respect for his desire for privacy? Or were they just happy that it was the school nurse and counselor who had to deal with it, not them?

"You're not allowed to hide within the hiding place," Avery says, drawing Ryan back from his thoughts. "What's on your mind?"

"I'm just very happy to be here," Ryan replies.

Avery reaches out and pulls Ryan closer. Soon they're kissing quietly in the hiding place, kissing like their kisses are a secret they're sharing.

Ryan loses track of time, but Avery doesn't. After they've been making out for about fifteen minutes, he pulls back and says, "I really should go to sleep."

"I know, I know," Ryan says, nestling into his pillow. He's forgotten that this isn't where he's supposed to sleep.

Avery looks at him again in the blanket starlight.

"What?" Ryan asks.

"I just want to figure out how to help you," Avery answers. "That's all."

It's like Avery's words are a key to a lock Ryan didn't

know was inside him. And when it turns, emotions come out. Powerful emotions. Because Ryan realizes this: He isn't used to a boy wanting so wholly to tell him the truth, to be on his side.

"I appreciate that," he says, trying to control the mix of gratitude and confusion in his voice, trying not to overwhelm Avery with how overwhelmed he feels. "I appreciate you taking me in. I appreciate you inviting me to see your show. I appreciate you building me a hiding place. I appreciate all of it."

"You deserve nothing less," Avery tells him. Then they hug again, and kiss again, until tomorrow's obligations once more intrude.

Avery is the first to slide out of the hiding place. Reluctantly, Ryan leaves, too. He helps Avery disassemble the fortress, turning the sofa back into a sofa and then into a bed. Avery helps him unwrap his toiletries, and they go brush their teeth together.

When they're done, Avery says, "I probably won't see you in the morning. I have to leave here before seven. And I don't want to see how you'd react if I woke you up that early to say a quick goodbye."

"You could."

"I won't. Nor should you ever, ever do that for me."

"Got it."

They share a goodnight kiss. Then they say the words they can usually only text.

"Sweet dreams."

"Sweet dreams."

Ryan tiptoes down the hallway, no idea if Avery's parents are still awake or can be easily awakened. Back on the sofa, he can't help but feel he's still in a place that Avery's built, a shelter offered, an enclosure with soft walls. Even though they're not in the same room, Ryan imagines Avery breathing beside him. It feels better to be closer to him. So much better to be so much closer.

This must be what it's like to fall in love, he thinks.

Then he corrects himself.

No.

This must be what it's like to be in love.

River, Be My Friend

(the second date)

Ryan hasn't experienced this since he was a Santa-believing kid on Christmas Eve. But the symptoms are clear, as is the cause.

He is too excited to go to sleep.

This boy he's just met—Avery—only left a few hours ago.

And in a few more hours, he'll be back.

Date number two.

When he left the dance, he wanted to call right away, continue the conversation even though Avery was driving. He cautioned himself to be cool, to take it slow . . . but that only lasted two hours, tops. He called. And when he heard Avery say hello on the other end, it was a lifting of clouds, a power surge within his nervous system. How else to explain why he invited Avery back to Kindling the next day? And Avery's response—so welcoming, so eager.

"I warn you," Ryan said. "There isn't much to do here."

Then he went on and on about how little there was. He could've gone on even more, but Avery interrupted and said, "As long as you're there, it will be enough."

Who says that?

More specifically: Who says that *to Ryan?*

Nobody. Ryan is positive of this.

The unreal part isn't that he's found someone awesome.

The unreal part is that someone awesome wants to see him again.

This is what keeps him up most of the night: He has no idea what he did right at the prom, and because he can't figure that out, he doesn't know how to do it again. He is sure he'll be a disappointment to Avery, because at heart he believes he's been a disappointment to everyone else, including himself. It doesn't occur to him to question why something to get excited about also provides a reason to beat himself up. The two things should be separable, but in his mind they aren't.

The only reason he invited Avery back to Kindling was because there was no way he could invite himself over to Avery's town. But now he's stuck, so stuck, because there's nothing at all about Kindling he wants to share.

He can feel his heart beating faster, and knows it isn't love but fear stomping on the accelerator.

Calm down, he tells himself. *You have to calm down.*

Like other nights when he can't sleep, he imagines himself away from his bed. He imagines himself floating on his back, riding slowly down a river. He feels his limbs untense.

He feels his mind getting control of his heart. He rides it along and along . . . and there, right before he finally falls asleep, he realizes what they're going to do.

Avery drives to Kindling the next morning with the fervor of someone retracing his steps to pick up something important he's left behind. Only it's not his wallet he's going back to get, or a suitcase. No, it feels a little like his future fell out of his pocket as he was driving away last night, and now he needs to go back to reclaim it.

On one level, he feels ridiculous, upending his Sunday to see a boy he's only just met. There's homework he needs to do. There are lines he's supposed to be learning for tomorrow's rehearsal. He isn't being responsible at all.

But, truly, he doesn't care about any of that.

He is trying desperately not to overthink it, anticipate what will happen, or script what he'll say ahead of time.

No. He's riding a spontaneous tide here, a tide that didn't hit last night as much as it welcomed them both in, carried them onto the dance floor and then into conversation.

What he feels is faith. Faith that Ryan likes him, too. Faith that Ryan is a gentle soul who won't hurt him with games or lies. Faith that when he gets to Kindling, the future will be there, right where he left it.

He is nervous to hope. Nervous to expect.

But underneath the nervousness is the tide, and the tide is telling him he's driving in the right direction.

Hope needs to be earned. But you can't know if it's earned until you offer yourself to it and see what happens.

Ryan doesn't know what kind of car Avery drives, but he's pretty sure there's no one else with pink hair who'd be pulling into his driveway.

His parents are off at church, which is about enough to make Ryan believe in God. There's been no one to witness his vigil at the window, the number of times in a minute he could check his phone to see that a minute hadn't yet passed. And now he alone is here to welcome the car, to welcome the driver.

He walks up as Avery steps from the driver's seat. Both of them are too happy to realize they are smiling.

"I just happened to be in the neighborhood . . . ," Avery says.

"I'm glad you dropped by," Ryan replies.

Then they teeter, because they're in front of each other now, and neither is certain of the second-date protocol. It's Avery who widens his arm, making Ryan smile even wider, because, yes, here it is: the welcome hug, the reunion hug, the this-means-something hug. They've passed the point of anticipation.

"Do you mind driving?" Ryan asks.

"Not at all," Avery says. "I love to drive."

There's no clear logic behind this decision on Ryan's part. Maybe in Avery's car, they'll be more anonymous, more free.

And also, Ryan secretly admits to himself, if Avery's driving, then Ryan can watch him, and not the road.

"Where are we headed?" Avery asks once they're both strapped into their seats. "What's the best Kindling has to offer?"

It would make sense to start the day with coffee, to go to the Kindling Café. But there are bound to be other kids from the high school there, and Ryan doesn't want to see any of them, friend or foe.

Avery is honestly expecting Ryan to suggest coffee, or maybe a diner. So he's surprised when Ryan says, "The river. How do you feel about heading to the river?"

"I feel great about heading to the river," Avery replies. "Show me the way."

Ryan tells Avery where to turn, and also apologizes, because there's a call he needs to make.

"It's related to our plans," Ryan assures him.

Avery appreciates how sincere this is. "It's fine. Go for it."

Ryan knows Aunt Caitlin is bad about checking texts. Now that the plan has been sanctified by Avery's enthusiasm, it's cool to make a call.

"Hello, dear nephew," Caitlin answers. "What's up?"

"I'm riding here with my friend Avery, and I was hoping we could park in your yard and take the canoe onto the river. If you're not using it today."

"Of course. Have I met this friend Avery?"

"Um . . . no."

"Is he from Kindling?"

"Nope."

"Ryan . . . are you on a date?"

Ryan could just say yes. But instead he draws it out, so Avery can hear it. "Yes, it's a date."

"Well, that's exciting. When you're done, if you want to drop by for a snack or something, please do. I'll be around."

"Sure thing."

"Love you."

"Love you, too."

Avery is completely taken with the sound of Ryan's voice as he says this. He has no idea who Ryan's talking to, but the affection he has for them is abundantly clear.

If you are hoping for someone's affections, understanding that they have the capacity to be affectionate is always a good start.

"That was my aunt," Ryan explains after hanging up. "We're going to borrow her boat."

"You two are close?"

"I honestly don't know what I'd do without her."

"That's awesome."

"I know. Oh—you'll want to turn right on the next street."

When Avery imagines rivers, he pictures Mississippis and Hudsons, or maybe white-water rapids with death-defying challenges at every turn.

The river Ryan is offering is nothing like any of those.

Those are highways and this is a country road; Avery takes it on faith that it's actually a river, but to his eye, it's more like a stream.

Still, even though the current isn't strong and the space between the shores isn't wide, the presence of water registers, that alchemical interaction where your body feels like a tributary and your heart eases into the pace of gentle waves.

Avery immediately understands why this is a place Ryan loves, and is glad to have been brought here.

Ryan remains too nervous to read Avery's contentment as Ryan walks them over to the canoe, a boat big enough for two. Together they carry it to the makeshift dock Caitlin's put at the edge of her yard, and then Ryan supervises as they lower it into the water and step inside.

"No life jackets?" Avery jokes.

Ryan, not realizing it's a joke, looks stricken, and says, "It's really not that kind of river. But if you feel uncomfortable, I can go see if Caitlin has one."

"It's totally fine," Avery assures him. "I trust you to dodge the rapids."

"Dodge the rapids. Check," Ryan says, scribbling it on an imaginary list and, yes, checking it off.

Avery sits in the front, Ryan in the back. There are two paddles in the bottom of the boat. Avery is excited by the feel of one in his hands.

"Do you prefer the left or the right?" Ryan asks.

"I'll go left," Avery replies, putting the paddle in the water.

"Excellent. Let's go."

Ryan has faced them upstream to begin; at this hour, there isn't much resistance, and it's always better to have the current on your side on the way home.

They head off, and fall easily into a rhythm. Avery delights in guiding the paddle through the water, the way he can feel his arms working, the pull that's required to leverage against the water and the release when the boat glides under their lead.

Ryan is the one keeping pace, measuring his strokes against Avery's to keep them in sync. While Avery moves his paddle like a spoon, Ryan directs his more like a knife. The light hits Avery's hair in fascinating ways, sometimes making a halo, other times a cloud.

There isn't much for them to see at first. Mostly the backs of houses, the detritus of backyards. In the past few years, the river has risen above its banks a few times; not a flood, really, but definitely a warning. Some people like Caitlin have pulled back from the river, shored up their possessions. Others let things fall where they fall, so you can't tell whether the river took them there or whether it's just the flotsam of human laziness.

Ryan feels he isn't being a very good tour guide, so he tells Avery a little bit about the river's rise. Then Avery says, "Wow, what's that?" and Ryan looks to his left and sees the only yard around here that looks cultivated, deliberate.

"That's The Garden Lady's house," he explains. "For all I

know, she's a witch, because she can get just about anything to grow, even after the soil is flooded."

"A good witch, then."

"Definitely a good witch."

"And you call her The Garden Lady?"

"Yeah. I have no idea what her real name is."

Avery holds up his paddle and points to another yard. "Who lives there?"

"I have no idea. This isn't my neighborhood."

"Well, *I* know who lives there."

"Do you?"

"Yeah, that has to be the home of Wheelbarrow Dude."

Sure enough, there are at least five wheelbarrows in various states of disrepair in the neglected grass.

"Of course, Wheelbarrow Dude," Ryan says.

This is how it starts. Soon they're looking into the lives of The Clothesline Fanatic, Gnome Addict, The Bicycle Thief, Hump Grump, The Fire-Pit God, and The Indifferent Ruler of Disowned Toys. When the houses grow less interesting, Avery lifts his head and sees The Bird Castle floating white and semipuffy in the sky above them. Ryan isn't sure—he thinks it might be the home to The Angular Boatman.

It's an enjoyable stroll through words, but it's not, Ryan feels, conversation. He's grateful when the river steps into the woods, broadening to a shallow inlet.

"Stop padding for a second," he tells Avery. He steers

them to a place where the water settles into a murmur so they can settle, too.

"Here," Ryan says. "A drifting spot."

Ryan puts his paddle in the bottom of the boat, and Avery turns and follows suit. Now they're facing each other. Avery feels very sweaty and very satisfied. He smiles at the blue-haired boy looking at him so openly.

"Hi," Ryan says.

"Hi," Avery says back.

"I would've brought fishing gear, but it's just so mean to the fish."

Avery leans over a little, spreads his fingers in the water. It feels good to create a current, however small. The air is light and the water is quiet, the trees bending from the shore to listen to the tiny waves. The boat rocks gently.

"So what's your story?" Ryan asks.

Avery looks up at him, hand still in the water. "My story?"

"Yeah. Everybody has at least one."

For a few uncomfortable seconds, Avery worries that Ryan thinks he's a mutant, thinks he's a faker and wants him to come clean. But then Avery realizes from Ryan's expression that, no, it isn't about that. Ryan is trying to craft a conversation, and wants it to be a meaningful one. Because what's more meaningful than listening to a person's story?

"I can start if you want me to," Ryan volunteers.

"Sure," Avery says. "You start." Because it's a little safer that way. Avery doesn't know how he can tell a story without telling *the* story, and he wants to be sure Ryan was really looking for something that big when he asked his question.

"Okay," Ryan says. "Here goes." He takes in an endearingly nervous breath, then dives in.

"I guess it all starts here in Kindling—although God knows I hope it doesn't end here. All my family is from here, and with the big exception of my biological father, none of them have ever left."

Now Ryan stops. Is this really the story he wants to tell? Does he really want to show so much of himself so soon?

He looks at Avery, who isn't going to rush him, who is okay just floating along.

He keeps going.

"I don't talk about this stuff a lot, because there aren't many people to talk about it with. Most of my friends grew up here, too, so it's not a story I have to tell them, because they were around. And because I don't really think about it a lot, they don't, either. Does that make sense?"

"Totally," Avery says.

"Okay. So . . . Dad 1.0 left when I was three, so I don't really remember much about him. I just know he was a jerk to pretty much everyone. When I got old enough, Aunt Caitlin told me I was the best thing that ever happened to my mom, Dad 1.0 leaving was the second-best thing that ever happened to my mom, and Dad 2.0 coming into the picture was the third-best thing that ever happened to my mom. Dad 2.0 is Don, who sort of swept in and made things better, by all accounts. I honestly don't think of him as Don, or even Dad 2.0. He's just Dad. And like with all parents, I didn't really get to choose him. He's not bad, but he and my mom are both pretty rigid. They sync up that way. So I'm kinda the odd guy out. Pun not intended, but there it is. Is this at all interesting to you?"

"Of course it is."

Ryan realizes he's been picking at his cuticles as he's been talking, and tries to stop. "So yeah. That's the background. I grew up here, and I get into fights sometimes with my parents. Caitlin saves my life on a daily basis. Okay, that's an exaggeration. She saves my life on a weekly basis. She totally called it on me being gay. My mother was too lost in herself to notice, and Dad didn't want to see it, so he ignored it. Caitlin waited for me to catch up to her. I had other things to think about at first—mostly just trying to fit in, you know. Little League, that kind of thing. But eventually I noticed who I was staring at, and it wasn't the girls. I'll be honest—it freaked me out. I tried to like girls instead. I really did."

"How'd that work for you?" Avery asks, letting his voice joke a little.

Ryan mocks up a sigh. "Well . . . I went out with Tammy Goodwin for almost all of fourth grade. Really serious. I mean, we bought each other stuffed animals on Valentine's Day. That's practically marriage, right? By high school, I knew who I was. And by the time I told Caitlin, I wasn't even surprised by how unsurprised she was. She took me out on this river, in this canoe, and we'd talk about things.

She's not that old—she's about to turn thirty-three—and she's had about as much luck with guys as I have. She's the one who convinced me I shouldn't try to hide. She said hiding never worked. She told me Dad 1.0 spent so much time hiding that it was impossible for him to be happy here. He isn't gay—I guess that makes it sound like he's gay. He isn't. But he didn't want to stay here. He never wanted to stay here. He just wasn't strong enough to tell my mom until it was way too late."

"Do you have much of a relationship with him now?" Avery asks.

"Nah. Maybe because I was so young when he left, there can be long stretches when I forget he even exists. He's just not a part of the equation, you know? Sometimes he'll call on my birthday. And when I started high school, he added me onto this group email where he sends jokes to his friends, and I was like, *this is too weird,* so I asked him to take me off. He never responded . . . but he did take me off. I visited him once in California, and it was a disaster. This was a year or two before the joke email—I was twelve, but he planned it out like I was seven. Like, he genuinely thought I'd be excited to meet Mickey and Donald and Pluto, not ride the 'adult' rides. I mean, I could tell he was trying hard, but in the wrong ways. He thought Disneyland could make everything better. Like, I'd be able to overlook his basic absence in my life and run back to my mom and tell her what an amazing job he did. We ran out of things to say pretty quick. I emailed him when I was coming out to everyone,

195

and his reaction was actually one of the best ones I got. He told me to do what I wanted to do. But part of me felt like it was easy for him to be okay with it because he'd given up on me a while ago. He wasn't as invested as everyone else."

Ryan realizes he hasn't been looking at Avery, or anything, really. He's been staring off, his eyes shut to the scenery as his head goes back to Disneyland, goes back to sitting at the computer, reading his father's email.

"Gosh," he says, "I'm talking a lot." He almost adds, *What have you done to me? I never talk like this.* Because the look Avery's giving him—the only other person who looks at him with such regular encouragement is Caitlin. And damned if it isn't encouraging.

"No," Avery says. "Go on. How did everyone else react?"

This time Ryan almost asks, *To what?* Then he remembers what he was talking about.

"Oh, you know. Mom cried. A lot. Dad was angry. Not at me, exactly. But at the manufacturer for giving him a defective son. Most of my friends were fine, though. I mean, a couple of them flailed a little in their first reactions—some of the guys were wondering if I was secretly in love with them. Which was only right in *one* case . . . but that went nowhere. The girls were cool, even the churchy ones. Well, with one exception there, too. The inevitable rumors started, and I decided the only thing to do was confirm them, so I dyed my hair and started putting *Steven Universe* buttons on my bag. I didn't resist when the Rainbow Alliance pretty much recruited me for their club. The advisor, Mr. Coolidge, is super cool, and has gotten a lot of things done, including the dance last night. That was his idea. The gay prom. He contacted every other alliance in the area. Is that how you heard about it?"

"A friend saw a post about it," Avery says. "We don't have a Rainbow Alliance, but we do have a school play. A bunch of us in the play decided to go."

"Well, whatever got you there, I'm glad you made it. I guess that's the latest plot twist in my story, isn't it?"

Avery takes it as a responsibility, to be a part of someone else's story. He knows Ryan is saying it playfully, not heavily. He knows Ryan is saying it to show that he's done with his own storytelling, which means it's time for Avery to start. Avery isn't sure that Ryan is a part of his own story yet, but that could be because he doesn't feel anyone can be a true part of his story until they hear it and accept it.

They're drifting on the water—not much, just a gradual pull. Avery finds himself drifting to a small part of Ryan's story, an image that's stayed buoyed in his thoughts. He knows Ryan is watching him, waiting to see what he'll say next. He goes to the buoy and starts there.

"I was just thinking about you and your aunt in this canoe," Avery says. "How nice that must have been, to talk here. For me, it was like a kitchen-table war council. Us against the world. Coming up with a plan."

"That sounds stressful."

"Yeah, but at least everyone in my house is on the same side. I know how lucky I am about that. And unlucky in other ways."

"Unlucky how?"

And this is it. This is where Avery must decide how much to tell, how much to let Ryan in. Like everyone else, Avery considers his inner world to be a scary, convoluted, inscrutable place. It is one thing to show someone your best, cleanest version. It's quite another to make him aware of your deeper, jumbled self.

Here in the daylight, does Ryan already notice? Does he already know? If he does, it doesn't seem like he cares. Or maybe that's just more hoping on Avery's part.

Enough, Avery tells himself. *Just talk to him.*

"I was born a boy in a body a lot of other people saw as a girl's," Avery begins. Then he stops, takes in Ryan's reaction.

Ryan is surprised. Not by the information Avery is conveying—while there are particulars that are still a mystery to him, the fact that Avery is trans is not. The thing that's surprised Ryan is that Avery is going there so quickly, that he trusts him so immediately to explain something that no one else needs to know. Ryan is surprised that Avery already feels he's deserving of this story. And in this way, he, too, feels a responsibility.

Avery notes Ryan's pause, notes Ryan looking at him, and he feels like a body on display. It's an extra level of self-consciousness—the difference between the other person having normal vision and an X-ray.

"Go on," Ryan says. His tone is encouraging.

"I think it was obvious to everyone from the start. And my parents are very . . . liberal, I guess. Practically hippies. So they actually tried to make it seem like I wasn't going through anything out of the ordinary. Now I can see the strain, and how much easier it would've been for all of us if I hadn't been born misgendered. But they never made me freak out. It was everyone else. Well, not everyone. There were some people who were great. But there were a lot of people who weren't as great. I was homeschooled a lot. We lived in a few places, trying to find the right doctors. Eventually we found them, and I found other members of my tribe. Mostly online. But my parents and I go to conferences as well. They put me on hormones early, to sort of stop me from going through the wrong kind of puberty. Is this TMI? I'm sure you don't want all the details."

Ryan leans toward Avery, the boat rocking back and forth as he does. Avery grips the side, and Ryan puts his hand on top of Avery's.

"Tell me whatever you want to tell me," he says. "It's cool."

Avery shudders, and can feel the shudder travel through the boat, through the water, until the water becomes smooth again, until he feels his nerves become smooth enough to continue. It's too much, too soon, but now that he's talking, he can't stop. He's talking about the treatments that have happened and the treatments that are going to happen, and all along pretty much the only thing that's filling his head is the question of whether Ryan is seeing him as a girl or a boy. Now that Ryan knows, is Avery still a boy in his eyes?

Ryan is measuring his next words carefully—in fact, he's been weighing them, trying them out in his head, even as Avery's been talking.

Finally, he says, "I like whatever it is that makes you the person you are. And although I'm sure it was really hard, I'm really glad you found a way to be true to the person you are." It's like something Aunt Caitlin would have told him, back when he was figuring things out. "Meanwhile . . . what else? Any siblings?"

"No," Avery says. "It's just me." He appreciates what Ryan's just done; instead of changing the subject, Ryan's broadened it. It's not dismissive at all of what Avery's just told him, but instead acknowledges there's more to knowing Avery than knowing his gender history.

They talk about being only children, including how weird it is to have their parents to themselves. Both Avery and Ryan have wished for siblings, if only to share the spotlight, fraction the focus.

As their conversation drifts, so, too, does the boat. Avery expresses a brief concern about this, but Ryan assures him it's fine; there aren't any dangerous waters to cross into, no threat that awaits if they drift too far. So Avery settles into the drift, maybe not as naturally as Ryan, but close. The sun makes his skin feel a little glow. The breeze and the water seem to be following the same languid metronome. It's so much easier to not have a care in the world when the world doesn't seem to have much of a care, either.

"Take it all in," Ryan suggests. He closes his eyes and indulges his senses. It's not a perfect peace—someone is mowing or plowing in the distance, a thrum of machinery that revs and falls, and the sun can't stay away from the clouds, performing a shadow play that turns the temperature indecisive. He wishes Avery was on his side of the boat, his back against Ryan's chest, Ryan's arms around him.

Avery watches the light play in Ryan's hair, sees the blue shift from day sky to night sky, glimpses the roots as the ground beneath those skies.

When Ryan opens his eyes, he catches Avery looking.

"Your hair," Avery says, knowing he's been caught. "I was checking out your hair."

"I was checking out yours earlier. It's fun in the light. Why so pink?"

How many times has Avery gotten this question?

So many times.

And most of the times, it's asked with an ax behind it, or at least with an edge. That's not how Ryan is asking, but the usual response instincts kick in.

"I know, strange color choice, right?" Avery says. "For a boy once seen as a girl who wants to be seen as a boy. But think about it—it just shows how arbitrary gender is. Pink is female—but why? Are girls any more pink than boys? Are boys any more blue than girls? It's something that has been sold to us, mostly so other things can be sold to us. My hair can be pink because I'm a boy. Yours can be blue because you're a girl. If you free yourself from all the stupid arbitrary shit that society controls us with, you feel more free, and if you feel more free, you can be happier."

"My hair's blue because I like blue," Ryan says.

"And mine is pink because I like pink. And I totally didn't mean to lecture you. It just makes me mad. All the stupid arbitrary shit."

"It makes you want to overthrow the world."

"On a daily basis," Avery says. Then he looks at the river, looks at Ryan on the other side of the boat, really takes him in as the water gently rocks them both. "The world from here isn't that bad, though. This right now is a world I can live in."

"Shall we explore some more?" Ryan asks.

"Yes," Avery replies. "Let's."

Ryan picks Avery's paddle up from the bottom of the boat and hands it to him, then takes up his own. He's sorry when Avery has to turn around to get things moving again, but not sorry when the movement really kicks in, when they are gliding at something that feels like true speed. There's no talking now, just the tandem of their arms, the common delight of their effort. What better race than one with no competitors, no spectators but the trees and the houses and the memories forming? Time loosens from its spool. Thought gives way to sensation. Avery, who rarely lets himself feel strong, feels Olympian as his paddle wrestles the water. Ryan, who rarely lets himself feel in control, watches the point of the bow and course-corrects when needed. When he senses it's time to turn around, he calls on Avery to slow, then veers them so they align with the current. They begin their way home, with the same fervor they used for the way out.

By the time they return to the makeshift dock, the sun is well beyond the halfway mark in the sky. It's only when they stop paddling that they can truly feel the exertion of their effort.

When they get back to Caitlyn's yard, they both have to wipe the sweat from their foreheads. Ryan jumps out first and holds out his hand to Avery. Even though he's an overheated mess, Avery takes it. Ryan pulls him onto land and keeps hold. They stand there, face to face, toe to toe.

"That was fun," the blue-haired boy says.

"It was," the pink-haired boy replies.

Both feel these words are inadequate.

For hours, Avery has been thinking about kissing Ryan. Impossible to do in the boat without a lot of awkward rocking to get there. But now . . . now . . .

Ryan thinks it's like they never left the dance last night. It's like they're still dancing.

"Hey!" a voice calls out—Aunt Caitlin, coming down from the house. "How was the river?"

She walks a little closer, sees how they've moved a little bit apart, but are still holding hands. They're not looking at each other now; they're looking at her.

"So, Ryan," she says, "are you going to introduce me to your friend? I'm guessing you boys are thirsty. I have just the thing. Pull that canoe up to where it was, okay?"

The canoe. Ryan feels like an idiot; they left it in the water, and it's fortunate the current was so gentle that it wasn't carried off. After Ryan makes a quick introduction between his aunt and his date, Caitlin goes back inside and he and Avery lift the canoe and dock it in the enclosure where Caitlin keeps it.

"You up for a drink?" Ryan asks Avery.

Avery is wiping the sweat off his forehead again. "Hell yes," he says.

Even if Ryan and Avery had no sense of time on the river, no sense of when they'd arrive back, Caitlin somehow knew. Because not only is there pink lemonade ready in a pitcher, but there are oatmeal raisin cookies only minutes out of the oven. Countless times, Ryan has sat at this kitchen table when the world has felt like too much for him, when he's wanted to sit inside a house that fully feels like a home. This table, he thinks, has seen so much of his anguish. But now, with Avery, it's witnessing the opposite of anguish. The table's presence makes it more real, because it makes it more a part of Ryan's life.

Avery wants to make a good impression, and is too nervous to realize this won't be hard. When Caitlin asks how they met, he turns it into the longest story in the history of humankind, telling her everything short of the amount of gas that was left in the tank after he and his friends drove home to Marigold. Halfway through, he knows he's talking too much, but Ryan and Caitlin don't seem to notice it as much as he does, so he goes on. When it's over, Caitlin asks, "And this was how many weeks ago?"

It's Ryan who smiles and says, "This was all last night."

"It makes sense," Caitlin says. "With some people, the minute you start talking, it feels like you've known them for years. It only means that you were supposed to meet sooner. You're feeling all the time you should've known each other, but didn't. That time still counts. You can definitely feel it."

Avery knows he should be trying to get Ryan away, should be trying to get him alone, get him close enough to kiss. Time is quietly ticking down to the moment he'll have to leave—he promised his mother he'd be home before dark. But he is enjoying the company, the lemonade, the cookies. He feels it's probably wrong to think of this as more worthy than kissing and making out. But right now, it is.

"Do you want to see some embarrassing photos of Ryan dressed up as Britney Spears for Halloween?" Caitlin asks.

"I was six, and I was playing dress-up," Ryan clarifies. "I didn't go out trick-or-treating as Britney."

"Because if you had—"

Ryan groans. "Maybe we would've figured out things sooner?"

Avery laughs and says he'd still like to see the pictures.

Caitlin runs to her room and comes back with a few snapshots—some embarrassing, some sweet. Avery enjoys this, but also has the tug he sometimes gets when he knows that if the situation were flipped, he'd feel very different about Ryan seeing photos of him early on.

He doesn't feel any scrutiny from Caitlin. Or any from Ryan, either, after all he said in the boat. While intellectually he understands this is possible, emotionally he's still not ready for it, and has to accept it gradually rather than immediately.

What's clear to him, as three of them eat cookies and two of them feel the satisfying soreness in their muscles, is something both simple and extraordinary, something that exists beyond doubt: Last night, Ryan appeared in his life . . . but today, he has truly entered it. And Avery has entered Ryan's life as well. The rest is still to be determined.

Avery can try to ignore the clock, but it's harder to ignore the sun lowering outside. Avery asks where the bathroom is, and once inside calls his parents, asking for an extension. But it's pointed out that he's only had a license for a little while, and he was already out late last night.

"I think I have to head home soon," he says when he gets back to the kitchen.

"It's been so wonderful to meet you," Caitlin says. "Here, let me give you some cookies for the drive. And do you want a Coke, too, for some caffeine?"

Avery thanks her a few times, accepts her care package. He and Ryan both hug her, then head to Avery's car so Avery can drive Ryan home.

The ride goes too fast. It feels like all they've managed to do is sum up the day, talk about how well it's gone, without a chance to really add to it. Ryan asks Avery to pull over a few blocks away from his house. He'll be coming from the direction of Alicia's house, which is where he'll say he was, if his parents bother to ask.

"This is a good spot," he tells Avery. "I don't want to say goodbye in front of my house, if you know what I mean."

Avery thinks he knows what Ryan means, knows what Ryan wants to do, and immediately all his senses are reaching out for it. The radio is on low, the dashboard glowing dimly in the increasing twilight.

"I've had a great time," Avery says, because he feels it needs to be said again.

"Me too," Ryan murmurs.

It is the shift into that murmur that marks the turn. Avery suddenly feels like he is breathing electricity, and it is through this air that Ryan is leaning. Avery leans into it, too, leans into all of it, and that is when their lips touch for the first time, that is the consecration of everything they've already known. Every serious kiss says at least ten things at once—*I want you* and *I'm afraid* and *I want this* and *I hope this isn't all there is* and so many other feelings. All of those are present in this kiss, but one word rises above them all, one word moves from one boy's lips to the other's, and back again.

Welcome, the kiss says.

Over and over. Back and forth.

Welcome.

The Cast Party

(the ninth date)

As Avery takes his calculus exam, and again as he takes his history exam, he tries not to be distracted by the fact that right now Ryan is alone in his house. He feels he's getting to know Ryan well, and he certainly knows his house well, but somehow his imagination fails when he tries to put the two of them together.

Ryan was still asleep when he left, and Avery didn't have the heart to wake him just to say goodbye. Instead he did what any young lover would do—he stood beside the door for a very short time and watched the object of his affections softly dreaming. Even asleep, Ryan had an expression of mild surprise, his eyes closed but his mouth looking to be on the verge of speech. His arms curled one way (gathering) while his legs curled the other way (a leap). His blue hair pointed in what felt like an infinite number of directions.

When we speak of tenderness, sometimes it's caused by the raw vulnerability of the person being seen, and sometimes the source is the raw vulnerability of the person who is seeing. Ideally it is a match between the two, where the open weakness in one inspires an open weakness in the other. That's what Avery felt, seeing Ryan asleep on his couch, the uninvited guest he wanted to make perfectly at home.

But was that possible? As Avery goes through calculus and history, he knows that Ryan's reprieve is only temporary. At the end of the weekend, he'll have to go home. And now Avery feels the exasperation that lines the pockets of love, frustration that even if he gives Ryan all the affection he has to offer, he cannot control how much affection anyone else provides. He can give Ryan a home for a weekend, but when it comes to Ryan's real home, Avery is powerless. And that gets to him.

His friends see that he's distracted, and they assume it's because of the play. At lunch, Avery texts Ryan and finds he's been getting assignments from his friends, starting homework now so he doesn't have to do it the rest of the weekend. Ryan asks Avery if he's getting preperformance jitters, and Avery is surprised to realize the answer is no. Possibly this is because of denial—it seems unbelievable to him that in a few short hours he will be on a stage with an actual audience. But also, he feels ready. Ready to be up there. Ready for Ryan in particular to see him, to take this further step into his ridiculous world.

"When will Romeo Ryan be here?" Pope asks.

"Tonight," Avery answers. "He'll be in the audience tonight."

Ryan texts Alicia throughout the day. Besides conveying what happened in his classes, she is full of advice.

Whatever you do, don't seek out his diary. That never ends well.

and

Even if they say to help yourself to whatever's in the fridge, don't take too much and don't zero in on anything that's expensive, because odds are they're saving that for themselves.

and

Even if you're sleeping there again tonight, make sure you take the sheets off the couch before they come home, so if they look in, it will look like their living room and not like your campout site.

He has no idea how she knows these things, but the advice feels sound, so he follows it.

There are also texts from his mother. He doesn't read those.

When Avery's parents come home, Ryan knows he has to put his phone away. They tell him they'll be leaving for dinner at five-thirty, since the show starts at seven-thirty.

Ryan is comforted by the fact that when it's just the three of them in the car, they don't seem any more acclimated to the situation than he does. Years of carpooling have put Avery's mom more at ease, or at least more able to project ease from behind the wheel. Avery's dad, though, can't help but study Ryan every time he turns to ask an innocuous question.

Ryan is glad he bought a new shirt to wear, because the

restaurant they go to is a pretty nice Italian place, much nicer than anywhere his own parents would take him and his friends. It's a table for ten, and soon they're joined by Avery's aunt and uncle and two young cousins, as well as three family friends. When Avery's mom introduces him by saying, "This is Avery's boyfriend, Ryan," Ryan has to try hard to keep it together. It's not only that her saying it makes it more real (which it does), but he also can't imagine a universe in which his mother introduces Avery in the same way. It's a lot. And maybe Avery's mom sees this, because after hands have been shaken and the introductions are over, she reiterates, "It's really wonderful to have you here, Ryan."

He knows that this is Avery's stage debut, but seeing everyone else's reaction to that fact really brings it home. Avery's mom, so calm in the car, is more nervous now. The cousins, ages seven and nine, are bouncing with excitement. The other adults are saying everything's going to be fine, that Avery conquers any challenge he sets himself. They don't ask Ryan for his opinion, and he doesn't volunteer it; he agrees, but that agreement is based on guesswork, not history.

Ryan notices that the younger cousin is wearing Poké-mon sneakers, so that opens up one conversational path, and by the time his main course arrives, Ryan feels secure that he's won over at least two members of Avery's family.

One of the family friends asks Ryan if he's an actor as well, and Ryan laughs in response, then quickly explains that performing in front of other people is the last thing he'd ever want to do.

"I can barely get out the words when they're my own words," he tells the table. "As you can see."

One of the family friends says, "I used to think that, but," and then launches into an account of her "blossoming" during a community theater production of *The Miracle Worker*. Ryan listens politely, but he enjoys the way Avery's mom rolls her eyes, having clearly heard this story many, many times before.

Avery's dad asks if anyone has seen *Don't Forget Your Shoes!* before.

"I think our great-great-great-great-great-grandmother was in a production when she was a girl," Avery's uncle jokes.

"Wasn't there a movie?" one of the family friends asks. "With what's-his-face. You know. The one who isn't Clark Gable."

"I'm sure it's going to be wonderful," Avery's aunt says.

"*I'm* Clark Gable," Avery's younger cousin proclaims.

Ryan settles into his food, happy to overhear for the rest of the meal.

It is chaos backstage. Controlled chaos, but chaos nonetheless.

With only half an hour until curtain, Pope's dowager wig can't be found, the living room settee is refusing to roll smoothly, Tara James is cramming lines because Sara Lane has the flu, and Dennis is driving everyone up the wall with his "vocal exercises," which sound a lot like the chorus of "Old MacDonald Had a Farm" fed through a meat processor. Mr. Horslen, who never yells, is yelling. Only Liz Macy seems unfazed by the hullabaloo, so Avery makes his way over to her.

"It's even worse with the spring musical," she tells him after they both take a look around. "People are even more insecure and precious about their singing. But don't worry—everything will sort itself out. We just have to stand out of the way of the mayhem and let the clock take care of it."

They finish getting into costume—Liz puts on her stockings, and Avery clips on his tie. (He wants to put on his fedora as well, but he doesn't need it until the croquet scene.) True to Liz's word, the clock sorts things out, because while curtain time can be held for seven minutes so people can get to their seats, it can't wait much longer than that.

Avery offers a passing thought to who's in the audience, and he certainly hopes that Ryan has survived dinner. But his phone is back in his locker and his mind has now entered the play. The curtain rises, and the family in the audience is no longer his family. No, this misfit ensemble, from Lavinia Stranglehold down to Baby Winston, is his family. He is now, he thinks, happily engaged to a woman who will end up in an attic.

They get laughs. Sometimes intentional, sometimes by mistake. But what a good feeling, to hear people laughing in the dark. While Avery's head is in the play, his heart feeds off this laughter, and the satisfaction when the dialogue zings the way it was meant to zing, and the physical comedy is pulled off without anyone losing an eye.

The only missed stitch is Dennis, who continues to rage like a thespianic plague. The laughter makes it worse, because laughter has never been Dennis's goal. The more the audience laughs, the angrier he gets. When the confrontation scene arrives and Lucius and Laurent discover both-and-neither of them are affianced to Betty Lou, Dennis is channeling all the fury of Medea, to a degree that Avery wants to tell Baby Winston to hide, even though Baby Winston isn't the object of Dennis's onanistic volcano of *acting*. Avery must stand his ground as Dennis spits and rends and howls. He is only saved when Pope-as-dowager runs in and says, "What in tarnation is all this commotion?" This gets a big laugh, and Avery expects Dennis to rip the couch from the stage and throw it at the audience.

Somehow he resists.

Ryan doesn't really know what to do with what's playing out in front of him. As a kid, it was always much more fun to play dress-up than to watch other people play dress-up . . . and isn't this dress-up? He's not entirely sure why a high school would put on a play where nobody is even remotely high school age. There are laughs, for sure, but when Ryan is laughing, it's mostly when things are going wrong, or when

Pope does such a spectacularly out-there version of dress-up that the showbiz gods are summoned.

Every now and then, Ryan sneaks glances at the rest of their party, to see if he's the only one feeling this way. Avery's father looks perfectly happy and Avery's mother looks a mix of nervous and happy. Avery's uncle looks bored and his aunt looks utterly charmed. The most enthusiastic are Avery's cousins, because they figure all high schoolers are adults, so it makes perfect sense for them to dress up as other adults. Every time Pope puts some whipped cream and cherries on top of a line reading, the cousins eat it up.

The one thing Ryan does love is how queer the play is. With no disrespect meant to Avery or his performance, it's very clear to Ryan that the whole kit and caboodle—the fiancée, the inheritance, even Baby Winston—should be given to the sarcastic lesbian aunt. (They keep calling her a spinster, and because he's never heard the word *spinster* before, Ryan imagines that in her free time she does something involving thread, like Penelope from *The Odyssey*, or the princess in "Rumpelstiltskin," whose name he can't remember.)

It's fun to see how much fun Avery is having. But it's starting to seem like a bad idea to sit through all four performances.

As soon as the standing ovation is through, as soon as the curtain closes after the final bows, everyone in the cast starts hugging each other, euphoric. They've done it. Somehow all the cogs, all the gears, were in working order. No lines were majorly flubbed. No entrances were majorly missed. No scenery fell, and Dennis didn't pop any of his own arteries.

It's a success, and everyone's giddy to do it again, twice tomorrow.

They change back into their street clothes quickly, handing over the sweatier parts of their costumes to Penny's mom and dad, who are in charge of cleaning the wardrobe. (Penny hasn't been able to do anything to stop the rumors that her parents' dry cleaning business was the reason she was cast as Baby Winston, and her parents' presence backstage makes matters even worse.)

More than half the audience is waiting by the stage door. Even though Ryan's hair certainly makes him stand out, Avery finds his parents first, based on his longer history of spotting them in crowds. Then he sees Ryan beside them, talking to his cousins. Because it's opening night, there are lots of flowers being given and photos being taken. Avery's cousins mob him like he's a celebrity, and soon his mom, dad, aunt, and uncle are congratulating him, too, with his mother passing along her friends' congratulations. (They had no desire to stay around.) Finally, Avery gets to Ryan, who gives him the widest smile and tells him how great he was. Avery, still euphoric, hugs him like a fellow cast member and then kisses him like a boyfriend. Other people around them notice, for sure. But for once, Avery doesn't notice them noticing, at least not until his younger cousin, grossed out by kissing of any kind, yells at him to stop it. This, in turn, horrifies Avery's aunt and uncle, who assure him and Ryan that Johnny's display has nothing to do with their gender. Avery hugs Johnny tight and says he knows, then punishes Johnny with wet, slobbery mock kisses until Johnny is practically peeing himself from laughter.

Ryan tries hard to feel like a part of this.

It isn't until Avery's in the backseat of the car that exhaustion sits upon the switch, and he feels his energy level shift from *on* to *off*. He and Ryan are holding hands, something Avery's never done with a boy before in his parents' car. It feels quietly monumental, offhand major. Ryan is staring out the window, staring past his reflection while Avery stares at it.

When Ryan turns again to Avery, he squeezes his hand, as if to say *I'm back now*. But then he says, "I just remembered I have to go to work tomorrow. I have a shift, and I forgot to arrange for a sub. But the good news is, I'll be done by four, so I can be back for the night performance, if that's okay."

"What time will you have to leave?"

"Early? Around six, I'd guess. But that's fine. I figure you have to go in early, right?"

"Not until noon."

"Oh."

Avery squeezes Ryan's hand again. "It's okay. We'll still have most of Sunday. And you can come to the cast party, right?"

"Of course."

Avery's too tired to put up much resistance. He doesn't want Ryan to lose his job. And he also feels that nobody, not even family, should have to see the play all four times.

When they get back to the house, Ryan has to practically carry Avery inside, he's so sleepy. He's yawned about eighty times, and his eyelids are closing curtains. After apprising his parents of Ryan's new plan (they seem neither put off nor pleased by the fact that they won't spend tomorrow with him), Avery goes to the living room with the total intention of staying up with him . . . but eighty more yawns later, Ryan releases him to his own bed, saying again how much he enjoyed the show, and how much he's looking forward to seeing it tomorrow.

Once Avery has gone to bed, Ryan unfolds everything he folded so finely this morning, and re-creates everything he dismantled. He tugs himself to sleep, then startles to the pre-dawn alarm. He makes the room a living room again, then steps quietly through the door. He is grateful that he hasn't woken anyone up. He is grateful to be able to leave without saying a word.

It's not that he doesn't feel the urge to stay. As he drives away in the ease of a Saturday-morning highway, he longs to go back, to have breakfast with Avery and his family. But this way, he tells himself, he won't wear out this welcome, and can swing back this evening without any endless hours stretching out to make them realize how much he's asking of them.

He does not text his parents to tell them he'll be back in town; he's hoping his mother won't decide to do any shopping this morning, although that was always going to be a risk. By the time he gets to the grocery, he is fully caffeinated, and talks to his coworkers as if he slept in his own bed last night. Once it's an acceptable hour, he texts Alicia to tell her he's around, and she drops by during his lunch break. They sit in her car with ready-made sandwiches, and he talks about what it was like to be there, to be introduced and accepted as Avery's boyfriend and see him having such a good time onstage. Alicia asks if Ryan's talked to his parents at all, and he shakes his head.

"You know you're going to have to, right?" she says.

"After the weekend," he tells her.

"Okay. After the weekend. I want to see you in school on Monday. I am not allowing you to run away, no matter how nice Avery's parents are. Frankly, I'm nicer."

Ryan swears he'll be in school on Monday. He hasn't even let himself think any further than that. Once his shift is over, he wishes he could stop off at his house for more clothes and a shower, but that's not really an option. (There have been more texts from his mom, asking when he's going to be home. He hasn't answered yet.) He cleans himself up in the employee restroom as best he can, throws his work vest in the communal hamper, and heads back to Avery's town. There's a little more traffic now—mostly trucks on long hauls, but also some people going Saturday-night places. The plan is for him to meet Avery's mom at the high school. (Avery's dad took the matinee.) Ryan arrives in Marigold early, so grabs a bite at Chipotle. While he's there, he sees a few tables of kids his age. Some of them could be going to the play. Others, he's sure, wouldn't be caught dead going back into the school building on a weekend, for whatever reason. Some of them might be friends with Avery. Some of them might have given Avery a hard time. Ryan realizes he knows a lot about the people in the play, and not a whole lot about anyone outside of it. Nobody in the Chipotle seems to have noticed him at all. Because he's sitting alone, it's like he doesn't exist.

It was way too awkward to even think of asking Avery for his mom's phone number, so Ryan scans the parking lot for her, and then does the same when he gets to the lobby. Finally, he finds her talking to two kids who must be friends of Avery's. They are clearly a couple; not just because they're holding hands, but because they seem to check with each other before answering anything Avery's mom asks.

Avery's mom smiles when Ryan comes into view.

"There he is!" she says. "I'm so glad you made it—I realized way too late that I don't have your number, and I think Avery's phone is locked away somewhere right now. Do you know Aurora and Dusty?"

The couple turns as one and says hi as one to Ryan. He realizes this has to be the pair of friends Avery told him about, who always do everything as a couple. Aurora has shampoo-commercial hair and a friendly smile. Dusty seems strangely familiar to Ryan, with a broad forehead and broad shoulders. As they shake hands in greeting, Ryan figures he's generic enough in his type that he probably just reminds him of someone who goes to his own school.

"We're so excited to finally see Avery onstage!" Aurora bubbles. "He's always been so good at acting!"

What does that *mean?* Ryan wonders. He sees the question flash across Avery's mom's face, too.

"Isn't that right?" Aurora asks Dusty. But Dusty has been busy looking at Ryan.

"Totally," Dusty says, turning back to his girlfriend. But not before Ryan notices the attention that's been coming his way. Almost like Dusty recognizes him from somewhere.

He doesn't have much more time to think about it, because Aurora and Dusty say they need to go get their seats—not as part of a larger group, just the two of them. That leaves Ryan with Avery's mom, who asks him about the drive, about work, about everything except the part she's probably most curious about: the unanswered texts from his mom.

"Thank you for leaving the family room in such pristine condition," she says as they walk to their seats. "I just wanted you to know I appreciate that."

"It was my pleasure," Ryan replies, immediately finding his own words to be pretty dumb. His pleasure? Really?

But he seems to be the only one who finds it a weird response. Avery's mom says, "It's wonderful that you could be here this weekend. I know it hasn't given you and Avery a whole lot of time together, but I'm sure he appreciates it. And hopefully you'll come back another weekend when there isn't quite so much theater to attend."

"Definitely," Ryan says as Avery's mom leads him into a row. "Thank you."

He notices there is no opening here for him to ask to stay beyond tomorrow, to be taken in as anything besides a guest. But that certainly matches his expectations. He thinks it's remarkable to have an invitation to come back, given so easily.

Some announcement must be made in the lobby, because soon everyone is flowing toward their seats. Ryan looks around and sees it isn't nearly as full as it was last night—but he figures that's to be expected, with opening night the big draw. He spots Aurora and Dusty a few rows ahead, across the aisle. As if summoned, Dusty turns his head and they make eye contact for a second, until Aurora says something and Dusty is summoned back to her. Canned curtain music begins, and the lights in the auditorium dim. The curtain rises to show the ground floor of the LeFevre residence. Ryan looks back at Dusty one more time, and that's when the recognition kicks in.

After Ryan first realized he was gay, he thought this realization would enable him to realize who else was gay, too—but in Kindling, this theory didn't particularly hold. After his lightning flash of a relationship with Isaiah, he decided he probably needed to extend his search radius in order to find someone more on his own wavelength. So at sixteen he joined Tinder and said he was eighteen (choosing Tinder because it seemed to be about dating, not sex). It was depressing how few fish this net caught. His settings were only for other eighteen-year-olds, figuring a few of them might also be in high school. He set his radius for five miles. Nothing. Ten miles. Nothing. Twenty-five miles. A few photos. Fifty miles. A few more. A hundred miles—with a few minor cities involved, suddenly there were a few dozen kids his age (or thereabouts). He became expert at cross-referencing with other social media, to make sure it wasn't an adult in disguise. And one of the very first people he matched and messaged with was undeniably Dusty, going by his initials, DB.

Things didn't get very far. DB wasn't out to anyone, and Ryan had just been through that with Isaiah. Still, DB was normal, at a time when Ryan really needed some other normal gay kids in his life. They messaged about crushes on Troye Sivan and Timothée Chalamet, and came up with a conspiracy theory that Troye and Timothée were actually the same person. Ryan shared how tough it was sharing his identity with his parents, and DB sympathized, implying that the reaction he'd get from his own parents would be similar. DB's full-face pic wasn't on Tinder, but he'd sent it to Ryan early on, an offering of trust. Ryan didn't feel a romantic spark, but figured they'd get together at some point to commiserate in person. Then one day he checked the app and DB was gone, completely gone.

And now, here he is.

* * *

If Ryan is distracted in the audience, Avery is also distracted on the stage. He doesn't feel good about the fact that if given a chance to kill Dennis Travers, he just might take it. *Don't Forget Your Shoes!* is only one plot point away from being a murder mystery, so why not open a trapdoor on the stage for Dennis to fall through and make the transition official?

He is not the only one feeling this way. As they wait in the wings, Liz Macy reports that Mr. Horslen seems to be ready to stuff Dennis in a locker and call it a day. Dennis overcaffeinated before and after yesterday's evening performance, leaving him largely sleepless for the matinee and then bolstered by another manic jolt (a Pamplona worth of Red Bulls) prior to the performance at hand. As a result, he seems to have wandered into the farce by way of *Long Day's Journey into Night,* and no one can mitigate his unhinged affectations. In a light scene where Lucius is meant to occupy Baby Winston with a game of horsey, Dennis managed to bring *The Godfather* to mind. Penny, playing Baby Winston, had enough and pounced on him harder than required (garnering her the nickname Sweeney Toddler, which will stick for years).

When Avery and Dennis get to the big confrontation scene tonight, Dennis flails so much that Avery must physically dodge his gesturing—which gets a big laugh from the audience. Dennis doesn't seem to hear them, and instead falls to the ground after his monologue about losing his fiancée. This is not in the script, nor has it been rehearsed. Avery is supposed to exit at the same time as Dennis, but after waiting for a few seconds, he gingerly steps over Dennis— another laugh—and the stage crew goes to blackout to give Dennis cover to crawl offstage.

Avery figures the confrontation has ended, but when the show is done, Dennis storms over in a barrage. Avery can't tell if he's still in character or not, until Dennis snaps, "That was the work of an *amateur*! How dare you! This might not mean anything to you, but this is my future you're messing with, and I do *not* appreciate it."

Liz Macy, standing nearby, says, "Whoa, Dennis. You need to chill."

Dennis turns on her then. "I do not need to chill! It's the rest of you who need to wake up. I'm the only one here willing to give it two hundred percent. And the audience notices."

"They certainly do," Emerson Crane, who has a bit part as the butler, murmurs.

Dennis either doesn't hear this or ignores it.

Avery is tempted to repeat it . . . but then he sees that Dennis is legitimately upset. He's been made to look bad in front of a Saturday-night crowd.

"Look," Avery says, "I'm sorry. I was improvising to get the laugh, but there was probably another way to recover. It won't happen again."

His conciliatory tone is not returned.

"It better not!" Dennis proclaims. Then he storms off in the same way he stormed in, a storm without an eye.

* * *

Avery reenacts this scene for Ryan later that evening, in Avery's bedroom.

"You amateur!" Ryan chides, laughing, when Avery is done.

They are hovering in the middle of the room, conscious of the fact that Avery's parents are still up, still walking around, and could poke their heads in at any minute to suggest it's bedtime. Avery dares to throw his arms around Ryan's waist, smiling. Ryan does the same.

"What are we doing?" Ryan asks. "Dancing?"

"Swaying," Avery replies. "We're just swaying."

Their arrangement is loose at first, then draws closer.

"Well, hello," Avery says.

"Howdy, pardner," Ryan says. He has no idea where that comes from. But it makes Avery smile some more, so it must be a right thing to say.

The door is open. Ryan can't believe that Avery isn't aware of that, or that he doesn't care what his parents might see.

Avery rests his cheek against Ryan's chest, hears his heartbeat, the music beneath the sway.

"I don't want to leave tomorrow," Ryan says quietly.

"You'll be back," Avery answers, not opening his eyes.

"I know." Ryan takes a deep breath, and Avery can feel it, the rise and fall. "But still, I wish I could stay."

* * *

The next morning, Avery's parents make such a big breakfast that Ryan assumes more people are coming to join them.

"We've got to celebrate the grand finale!" Avery's dad says as he delivers a plate of waffles to the table.

"Do you mean we're celebrating my accomplishment or the fact that you never have to see the play again?" Avery asks.

"Both!" his mom and dad chime out at the same time. Then all three of them crack up.

Ryan tries to remember the last time he laughed with his parents. He knows it has to have happened; his parents aren't ogres or robots. But it's like he lost their natural laughter as soon as his hair lost its natural color.

"Hey," Avery says.

Ryan looks up from his plate and sees all three of them looking at him.

"If you'd rather have your egg sandwich on a croissant instead of a biscuit, that can be arranged," Avery's dad says.

"No, no. Sorry," Ryan replies.

"No need to be sorry," Avery's mom says. "About anything. We're happy to have you here, Ryan. We're happy to feed you and give you a fold-out couch. It's the least we can do for someone willing to brave a school play three separate times."

"Mom!" Avery protests. But he's smiling.

It's only when Ryan is alone again with Avery's parents, when they are driving to the matinee, that he remembers what he's forgotten. His first impulse is to let it go, but his second, better impulse is to at least ask the question.

"Excuse me," he says, leaning toward the front seats. "Do we have time for a stop?"

Avery's father looks at him in the rearview mirror. "It's only about five minutes to the school," he says. "Can you hold it in?"

"Oh! No. Not that. I was, uh—is there somewhere to stop for flowers? For Avery? I wanted to get him flowers."

Avery's mom, in the passenger seat, turns her head and says, "What a lovely thought. We still have plenty of time." Then she turns to her husband. "Honey, can you make a quick stop at the florist?"

"Sure, but . . . uh . . ."

Avery's mom again turns to Ryan, this time making eye contact. "You are now my witness: He has no idea where the florist is. I've always suspected."

"I get you flowers!"

"I know, dear. At the same place you get your cereal and your beer."

Ryan can't entirely tell if they're joking with each other or not. He senses Avery's dad might not know, either.

"Turn left," Avery's mom says, guiding them to a parking spot in front of a flower shop.

"I'll be right back," Ryan says.

"Would you like me to go in with you?" Avery's mom offers.

"No, thank you."

The inside of the shop is fancier than he's expecting . . . but he's not sure why he was expecting anything because he's not sure he's ever been in a flower shop before. A woman in a dress that's practically triangular comes out from behind the counter and asks him if he needs any help.

"I need flowers," he answers. Then, realizing this isn't quite enough, he adds, "It's for someone in the high school play. It's their last show."

The woman smiles. "Is this someone a someone special?"

"Yes."

"Lucky girl!"

For a second, Ryan thinks about letting it slide. Life will be much easier if he lets it slide, if he just goes along with her assumption. Flowers are flowers, and whatever she suggests for the "lucky girl" is bound to be okay for Avery, too.

But . . . it's also wrong. And it feels wrong to let this woman picture one thing when something else is true. If he doesn't say something now, the flowers will be pointless, because even if Avery never knows, Ryan will know he let them both down because it was easier to do so.

"Lucky boy," he corrects.

The woman's smile falters for a second, and Ryan can't tell if it's from surprise or disapproval. He isn't sure whether or not she'll politely chase him out of the store, not until she says, "Well, do you know what kind of flowers he likes? You can't go wrong with roses."

Ryan thinks for a second, then says, "His hair is pink. What's the pinkest flower you've got?"

Gearing up for the final performance is strangely emotional for Avery. He's gotten used to being Laurent LeFevre, and he's not ready to stop being him for a couple of hours each day. But more than that, he's gotten used to this new supporting cast in his life. It's hard to imagine not seeing them after school every day.

He's certainly not the only one feeling this way—there's some hugging, a few tears. The only one not succumbing to the fits of prenostalgia is Dennis, who has locked himself into a stall in the boys' bathroom so he can "fully find" his character and "block out the childish distractions" backstage.

Before the curtain goes up, Mr. Horslen gathers everyone together and tells them to have fun out there—and, with the predictable exception, they do. The lines zing and the body language zags, garnering more laughs than ever before. Avery's having a blast . . . except when he has to share a scene with Dennis, who has all the lightness of a tank and all the humor of a sinkhole.

Avery tells himself to not let it get to him. And it doesn't, not really. Not until the confrontation scene. Perhaps mindful of his fall during the previous performance, Dennis comes on strong, spitting out his lines and acting like Laurent's theft of Lucius's beloved is the most egregious betrayal since Judas puckered up.

"How can you just stand there as my love flashes before

my eyes?!?" he wails. Then he pushes forward, getting in Avery's face. "How." Pointing accusingly. "Dare." Thrusting the finger forward. "You!" Jabbing Avery in the chest.

This sends Avery reeling. He is sick of Dennis and his raging bullshit. He is not going to stand in front of an audience including his boyfriend and parents and let some asshole poke him in the chest. If Dennis wants to improvise, so be it.

"You need to calm the fuck down," Avery spits back. "You need to stay away from this family because we all hate you. Betty Lou was never going to marry you. You *exhaust* her."

There is some laughter, and a few of the less gentle people in the theater applaud. Dennis looks for a moment like he's going to deck Avery, right there in front of the audience. But instead he stomps off before his final lines.

"Betty Lou!" Avery calls out. "The coast is clear!"

Kim Elias comes onstage, and she and Avery pick up the scene.

He hopes no one can see how much he's shaking.

Ryan wants to cheer—as far as he's concerned, Avery's just stolen the show. The second Dennis poked Avery so offensively, Ryan could feel himself tense, and could see Avery's mom and dad tensing in the seats next to him. Only when Avery pulled back could they let out their collective breath. And then Avery cut Dennis down to size with a few sentences. Suddenly Ryan's enjoying himself . . . until he realizes that Avery's parents aren't laughing or applauding, and that the collective feeling before has now unraveled, and what they're feeling isn't the same as what he's feeling. He's proud of Avery, but they don't seem to be.

Luckily, Dennis's character isn't in the final scene. Ryan wouldn't particularly want to see this play ever again, but at the same time he feels almost nostalgic about the fact that this is it, the end of the run. Everyone onstage seems to feel it, too, delivering their lines with more feeling than they deserve. When they get to the last line—Baby Winston taking his first steps and waddling offstage, with Lavinia Stranglehold calling after him, "Don't forget . . . your shoes!"—half the cast members are grinning and half have tears in their eyes. The standing ovation begins even before the curtain falls. When it's time for the proper curtain calls, Dennis and Avery are as far apart as can be, Avery delighting when he gets a raucous chorus of whoops for his bow, and Dennis acting completely unfazed by the cheers that greet him, too. The ensemble bows once, twice, three times, and then, when the curtain falls for the last time, the audience can see them turn to each other for hugs and congratulations and the throwing of wigs as if they were graduation caps.

The drama teacher makes an announcement that to avoid too much congestion in the hallways, friends and family will be asked to stay in their seats to wait for cast members to emerge from backstage.

"Well, that was . . . something," Avery's dad says to Avery's mom.

"A little too improvisational on all fronts," Avery's mom comments. She looks around the theater for a moment. "I don't see Dennis's mom. Otherwise, I feel I'd have to go over and apologize."

"Yeah, I hope she missed this performance," Avery's dad says.

Ryan wants to defend Avery—after everything that's happened in all the performances, what Avery did was practically self-defense. But the notion that Dennis's mom could have been in the audience keeps his mouth shut. It's not like he wants to pick an argument with Avery's parents, anyway.

The seats between Ryan and the aisle have been vacated, and now a girl his age is shuffling sideways toward him.

"You're Ryan, right?" she says when she arrives.

Ryan wants to ask, *Do I know you?* But he also doesn't want to be rude, so he just says, "Yes."

"I was told to look for blue hair, and you were the only candidate," she says. "I'm Hannah. Liz's girlfriend? She's the one who played the aunt? I came alone, and Liz and Avery texted me to say to look for you, because we'd all be going to the cast party together. Maybe they didn't tell you?"

"No, but that's awesome. I don't know anyone else here besides Avery's parents. Do you know Avery's parents?"

Hannah leans around Ryan and says, "Hi, Avery's parents!"

Ryan is about to attempt further introductions, but there's a commotion as a few of the performers come out onto the stage in their street clothes, jumping down into the audience to entertain their admirers. Avery and Liz come out together and head straight over. Hannah practically jumps into Liz's arms; Ryan, meanwhile, reaches under his seat and holds his odd pink bouquet out to Avery.

"What are these?" Avery asks.

"Snapdragons!" Ryan replies. "An applause of snapdragons."

He shakes the bouquet a little and it indeed looks like the flowers are clapping.

"I love them," Avery says, then kisses Ryan sweetly.

"That was quite a performance," Avery's mom says.

"Yeah," Avery replies, taking the snapdragons from Ryan and looking down at them. "That probably shouldn't have happened."

"What do you mean?" Ryan asks. "You were awesome. He deserved it."

"Thanks for saying that," Avery tells him. "But I kinda became the amateur he accused me of being."

"He'll live," Avery's dad says.

Avery's mom changes the subject to the cast party, and Avery explains they'll all be going over to Anna Anderson's house, and that her parents will be there to "curtail any untoward shenanigans." (This is a quote from the play.)

"Okay," Avery's mom says. "Just be home by eight. Ryan

needs to drive back tonight, and I don't want him getting home too late."

"We'll be fine," Avery assures her as the phrase "home too late" reverberates within Ryan like a game-show buzzer signaling that time is up.

Fortuitously, Hannah and Liz lean in then to send some Sapphic *let's get going* vibes. Avery gives his snapdragons to his mother for safekeeping, and Liz, Hannah, Avery, and Ryan decide to pile into Hannah's improbable choice of vehicle—a red 1990 Miata she tells Avery and Ryan she won in a bet. (She actually bought it used with a year's worth of carefully saved babysitting money.) The backseat only has enough legroom for a small toddler or a medium-sized dachshund, so Ryan and Avery end up lying atop one another like they've been stacked in some romantic cargo ship. Avery assures Ryan their destination isn't that far away.

Ryan expected Avery to be either exuberant or exhausted once the show was done, but instead he seems preoccupied. Ryan knows him enough now to have a suspicion why, but not enough to make an assumption. So it's a question he asks—

"Are you still thinking about what happened with Dennis?"

"Yes."

When you start dating, you feel like emotions are the roll of a six-sided die, and you read for the basics, react to the elemental. But the more you talk, the more time you share, the more sides the die takes on, and while you know you'll never master the response to every momentary roll, you do start to understand what the numbers mean. Ryan has never seen Avery like this, caught in the hinge of regret. He is sorry Avery is feeling this way, and at the same time, it helps him understand Avery a little bit more.

From the front seat, Liz says, "Don't worry about it. He totally deserved it."

Another roll, and the thirty-sided die becomes a forty-sided die. Avery doesn't dig in, but he also doesn't let Liz pull him out.

"In some ways, he did deserve it," he says. "But in other ways, he didn't."

"He won't be at the party, will he?" Hannah asks.

"I doubt it," Liz replies. "I don't think he liked any of us very much."

And now he knows what you all thought of him, Ryan thinks, but doesn't say out loud, because he knows it's the last thing Avery wants to hear.

Pope has decided to keep Lavinia Stranglehold's makeup and wig on for the cast party; the disconcerting part is that they are not wearing their costume, but instead have found a muumuu covered in pictures of dancing cats. They welcome Ryan, Avery, Liz, and Hannah as if it were their own home, which it is not.

"Make yourselves comfortable . . . but not so comfortable that they'd need to dry-clean the cushions after," Pope says. Then, somewhat to Avery's horror, they wink at Ryan.

Ryan knew the cast party wasn't going to be a rager, but he's still amused by the scene he discovers inside: The refreshments and CONGRATULATIONS banner would be at home at a fifth grader's graduation party. There's a "chip bar," where Tostitos and Lay's appear in their seemingly infinite varieties of dusting and shape. There is plenty of unjacked Coke and unscrewdrivered OJ. Pizza boxes wait like flattened lapdogs with eager mouths. A coffeemaker burbles at the edge of the beverage table, like the bad kid at the back of the bus.

Despite the lack of intoxicants, there's a certain kind of intoxication in the air. Casting, rehearsals, performance—it has been a very small era, but it's still the end of one.

Ryan still feels like part of the audience here. He might as well pull a chair to the corner of the living room and watch what unfolds. He expects Avery to jump into the fray and leave him behind—he would totally understand this course of action, because he is a guest, maybe even an interloper. The girl who played the baby is calling out to Avery from the sofa, patting the cushion beside her. The permission is sitting on Ryan's lips. *Just go ahead. I'll stay here. Have fun.*

But Avery doesn't leave him, doesn't step away even when he's beckoned. Instead he leads Ryan over to the pizza, which is exactly where Ryan wants to go. They load slices onto paper plates that offer them congratulations in balloon lettering. Liz and Hannah follow, and when the four of them have gotten sodas as well, they leave the living room for an adjacent, quieter den, where two couches sit catty-corner to one another. Avery and Ryan take one and Liz and Hannah take the other.

It's Hannah who says, "It's like we're on a double date!"

To which Liz adds, "Yeah—in someone else's house."

Avery leans over and dangles his pizza slice in front of Ryan. Ryan realizes he is supposed to take a bite. Lovingly.

"It's very romantic," Avery says. Ryan feeds him some pizza in return, which Avery responds to with exaggerated ecstasy. Liz and Hannah both crack up.

"How long have you two been together?" Avery asks them.

Hannah and Liz look at each other for a few seconds. Then Hannah says, "Four months, three days, and . . . two hours."

Liz pulls back and stares at her. "Really?!?"

Hannah feigns hurt. "How could you not know that?"

"You're bluffing."

"Are you so sure?"

Avery laughs, but Ryan is stressed out that this is a real fight. He only calms down when he realizes that Liz and Hannah don't seem too concerned about it. Hannah starts talking about how they met, her disbelief when an unrealistic crush suddenly became a realistic crush on a long bus ride home from a soccer match. Ryan is jealous at how easily they've dispensed with the moment of tension, how he seems to be the only person in the room still wondering if Hannah was making up the four months, three days, and two hours. Is it possible to be in love and to have forgotten the day it all started? Is it different when it's someone you've known all along, instead of someone you just met?

Avery leans into Ryan a little, and Ryan's thoughts come back to the room, to what's being said. Hannah gets to the end of her story just as Pope bounds into the room, proclaiming, "*There* you are!"

The party follows them into the room, as if they found the bookcase that was really a door all along. As other people come in, Pope sits down between Ryan and Avery, practically on their laps.

"I hope you don't mind," Pope says. "It makes me so happy to see you together at long last!"

Pope says this as if Avery has spent the past week toiling at school while Ryan fought a war in Austro-Hungary.

Ryan thinks it's a bit much, but Avery takes it to heart. Because it's only now that he realizes—the whole time they've been dating, he's been going to play practice. Now that it's over, he will get so much of his time back. Which means that Ryan will get more of it, too.

"Brave new world," Avery says, maneuvering around Pope to hold Ryan's hand.

Pope extends their arms and pats both Avery and Ryan at the same time. Then they stand and proclaim to all who will hear, "This dowager wants some dancing!"

With that, Lavinia Stranglehold exits the room.

Less than a minute later, a disco mix of "Defying Gravity" thumps against the walls.

The dancing begins.

It is always a challenge to a couple when one has the natural inclination to dance and the other does not. In the case of the couples on the couches, the preferences are evenly divided. Hannah jumps up immediately as more people follow Pope out. Liz groans a little, but lets Hannah pull her to her feet.

Avery can see Ryan settle farther back in the cushions even as the music and the excitement amplify. At a fundamental level, he gets it: This isn't a dark club or even the rec hall they first met in. This is someone's house and the sun isn't all the way down yet. The people who are dancing are doing it to continue the camaraderie they built over months of rehearsal and performance. Ryan isn't a part of that, and it will be hard to make him feel a part of that.

Still, Avery wants to try. No pressure, but still.

Ryan tries. Even though he would much, much rather stay on the couch, he sees that part of Avery is already in the other room, and the remaining part is asking Ryan to accompany him. Ryan gets up from the cushions, then holds his hand out for Avery to take. Even though Avery can certainly stand up on his own, he takes the hand, then keeps it that way as they emerge into the living room. Ryan has no idea what song is playing—a disco version of something about losing one's mind—but the music is almost beside the point. This isn't a dance floor like at the gay prom, with colored lights and a way to be able to hide yourself in the shadows. No, this is a living room with the lights on, and a bunch of friends dancing as unanonymously as possible. Everyone's eyes are wide open as they sing to each other and sway to each other and celebrate the moment they're within. Ryan tries to dance along to that as Avery tries to face him and face everyone else at the same time. But it's not really working. Ryan still feels like the audience member who's stumbled onto the stage during the curtain call.

He lasts a song, but then when the next song (the megamix from *Six*) comes on, he lets go of Avery's hand and says he's just going to step out into the backyard for a moment.

"Are you sure?" Avery shouts over the music.

"Yeah, you stay here and dance. I need some air. I'll be back in a few."

"Okay!"

Ryan goes over and takes a can of soda from the refreshment table, then slides open one of the doors that leads into the backyard. When he closes it behind him, the music becomes a quieter version of itself, the joy as played through a pillow. After walking a couple of feet, Ryan turns to watch the scene inside. Pope is proclaiming themself the king of the castle, and Avery is one of the members of their court, bowing gleefully.

It makes Ryan much more happy than it makes him sad to see this play out on the other side of the glass. It's not his joy, but he's glad it exists, that he can exist beside it, that he can know someone who's taking part in it. He doesn't feel left out, because he knows he's taken himself out, because that's what felt right to do. He doesn't feel separate from Avery here. If anything, he feels a little closer, to be able to see him as he'd be if Ryan weren't around, to know that his happiness isn't relying on Ryan, it's only complemented by Ryan.

"Who are you?" a voice asks behind him.

Ryan turns, and after his eyes adjust, he sees two deck chairs farther off on the lawn. Dennis is sitting in one of them.

Before Ryan can answer, Dennis leans forward, squinting, and says, "Oh, wait—you're Avery's boyfriend, aren't you? I've heard about you. I mean, nobody's actually *told me* about you, but I've heard things." There's a bottle of vodka at Dennis's feet, and when he sees Ryan noticing it, he picks it up and holds it out. "Would you like some? I can pour it right in your can. The Andersons have far too much trust when it comes to their liquor cabinet."

"Aren't they here?" Ryan asks.

"Upstairs. They're not going to interrupt. As I said, they have trust. Trusting *actors* . . . can you imagine? Here—sit down. Join me."

Ryan can't think of a compelling reason not to, so he goes deeper into the shadows, then sits down in the second deck chair. Now the living room looks like a scene on a screen, volume turned low.

He puts down his can for a second, which Dennis takes as an invitation, picking it up and adding some vodka to Ryan's Coke. Since Ryan knows he'll be driving later, Dennis has just rendered his soda undrinkable. But he doesn't say anything.

"So, what did you think of our little production? I saw you in the audience on multiple occasions. Surely you must have thoughts."

"I liked it," Ryan says, trying to leave it at that.

"You *liked it,*" Dennis repeats, as if Ryan's just handed him an epiphany.

"I laughed," Ryan adds, then instantly regrets it, remembering who he's talking to.

"You laughed! Well, of course you laughed. But tell me, Avery's boyfriend—did you *feel* anything?"

Ryan knows that *I felt proud of Avery* isn't what Dennis is looking for here. So he just keeps quiet, correctly assuming that Dennis will go on anyway.

"I suspected as much," Dennis says. Both of them are facing forward, the dancing still unfolding in a rectangle of light. "You see, *Don't Forget Your Shoes!* is, by pretty much any standard, a dreadful play. There are dozens if not hundreds of other plays that could actually speak to what's going on in our country. But no. The high school would rather we put our minds in mothballs. If we play it safe, if we don't make people feel anything, especially not discomfort, then no one will complain, and if nobody complains—well, that's the definition of victory in the administration's mind, isn't it? But here's the thing—I don't accept that. I know it's pretentious as fuck for high school students to consider themselves artists. But you know what, Avery's boyfriend? I'm an artist. Or at least an aspiring artist, because one of the first steps to being an artist is claiming it, devoting yourself to it. When given drivel like *Don't Forget Your Shoes!,* what does an artist do? I'll tell you—they see it as a challenge. The whole thing was designed to take people away from their cares, from their feelings. So what if you somehow turned it so they were forced back *toward* their cares, their feelings? Wouldn't *that* be art? Do you follow me?"

"Sort of."

"I'll take it. You have to understand—most comedies could easily be tragedies. Are you familiar with *Twelfth Night?*"

"Not really."

"Considered by most to be Shakespeare's greatest comedy, or at least one of them. It ends with two marriages. One involves a woman who marries a man she's never met before because she thought he was his sister disguised as a man. The other involves a man who marries a woman who he fell in love with while he was her boss, and while she was pretending to be a man. So I ask you, in realistic terms: Does either of these marriages strike you as particularly promising?

Or do you think that perhaps the dynamics at work here, and the sublimating of homoerotic desire, will lead to heartbreak, recrimination, and hostility? Same with *Don't Forget Your Shoes!* A young man has his fiancée, his fortune, and his dignity torn away from him by family members he always thought were on his side. Does that sound *hilarious* to you?"

"Only if you're not that young man," Ryan says.

"Exactly!" Dennis calls out, so loud Ryan half expects the people inside to turn to the window and look. But they keep dancing and laughing. "I tried to tell people about this, but they didn't want to hear it. Which only made me understand Lucius's rage even more. Now it's over, and all I can say is *good riddance.* Your boyfriend wanted me to calm down? I'm perfectly calm now. And look—he's searching for you."

Sure enough, Ryan can spot Avery leaving the dancing, peering out the window, not quite seeing them. Ryan attempts a wave. Dennis calls, "Out here!"

Avery isn't sure what to make of the scene in the shadows, Ryan and Dennis sitting like old friends at the edge of the party. It's too dark to read Ryan's expression, but his posture isn't relaxed.

"What's going on?" Avery asks. He tries to make it sound light, but he doesn't sell the line.

"Your boyfriend's been humoring me," Dennis replies. "And I appreciate that."

Ryan gets up from his chair as Dennis punctuates his appreciation with a swig of vodka.

"I'm surprised you're here," Avery says.

Dennis laughs. "So am I. But I figured it might help me step out of Lucius's skin, to be here and to see everyone back to normal again."

Avery realizes this is the most conversational Dennis has been since rehearsals started. He wonders if this is actually what Dennis is normally like.

Dennis goes on. "Look, no hard feelings about earlier. I was in the zone, you weren't in the zone, and as a result you took us all wayyyyyy outside the zone. Inside this meek little play we were handed, there's a Sam Shepard play waiting to get out . . . but I couldn't really free it myself. There were moments I thought I was getting you there—you've got the rage inside you, too, and I could see it flashing behind your eyes. But I understand now that it was me you were pissed off at, not Lucius. Fair enough. Can I offer you a drink? I don't have any cups, but I'll happily give you a swig."

"I'm good," Avery says. Ryan is now beside him. They exchange a look.

Dennis gets to his feet more steadily than either Ryan or Avery would have anticipated.

"No hard feelings?" Dennis asks.

And Avery thinks, no, the feelings he has toward Dennis are no longer hard. They are liquid now, easily digestible. The play is over; what use is there in being angry or annoyed?

"No hard feelings," Avery says.

Dennis takes this as an invitation to come in for a hug. Instead of backing away, as he would have onstage, Avery accepts it.

"Someday," Dennis says, "all this will be forgotten. But maybe some of it will be remembered."

Then he turns around and points to a spot to the left, beyond the backyard.

"See that? That, good sirs, is my house. I think I'll return there now, without this bottle in hand. My time here is done." Then he turns back to Ryan and Avery. "I think you two are a good couple. You're good, both of you."

With that, he puts the bottle down in the grass and walks gently into the night, stepping over the backyard fence as if it were a mere prop, not waiting to see if his exit garners any applause.

Ryan is honest with Avery.

"I don't want to go back inside yet," he says. "I want to stay out here with you."

Avery looks concerned. "Are you having a bad time?"

"No—it's not that. I'm having a good time, and I really want to hang out more with Liz and Hannah. It's just . . . I like getting to be alone with you."

Avery's concern dissolves. "I can't argue with that." He gestures to the deck chairs. "Shall we?"

Ryan sits back down in the chair he was in before. Avery

moves Dennis's old chair so their armrests overlap. Avery sits, and his and Ryan's arms overlap as well, palms kissing, fingers intertwining.

Inside, the dancing has turned to all-out singing. Ryan can't make out what song it is, but he watches as Avery's friends chorus into each other, exuberantly belting with unselfconscious glee.

Avery watches alongside, imagines what it must be like to see this scene as a near stranger.

"Nobody's ever going to mistake us for the popular kids," Avery says. "I can't say I mind that at all."

Pope is standing on a chair, using a pretzel stick to act as conductor.

"I've never had a group," Ryan says. "I have friends and everything. But never a group, not like this. There are groups I get along with, but I'm not a part of them, you know? You definitely have a group."

Avery rubs his thumb over Ryan's thumb. Just a little something to keep his heart warm.

"I'm new to groups, too," he tells Ryan. "And honestly? I don't think I noticed how much of a group we'd become until now. I can't wrap my mind around the fact that I won't be seeing them every day after school. It all passes so fast."

"I was thinking how you were just starting rehearsals when we met. That was one of the first things I learned about you, that you were in this play."

"Now here you are at the cast party. I'd say that's progress."

Ryan leans over and Avery leans in. They haven't found the exact right angle yet, but they're close.

"You know," Ryan says, "I've never been to a party as somebody's boyfriend before."

"An oversight on the universe's part," Avery observes. Then he asks, "How's it going?"

"It's going well. I'm not sure I ever would have imagined being here like this. And now I can't imagine not being here."

This is the most truth he's able to tell. Avery isn't a place he belongs yet. But Avery is definitely a place he could belong, one day. Because the people you love lead you to places you wouldn't have ordinarily gone. The people you love become places you wouldn't have ordinarily gone.

Ryan doesn't want to scare Avery away with his gratitude.

Good enough to hold hands, good enough to talk some more about the people inside. Good enough to have forgotten what's waiting for him at home. Good enough to feel Avery breathing as he leans imperfectly on Ryan's shoulder.

Pope bows from their conductor's platform. Ryan and Avery watch as the music shifts into something more conversational. The dance floor disperses, mostly to the refreshment table. Pope disappears into the den, then reappears. They ask Baby Winston something, and Baby Winston points to the back door.

"I wouldn't be as happy as I am now if you weren't here," Avery says.

Pope throws open the door with a flourish, unleashing all the voices inside to join Ryan and Avery in the backyard.

Ryan moves his free hand so it finds Avery's free hand. They join.

"There you are!" Pope calls.

Both Ryan and Avery hear the intention in Pope's sentence.

For the first time, they've become second person plural.

It fits.

Welcome to the Ocean

(the first date)

Ryan has never done anything like this before.

It almost feels like he's in the passenger seat as he steers his way to the community center. He can't exactly call his actions spontaneous—he's been going back and forth about whether to go for weeks. And even now, even as he's driving, at any moment he could still turn back. But back to what? That's the question.

So he lets the truck go forward. That's what it feels like. The truck is taking him there, not vice versa. Yeah, he's at the wheel, but really he's a passenger to something larger than his life. He's giving in to it, because he wants his life to become larger, too.

The radio tries to encourage him, the sad songs reminding him of now, the anthems reminding him of what's possible, the dizzying, glorious heights of self-assertion, of love. He is lucky to have a soundtrack for the war inside him— one side marching under an empty flagpole, convinced he

251

isn't worth much, and therefore deserves less; the other side carrying many flags, some of them rainbow, insisting that love is not only possible but inevitable, changing everything.

Your loneliness is not your fault, this side chants. *We are out there. You will find us.*

The velocity gives advantage to the voices of encouragement; being alone in your bedroom, staring at the ceiling and thinking that nothing will ever change, is very different from being alone in your truck, letting everything around you blur as you make an escape. He allows himself to think that maybe his loneliness *isn't* his fault. The love he wants, the belonging he craves, won't grow in the soil where other people have planted his life. But he is old enough now to begin the process of uprooting. This is it. This is him pulling himself from the earth at seventy-three miles an hour.

He doesn't have any goal in mind. He's not even sure he'll have a good time. Alicia will be there, and a few kids from town will be there, but if this night ends up being about them, he'll consider it a failure. He wants to prove to himself that he can be someone else, that his life can be something else, that the world will offer him somewhere else.

Even if it's just a community center dance in a small town, it'll be a start. Or not a start. This started long ago.

Not a start, but a step.

In Marigold, everyone goes to Liz Macy's house to pregame the gay prom. There is still widespread disbelief that it's happening at all—if Kindling is at all like Marigold, Avery figures there will be some people in town who'd rather burn down the community center than have it host a queer event. But apparently they don't get to decide. Avery chalks this up to progress . . . though he notes the progress may indeed be written in chalk.

Avery isn't sure who first said, "If we're going to go to a gay prom, we're going to have to really gay it up," but this philosophy has been adopted by most of the kids at Liz's house. Liz and Hannah are dressed in matching Elton John, neon-blue sequined tuxedos, special-ordered by the local tuxedo shop. Jesse Lukas somehow found a blue-and-pink-striped jacket to reflect the trans-nonbinary flag. Pope has bedecked themself in a velvet ensemble, and Lana Yip, who graduated last year but has driven back from college to attend, is wearing a ball gown her grandmother wore to *her* prom.

Avery is excited to have the opportunity to wear his suit, an item of clothing he's proud of but never really has an occasion to wear. When he wears it, he feels more seriously himself, more formally himself. Everyone in the store was sure it would need to be tailored in order to fit, but the moment he tried it on, he knew that wouldn't be necessary. It fit. It was meant for him, and he was meant to wear it tonight.

He puts on a white shirt, then the black suit. He doesn't have too many ties, but figures a black one will work. It takes a few attempts to tie it so that it doesn't have a tail. Then he heads to the kitchen, to show his parents. His mom becomes all emotional and goes for her camera. But his dad . . . his dad takes one look and says, "No, that's not right." Then he leaves the room, too.

Avery feels his emotions stutter. What is his dad talking about? Even though Avery is sure of his parents' support, he can't help but have that lingering fear that there is something he can do that will make it topple. Being human means never being entirely sure of other people, even if they're your parents.

But then his dad returns to the kitchen with the strange contraption from his closet, the hanger with special tabs that hold his ties in a bookshelf row.

"You need something more celebratory," he says. "Take your pick."

As a child, Avery had always loved this tie-sorter. Not just because of the colors and the patterns, but also because each tie seemed to have its own story, its own place in the chronology of his father's life. The ties Avery had picked out as gifts for Father's Day had their own special section, beside the tie Avery's dad had worn on his first date with Avery's mom, an ambitious paisley that seemed, years later, beamed from another world.

Avery's fingers touch these ties now in greeting as he by-passes a series of stripes and any tie that might most easily be described as *nautical*. His mother says, "There," just as he finds the right one: a pink tie with white polka dots. The pink perfectly matches his hair, as if a decade ago, his father or mother walked to the counter at Macy's and gave the salesperson a lock for guidance.

So that's what Avery's wearing now as he and his classmates pile into Lana's van to drive over to a town none of them have ever seen before, to a place promising a welcome it is rare for them to receive. At first, the van is full of music and conversation—the front seat calling to the backseat and the backseat calling back. But about halfway through, they all fall quiet. Hannah leans into Liz. Pope leans back, stretches out their legs. Lana leans into the steering wheel. Jesse leans into their seat belt. And Avery— Avery leans his forehead against the window and looks out, even though there's nothing, absolutely nothing, to see. For some reason, this gives him hope—and the reason is this: Already he knows that in order to get to what you want, you often have to cross a vast emptiness. How much nicer it is to cross it in a van full of kindred spirits, rather than crossing it alone.

Pope sits up abruptly and calls out, "Ohmygod, turn it up!"

A song has come on the playlist—a song that's rude and bombastic and the opposite of timeless, because it will be always married in everyone's mind to the year they first heard it. It will only take another year or two for them to be embarrassed by their love for it, but even as they're embarrassed, the love will thrive in a soft spot in their hearts. A one-hit wonder is still a wonder, and even when you get to the point of disowning it, a memory like the one forming for Avery right now will make you cherish it.

Lana and Jesse reach for the volume at the same time;

Jesse gets there first, but only because Lana is keeping an eye on the road.

Avery pulls back from the window and into the song. The bass throbs through the van so it feels like they're in the belly of a friendly, wild beast.

This is how Avery wants the night to be:

He hasn't come looking for love from one person. He's come to dance with his friends.

The municipal center looks like it always has to Ryan, blandness incarnate. That's actually what it says on the outside, MUNICIPAL CENTER, not COMMUNITY CENTER, as if to remind people it belongs to the town. The pool is in the basement, about as far away from the entrance as you can get, and yet when Ryan walks in, there's still a gust of chlorine, a tang of humidity. A local cop checks him out as he steps into the lobby; Ryan imagines it's for his security, but all he feels is an instinctive insecurity. There's a homemade banner hung over the front desk that says PRIDE PROM. The Magic Marker rainbow letters don't mark much magic for Ryan; it's surreal that his town is making this attempt, but less surprising to find it presented in such a ramshackle way.

Ryan knows he isn't being generous. This isn't how he'd phrase it to himself, but that's what it is: a lack of generosity to the people who worked hard to make this night possible, a lack of generosity to himself for being here.

There is music pulsing from the gymnasium, the promise of a heartbeat. There are teens in the hall, and Ryan doesn't recognize any of them. Some kids have really taken the queer prom thing to heart, wearing dresses that don't conform to the current decade—some puffy, some sleek; some bubblegum pink, some striped like animals who've lived to tell the tale. Gender has been rendered beside the point; people are wearing whatever they want.

It's an alternate universe. Ryan likes it and doesn't like it, feels encouraged by it and doesn't feel like he belongs here at all. He used to like it here, back when they called it the rec center. He and six or seven other boys would swim, then leave time to hang out by the vending machines before their parents came to pick them up. They were a pack. He was part of their pack. Until they grew up some more, until the jokes were less funny, until suddenly he was different, and they recognized it. They still have a pack, in a way. Ryan doesn't miss it, but he knows his life would be easier, maybe better, if he'd stayed inside it rather than been wary of it. Not afraid—never afraid. But wary. The thing is: None of them are here now. There's no way any of them would go near a pride prom, except maybe to throw some eggs at the windows. Instead there are all these strangers, traveling in their own packs, the kids in bold dresses hanging out with the kids in skinny ties and skinny jeans.

For the first time since he dyed it, Ryan's hair doesn't seem out of place.

He knows Alicia is here somewhere; she's texted him a few times, to see if he's arrived. Other kids he knows are here, too, probably dancing already, or standing to the side making comments about the kids who are dancing. Not in a homophobic way, but in a people-watching way. That's what they do.

Ryan knows they're around, but he doesn't seek them out, not yet. He detours to the bathroom first, startled, then amused, to find that the MEN and WOMEN signs with their sexless symbols have been completely covered by construction paper signs that say, simply, WHOEVER. The markers' magic is beginning to work.

Finally, Ryan heads into the gymnasium, which in the nighttime dim doesn't look like a gymnasium at all. The basketball nets have receded, unobtrusive chaperones. Colored lights have been borrowed and installed, so that everything has a purplish cast. A DJ spins where a referee might usually sit; the speakers aren't crystalline, but they do the job. Ryan sees Alicia and some other kids dancing in a corner, talking to each other as they jump and sway. He should go over to them. He knows he should go over to them. But he stops. He stays alone a little longer. He doesn't feel lost, but he's still waiting to feel found.

This night is supposed to be different. He needs it to be different.

He stands there waiting. He doesn't make his next move, because none is occurring to him.

Avery and his crew spill out of the van laughing. The number of cars in the parking lot is already a kind of amazement;

each of the kids from Marigold thought at some point in the ride it was possible that they'd show up in Kindling and find an empty prom. But no—queerness is representing. You can tell it from the bumper stickers and the items dangling from the rearview mirrors. Not with all of the cars. Not even close. But enough. More than usual.

As they get to the entrance, they find a school bus dropping other kids off. A school bus at night feels like a school bus on a secret mission, and in this case it has delivered its students closer to their authentic selves. Avery is relieved to see he won't be the only trans kid at the prom; at least two, maybe three, have arrived on the bus, looking dapper or delinquent, diva or dork. The group is chaperoned by two small-town drag queens in full regalia.

"Incredible," Pope murmurs, pronouncing it *incredee-blay*. Pope and Jesse and Hannah have never seen a drag queen in person before, and Avery, Lana, and Liz have only seen them a couple of times, mostly from afar at parades or rodeos. Close up, they are more intricately impressive. The illusion holds; you cannot picture anyone underneath, nor would you want to. But at the same time, you have to appreciate the achievement, the after has so thoroughly eclipsed the before. The queen has not erased herself to do this, but has instead enhanced herself into the character she's become.

One of the drag queens, Noxema La Crème, sees them staring, but knows it isn't a bad stare.

"Aren't you pretty in pink?" she says to Avery. "Now

don't go breaking Duckie's heart, you hear? That boy's been through enough."

Avery has no idea what she's talking about, but promises nonetheless to be an upstanding citizen of the heart. (Those aren't his exact words. Instead he tells the drag queen, "Okay!")

Before they get to the door, Pope tugs on Avery's sleeve.

"How do I look?" they ask. And on their face, Avery can see the thin ice that Pope's bravado skates atop. They've only driven to another county, but Pope is worried that suddenly their schtick won't work.

"You look divine," Avery replies.

Pope smiles, a little confidence returning. And Avery feels more confident, too—having to deal with Pope's insecurity has momentarily made him forget his own.

Nobody is going to use the decorations here as an argument for the concept of a "queer eye"—but the decorations, Avery feels, are beside the point. The point is the number of kids clustering within the lobby and the halls. The bus has brought a certain busyness to the municipal center that reminds Avery of an assortment of birds; it's almost cliché to think of gays as flamingos, but here he sees hummingbirds and pigeons and mourning doves and, yes, flamingos. Avery himself feels like an oriole; not as showy as the others, but still with a personality.

There is song in the way everyone is talking to each other, and there's also song spilling through the air that holds them.

"It's a pride prom!" Pope proclaims to their group. "We must partake of the dancing!"

From behind him, Noxema La Crème calls out, "Hallelujah and amen!"

This is when Avery feels it: His heartbeat suddenly has a whole lot of added bass. Nervous tremors cascade through his body. He knows he belongs here. He swears he knows he belongs here. But his body wants to show him the cracks in his thinking. *Do not put yourself out there. Do not make yourself noticed. Do not think you'll be happy, because that will only make you sadder when you're not.* He's not even hearing these words; it's like they're in his blood, in his nervous system. He wills himself to be steady, to feel worthy of this destination. *Just have a good time,* he tells himself.

None of the people he's with notice he's wavering. Part of him is relieved by this. Part of him wishes they knew him better, could see his signs.

Pope leads their group forward as if this is a club Pope's been to a thousand times before. Avery walks in the door of the gymnasium ten minutes after Ryan does. The DJ has just started a song that unlocks the dance floor, and kids are starting to turn the silence into a fray, moving their bodies decisively as the singer lets loose a *maybe*.

Three things happen in quick succession. Pope grabs the hand of the nearest person, who happens to be Jesse, and they plunge into the dancing. Hannah spots a few friends from school and leads Liz over to meet them. And Lana sees a boy she used to date and is so unprepared for it that she runs off to the restroom. Avery could follow any of them but instead he holds fast. The song shifts from maybe to yes, cutting from indecision to a feeling. The dance floor erupts in hand-clap euphoria.

Avery looks at the people in the crowd, then looks at the people who are, like him, ringing the crowd. He spots a boy whose hair is as blue as Avery's is pink. Instead of dancing, he is singing along, every now and then closing his eyes and swaying his head. Because he's been watching the crowd, it doesn't occur to him that anyone could be watching him.

It is not in Avery's nature to approach strangers, however cute. But this isn't an aspect of his nature he particularly likes, so he figures now is as good a time as any to alter it. He is drawn to the blue-haired boy—drawn by curiosity, drawn by empathy, drawn by the fact that neither one of them is their natural hair color. There's the thrill of not knowing who he is, and the thrill of possibly finding out.

It's as if someone's laid down a red carpet between them, a yellow brick road. No one gets in Avery's way as he walks over. The song remains and the dancers disappear. His heartbeat is still loud, but no longer an alarm. It's a musical instrument. He is writing this song as it's happening. He has started their story before Ryan even knows it exists.

Ryan turns a little, swung by the song, and sees Avery walking toward him. He doesn't realize he's this boy's destination—not at all. But he notices the travel, and the boy who's traveling. He sees the pink hair and smiles.

Avery smiles back, uses that moment to step into Ryan's life.

"Hi," he says.

"Hi," Ryan says back, a little confused. He doesn't understand what's happening—has this pink-haired boy mistaken him for someone else?

Avery, sensing confusion, says, "I saw you standing there and thought it might be a good place to be."

Ryan has no idea what to say to that.

"What town are you from?" Avery asks.

"I'm from Kindling. Here."

"Oh! I'm from Marigold."

"Awesome," Ryan says. Then: "I have no idea where that is."

"About two hours away."

"Wow. That's a far drive. Worth it?"

Avery is looking straight at Ryan when he says, "Yes."

It's only now that Ryan realizes . . . this pink-haired boy is flirting with him. This has never happened to him before. No boy has ever come up to him like this. Online, sure. But in person? There's nothing to hide behind, no safe pause for typing the next words. He has no control of the moment. He must give in to the moment.

"Do you want to dance?" he asks. This isn't a sentence that comes from his heart. It's a sentence that comes from movies, from fantasies, from fairy tales, from him grasping at how to fill the space in a way that will keep the flirtation going.

Avery aces it when he replies, "Yes. But first I want to know your favorite kind of dog."

"My favorite kind of dog?"

"Yeah. Just say whatever comes to mind first."

"A pug?"

"Excellent. Now ask me a random question."

"Um . . . what's your favorite . . . shape for a cloud?"

(Ryan has no idea where this question comes from. It's like it was unlocked by the word *random*.)

"A castle," Avery answers with a smile. "No—a dragon. No—a castle shaped like a dragon!"

"Is that your final answer?"

"Yes."

"Okay . . . what's your next question?"

"I think we're good, don't you? We know each other thoroughly now. I think we're ready to dance."

Ryan can't tell if Avery is kidding or not. Avery can't tell if Ryan is as into it as he is. There is a momentary teeter, a lurch of anxiety. Their consciousness of everyone else in the room returns—more acutely for Ryan, because it's his town. The interruptions will soon be closing in. In less than a minute, Lana is going to return from the bathroom, resolute, and Pope is going to look for Avery in order to gather their group together. In less than two minutes, Alicia is going to decide Ryan is being a drag, and will naturally attempt to drag him out of it.

The pink-haired boy looks at the blue-haired boy and sees he has no idea what to do.

The blue-haired boy looks at the pink-haired boy and asks him silently for help.

"Oh, wait," Avery says. "I forgot something."

Ryan thinks he means he's left something in his car. Or he's looking for an excuse not to dance, not to prolong this.

"Okay," he says. "If you need to go . . ."

Avery laughs. "No! I forgot to say, 'Hi, I'm Avery.'"

Ryan feels the seesaw of his heart dip low, then even out.

"Hi, Avery. I'm Ryan. But you can call me Ryan."

From Avery: that smile again. On a chemical level, Ryan already loves that smile.

"*Now* we know each other completely," Avery states.

"Guess we'd better dance, then."

The dance floor—the same floor as the nondance floor, really—is only a few short steps away. Ryan gives Avery an *after you*, and Avery returns with a *no, after you*. Ryan feels the impulse to take Avery's hand, to link. But he doesn't have that confidence in himself or the moment yet. They arrive together, separately. Separately, together.

A song has been playing the whole time, and it's the song, more than the dance floor, that they step into.

This is what it's like to dance with a boy you like, even if you are liking him for the very first time: The capacity of your awareness expands, but even as it expands, it only contains three things—you, him, and the music. Nothing is effortless, and this certainly takes some effort, but the effort has a joy to it. Even the awkwardness is a giddy awkwardness, because there is no room for shame here. Only hope.

Ryan is taller. Avery knows his body better. They are strangers and they are a pair at the very same time. Avery's hair gets in his eyes. Ryan can feel the sweat on his back. They cannot stop smiling. They pull into each other, their hands finding an easy way to hold. Avery sings along a few words, and Ryan sings a few words back. Everything is in agreement. Their bodies are in agreement. Their smiles are in agreement. The music is in agreement. It's so much more than they ever would have asked, and also exactly what their hearts deserve.

One fast song leads to the next, which leads to the next. Then the DJ bends the path, sends them into a slow song. Ryan hesitates; a slow dance is a lot to ask of someone else, and he doesn't know how to begin to ask it. But Avery smiles. Avery says, "Come here." And Ryan gives himself to that. He lets Avery introduce him to closeness. He lets Avery's hands tell his hands where to go. He lowers his head so his cheek can rest above Avery's ear. Blue hair on pink hair, pink hair on blue.

This.

It's—

Ryan is overwhelmed. By feeling. By holding. By knowing.

* * *

When you've never seen the ocean, this is what it feels like to see the ocean. You can only observe what's in front of you, which is impressive. But what alters your life, what leaves you at a loss for words, is knowing what's beyond. Standing there, seeing just a fraction of a fraction of its face, you know it can only lead to something enormous.

All they do is sway. It is the most natural motion in the world.

The wind does it. The tide does it. Other couples do it.

Ryan and Avery do it, too.

They have each found something, and they have each found someone.

Both at the same time.

"There you are!"

At first Avery doesn't hear it, but then Lana is at his side, asking where everyone else has gone.

Avery pulls back from Ryan, just a little bit. And Lana reacts as if Avery was hiding Ryan this whole time, as if he wasn't right there holding him.

"Oh!" she says. "Who is this?"

"This," Avery replies, "is Ryan."

The dance floor is too crowded for Ryan to retreat entirely, but Avery sees him shy away.

"Hi, I'm Lana!"

"Hi."

Lana turns back to Avery. "Have you seen everyone else?"

Avery takes hold of Ryan's hand, so he won't shy away too far.

"No," he tells Lana. "I've been here. And I'm going to stay here. I'm sure they're around, though."

Avery barely knows Lana. But he relies on her understanding.

He sees it click—Lana stepping out of her own situation to see Avery's.

She smiles. "Got it. If I see them, I'll tell them you're here. We'll let you know if there's anything for you to know."

"Thank you," Avery says. Then he turns back to Ryan, squeezes his hand, tries to return them to the song.

"Do you have to go?" Ryan asks. "I mean, it's okay if you have to go."

"But it's more okay if I stay, right?"

"I think so? I mean, if it's more okay for you, it's definitely more okay for me."

Teeter. Teeter. Emotionally, Ryan is the kid on his bike leaning on its training wheels. He doesn't know what will happen when they fall off. Will he fall, too?

Avery takes his other hand. The DJ returns to a fast

song, a song everyone loves. There's a cheer and an eruption of bright movement around them. They stand there looking at each other, their arms an imperfect circle.

"I'm glad I'm here," Avery says.

When the training wheels fall off, the thing you have to do is pedal forward. Pedal like you know it will work. That way, you don't fall. That way, you soar.

Ryan lets himself believe Avery.

Inside the song, they soar.

The DJ does not relent. He knows which songs have that magic to them, the ones that lift you to the mountaintop and show you the view. The dancers cede their heartbeats to the greater thrum. They are awash in smiles and sweat and soul. The sweetest deliverance is a shared deliverance, and in this ugly municipal center, about a hundred teens from a hundred-mile radius are reaching for the beauty and attaining it. Their cares, their fears, their petty dramas can't help but fall away as the music draws them to a pure elevation. For three minutes, five minutes, they can love the entire world, because the entire world is right here in front of them, and it's vibrant.

Ryan and Avery ride these songs together. Their touch, their hold, their smiles, the opening of their eyes and the closing—all of it makes these moments shared, makes their experience of each other inseparable from their experience of the music.

There is no better place to be.

Time can be counted in the number of songs that pass . . . but who's counting?

Finally, there is the comedown, the song that doesn't quite live up to the others. Ryan becomes aware of the sheen across his forehead, the trickle down his back. Avery catches his breath. They both look a little worn out, but not disagreeably so.

"Want to step outside for a second?" Avery asks.

"Sure," Ryan says. "I can give you a tour."

Immediately, he's worried he's going to run into people from town, people who'll want to stop and talk, who'll want introductions. (He doesn't know that Alicia, seeing what is happening with the pink-haired boy, has told everyone else to give them space.)

They stop at a water fountain. After Avery guzzles down as much as he can from its tepid offering, he asks, "Is there a pool here? Is that what I smell?"

"Yeah," Ryan says. "I'll show you."

It only takes a few turns for them to be away from everyone else, for the sound of the dance hall to move offshore. The first stairway they come to is locked, but the second one isn't, so Ryan can lead Avery down to the basement.

"Have you lived in Kindling your whole life?" Avery asks.

"Yup. So I've been coming here for as long as I can remember. A couple of the rich families in town have their own pools, but most of us use this one. I remember coming as a kid in the winter, and how weird it would be to step outside and have my hair freeze. I'm sure that wasn't healthy, but I'd do it on purpose, you know? Leave my hair wet, just so I could see if I'd get icicles when I stepped outside. I was that kid."

"Makes total sense to me." Avery can tell the pool is getting nearer because the chlorinated smell is overpowering, almost ammonia-level.

"We have to go in this way," Ryan says, gesturing to a door that says MEN'S CHANGING ROOM. Avery follows him in and it's super eerie—a bare-minimum fluorescence keeping the lockers and the shower stalls from total darkness.

"Who knew these rooms could get even scarier?" Avery jokes.

"Sorry," Ryan says. "We're almost there."

He hurries them forward to the source of the scant light—a swinging door that luckily opens when it's pushed. The pool is lit from below, so it first looks like it's the entire floor of the room, a gently wavering blue.

"Ta-da!" Ryan says. He sounds relieved to find it's still here, that he hasn't let Avery down.

"Lo and behold," Avery replies.

There isn't anywhere for them to sit; this isn't the kind of pool that people lounge next to in deck chairs.

Ryan feels self-conscious. Is this really the best he has to offer? What is he doing?

"I'm sorry," he says. "It's really just a pool."

"I like it."

"Why?"

Avery laughs. "I don't know why. I like that it's just us here. I like seeing you in this light."

"You don't have to be nice."

"What?"

Ryan feels like he might as well throw himself in the pool.

"I'm so bad at this," he confesses. Then he looks down, because he doesn't want to see Avery's reaction.

Avery steps closer. "I think we're at the point where you don't get to be the one who decides whether you're good or bad at this." He touches Ryan's arm; Ryan looks up. "I think this is turning out to be an amazing first date."

Ryan is so surprised, all he can do is echo, "First date?"

Avery takes his hand again. "Yes. And don't forget the other part. An *amazing* first date."

"But you live hours away."

"That's no reason to stop, is it? I mean, there has to be a second date, right?"

Ryan doesn't understand why he can't accept this, why he can't just say yes, of course of course of course. It's like he can't trust his own happiness. It's like he's already forgotten his ability to soar.

But. Something good must have happened, because something has enabled his hope to be stronger than his doubt.

Avery's presence certainly helps.

The response takes a little longer than either of them

would like. As Ryan's heart builds momentum, Avery's approaches a dip.

Just in time, Ryan says, "I would love a second date. Like, tomorrow. What are you doing tomorrow?"

Avery smiles. "I think I'm having a second date with you."

At this moment, two things happen: Avery's phone vibrates, and a light goes on behind a door on the other side of the pool, which Avery assumes is the women's changing room.

"Maybe we should go," Ryan says.

"Goodbye, pool," Avery says.

And Ryan, not holding back, takes on a goofy voice and says on the pool's behalf, *"Goodbye, Avery."*

Avery laughs, and Ryan loves the sound.

Back in the stairway, Avery checks his phone.

"What is it?" Ryan asks.

"It's my friends. I think they want to go soon. Because of the drive back."

"Oh."

"I'm going to tell them we're getting in one last dance."

Normally, the word *last* would make Ryan sad. But already he's feeling a strange trust in the future.

This time when they dance, they notice everyone around them. They recognize that they are a bunch of queer kids dancing in the middle of nowhere, finding somewhere. It ties them a little bit more to everywhere.

In two minutes, they will exchange phone numbers. In eight minutes, Avery will be back in Lana's van, everyone asking him for every detail about the blue-haired boy. In five minutes, Ryan will finally look at his phone and see that Alicia has been aware of him the whole time. In twelve minutes, she'll meet him out by his truck, will ask him how he is. At first, he'll just shake his head, not having any idea where to begin, but grateful that she, too, saw it, that there's no way it was only a dream. In fifteen minutes, Ryan will send Avery his first text, saying what a great time he had. In sixteen minutes, Avery will text back, seconding the emotion.

But now . . .

Inside the song that carries them, they find the word *free*. They dance to that word more than any other. At one point, they dance as if it's a slow song, even though it's a fast song. Then they return to the beat. They jump together, swirl together, hold together. Everything feels lighter than air.

It doesn't feel like a last dance at all.

Derivation

(the tenth date)

On his way home from the cast party, Ryan realizes there is no way he can go home. He has to see if it's possible to be happy without paying for it in sadness afterward. He can't step from time spent with Avery to time spent with his parents. He cannot put himself in a position of being so unrelentingly misunderstood. He's explained himself enough. They don't want to hear it. Which is why there's no going back.

He drives to Caitlin's. His texts to her have gone unread, so he rings the doorbell and wakes her up. She takes one look at him and knows exactly what the situation is. He's aware she's been trying to avoid the position he's putting her in. The door opens anyway. She hugs him before he can even put his bags down. They don't talk it over; she doesn't try to persuade him otherwise. She just gets the sheets from the closet and leaves them on the couch. She says she loves him, and that she'll see him in the morning.

He thanks her. He doesn't say for what, but they both know.

At two in the morning, Ryan texts Avery:

Are you free next Saturday to help me move my stuff to Caitlin's?

Avery's response is instant.

Of course.

Avery is supposed to spend Saturday with his own parents. After all the rehearsals and his time away with Ryan, they've been looking forward to some family time. Avery knows this. But he also knows he has to be in Kindling. Ryan is doing something momentous and wants Avery there. That matters more.

Avery assumes his parents will be sympathetic. Still, he waits until Friday at dinner to tell them what's going on.

He explains as much as he can without feeling like he's invading Ryan's privacy. He tells them he's been texting and talking with Ryan all week, preparing. Ryan's been trying to go through all the usual motions of school without thinking too much about the reckoning that's about to occur, but even Avery can hear its drumbeat.

"I said I'd be there," Avery lets his parents know. "I promised I'd be there."

In response, Avery's mom and dad share a long look,

and he understands that he has inadvertently continued a conversation they've been having without him. His dad puts down his fork; his mom looks at him gently, but also with concern.

"Honey," she says, "we've made plans for tomorrow, remember? For the three of us? We're going to take a drive to have lunch at that French place in Wickham that Ramona liked so much, and stop at Donna's studio to look at her new sculptures. She's looking forward to seeing us."

They could leave it there. It's enough of an argument.

Instead Avery's dad takes the conversational baton and adds, "It's not just that, Avery. Your mother and I both like Ryan a lot, and we're very happy the two of you have found each other. But because we're your parents, we also want to be sure that your relationship doesn't take over your life. We know how all-consuming love can be at your age, especially with the right person. But you can't let *anything* be all-consuming right now. You have to keep parts of yourself open, give yourself a little space to grow."

"You can see him next weekend," Avery's mom says. "You can invite him here. We'd love to spend more time with him. But this weekend, you need to take a break. You've already made plans with us—and even if you hadn't, we'd still be suggesting you take a break. It will make things better in the long run, I promise. And a long run with Ryan is what you're after, isn't it? That's certainly how it's seemed."

Avery knows how lucky he's been that his parents have always been on his side. Even though there were times he had to be patient with them, even though there were times they said the wrong things or even did the wrong things because they thought they were the right things, they never made him doubt himself at an existential level, never made him regret being who he was. But now, it feels, they're telling him he's going too fast.

"I know we have plans," he concedes. "And I'm really sorry about backing out of them. I wish I could be in two places at once. But we can go to the French place or go see Donna's studio any day—we could even do it Sunday! But tomorrow I really have to be with Ryan. He needs me."

Avery's mom's gentle tone doesn't change when she says, "I know it's hard to understand, but you haven't known each other long enough to need each other. Or at least you shouldn't need each other, not yet. I'm not saying it won't happen—I actually think it *will* happen for the two of you. But in time. Over time. As you get to know each other, as you get to know each other's lives, you will grow to need him, and he will grow to need you, until you get to the point that the need will be so much a part of your life that you will think of it as inseparable from who you are. Your father and I know what that's like. But that need—it can take so much from you, Avery. It gives and gives, but it also takes. Which is why we're asking you to approach it slowly."

Avery understands what she's saying, in the abstract. But what Ryan's going through isn't abstract. It's real.

"Mom, Ryan's not asking me to go to a party with him.

He's getting his things to *move out of his house.* Whether you like it or not, I'm his boyfriend, and I should be there."

"We like it, Avery," his dad says. "Listen to us, okay?"

"We sympathize with what Ryan's going through," Avery's mom continues. "Obviously. But what we're saying is that with something so big, he needs to be able to do it whether you're there or not. He's taking control of his own life, and that's a good thing. But he can't take control of his life fully if he's relying on you to help him do it. I know it's hard for you to see that—you wouldn't be you if you didn't want to be there, and that heart of yours is in exactly the right place. But you need someone outside that heart to give you some caution, some perspective. And that job falls to us."

It would be simple for Avery to scream. To let all the emotions amplify into a storm—incomprehension that his parents could be so wrong, anguish that he might actually let Ryan down at such a moment, frustration at waiting for so long to love someone only to be told to slow down. In a flash, Avery realizes that if he were Ryan, and these were Ryan's parents, that is exactly what he'd do: unleash the indignation and let it bite whatever it wants to bite.

But these are his parents, looking at him with a concern that is, at the very least, sincere. So he doesn't pound the table. He doesn't push back his chair. He doesn't even raise his voice when he says, "I need to be there. If you don't understand why, that's fine. I apologize again for screwing up our plans. I hope we'll still get to do them another day.

As for tomorrow—I don't think you're going to try to stop me, are you?"

Avery's mom and dad don't need to look at each other to consult.

"No," Avery's dad says. "We're not going to stop you."

"We're just going to hope you listen to us anyway. We want you to be careful."

"I'll be careful," Avery promises, even though he's not exactly sure what he's supposed to be careful about.

His parents are disappointed in him; he can tell. And he's disappointed in them, as they surely know.

The subject is dropped, but it remains the only subject in the room.

Avery won't tell Ryan any of this happened.

He doesn't want there to be any doubt.

He goes back to his room, and when he sits down on his bed, the first things he sees are the snapdragons Ryan gave him, a little ragged but still special. When they're gone, he'll replace them with a photo he took of them right after he got home from the cast party. Beside the photo will be the card that's now beside the flowers: *Here's to many more. Love, Ryan.* Avery hasn't asked whether Ryan meant many more shows or many more flowers. He'll never ask.

He'll always take it to mean both.

For years, Ryan felt his life was a mostly unspoken negotiation with his parents.

This week, it's become a more formal negotiation.

When Aunt Caitlin took him in, she stopped being a good go-between; there's no question now in his parents' minds which side she's on. She's tried hard to remain diplomatic—no, she's not saying they're bad parents or that their home is a bad place for Ryan, she's just saying that right now her house is a better place for him, etc.

Ryan's survival strategy has been detachment.

He's told Alicia that he's staying at Caitlin's, but hasn't said anything about moving out, because he doesn't want to have to deal with all the inevitable follow-up questions. School has always felt separate from life at home, so he leans into that now; it's not that he's suddenly happy to be in class, but it gives him enough reason to pause all his other thoughts, to believe like everyone else that the future is something that's happening next year after graduation, not tomorrow.

It's only in those moments when he's left with himself—driving in the truck, waiting for sleep, stocking shelves at work—that he does things like wonder about the difference between giving up and letting go. He feels his parents gave up on him a while ago, but they're not letting go. He's now given up on his parents, and trying to let go. But once he lets go, what does he hold on to? Caitlin? Avery? It's not the same. He knows it's not the same.

Caitlin tries to get him to talk. Says it isn't healthy to fall so silent. But right now, the silence is his protection. Like armor, he knows he can't wear it forever. He just wants to get through Saturday. Then he'll take it off.

Saturday. Caitlin says he needs to talk to his parents, but has agreed it doesn't have to be Saturday. She'll meet them for lunch somewhere, keep them out of the house. She's not going to lie—she's told them he's going to stop by to pick up a few things. *Like underwear,* he heard her tell them on the phone. And he thought, *Wow, this is what it's come to: My aunt and my parents are talking about my underwear.*

It would be funny, only it's not really funny.

That's the truth he keeps most hidden in the silence: the fact that while he knows he's making the right decision, it doesn't feel right at all. He can't stop doubting, even though he feels he doesn't have a choice.

Avery gets up before his parents. Or at least he thinks he does—for all he knows, they're awake behind their bedroom door, still hoping he'll change his mind and spend the day with them. They're not going to stop him, but they're not going to make him breakfast, either.

He keeps quiet, and they don't stir. He makes himself some cereal, grabs his car keys, and goes.

It's only when he's driving that he realizes how little thought he put into getting dressed, how unnervous he is about seeing Ryan again. He didn't have to cross that boundary of self-consciousness; the boundary was no longer there.

Would it be different if this were a normal date, if he were driving to a movie or a restaurant? Maybe. Probably. But the fact is, this isn't a normal date, and that is itself a marker of how far they've gone in so short a time. Even if his parents don't see it that way, or maybe even see it as a negative, Avery is sure that it is true, and it is good.

He knows that love can be all-consuming. He's seen friends erase themselves like that. But love doesn't have to be defined by what or how much it consumes. It can be providing as well. Not all-providing. But . . . providing.

That's what he wants from Ryan. That's what he thinks Ryan wants from him. A providing, supportive kind of love.

What Ryan's going through isn't something Avery knows anything about, really. But Avery is young enough not to recognize this, not to be too intimidated by this. He still thinks that building a relationship with someone is about finding the things you have in common, not about steadily navigating the things you don't.

Ryan texts to make sure Avery is on his way. At a stoplight, Avery sees this and texts back his estimated time of arrival. That's what the map app on his phone is good for now: predicting the timing. In terms of directions, Avery's got it down. This route has become personalized, familiar. Whatever happens, these roads will always remind him of Ryan, even though so many of the chain stores and chain restaurants he's seeing can be found on other roads in other towns. Even when things turn sparse as he approaches Caitlin's house, he smiles from a deep satisfaction when he knows exactly which way to turn. A left. A curve. A sudden right. Down a stretch of trees, water hiding behind but letting itself be found. Left onto her street. Another left into the driveway.

And there he is: Ryan waiting on the front steps. Now he stands, welcoming.

Ryan quickly explains that Caitlin just left, and will keep his parents busy so he and Avery can do what they need to do.

"She says hi," he adds at the end. "She's excited to see you."

"I'm excited to see her," Avery says. "But I'm gonna be honest—I'm more excited to see you."

This is when Ryan realizes that he needs to step out of his headspace long enough to kiss his boyfriend, to enjoy his company for a few minutes before they get to the business of extracting him from his home. The kissing is so success-ful that his headspace transfers entirely to kissing headspace, and it's Avery who has to separate them and say, "Don't we have to go?"

Yes, Ryan reminds himself. They have to go.

He hoists the duffel he has waiting by the door, and they walk to his truck.

It's not a long ride. Ryan has a lot to say, but he's not sure he wants to say any of it. He wants to apologize for drag-ging Avery into his mess. He wants to thank Avery for being here . . . but he also doesn't want to thank him too much, like it's a big deal. The thing is, it's good for Avery to be here, but it still doesn't feel natural for Avery to be here. When they're alone together, they are the leads of their own show. But put Avery here, in the middle of all this parent drama?

It still feels like he's a guest star. It still feels like Avery can't possibly know Ryan well enough to be comfortable here. So Ryan's uncomfortable, thinking about that.

He does some math in his head.

Avery's not really paying attention, just letting his thoughts drift off in the passenger seat, when out of the blue, Ryan says, "Sorry. I'm guessing this is not what you thought we'd be doing on our tenth date."

"Oh, wow," Avery says. "Double digits."

"I mean, when I've been to your house, it's been really nice. My house isn't going to be as nice."

"It doesn't have to be. And it's not your house anymore. Not if you don't want it to be."

"Depends on who you ask."

"I'm not asking your parents. I'm asking you."

Ryan takes his eyes off the road, looks at Avery.

"Honestly?" he says.

"Yes," Avery replies. "Honestly."

"I have no idea. I am so angry and sad right now that I don't trust myself to give an answer that'll last."

"Then that's the best answer for now."

"Okay. But none of that makes this a fun date."

Avery reaches out for Ryan's free hand. "Not all dates have to be fun. Not at this point. We have other priorities now."

"Like?"

"Like, real."

"Well, this will definitely count as real."

Avery is relieved when there aren't any cars in the driveway or the garage. When they get out of the truck, Ryan shoulders the duffel bag but doesn't go to open the garage door. Avery can see him taking that pause, steeling himself from the inside.

Avery reaches out his hand, but instead of the whole hand, he offers his index and middle fingers, pressed together. Ryan looks at him quizzically.

"Double digits," Avery explains.

Mission accomplished: Ryan has steeled himself, but not so much that he's lost access to his heart. He offers his fingers, and the two of them link. Like that, they enter the house.

The first impression the house makes on Avery is one of smell: As soon as they walk in, they're greeted by a scent that's much more an approximation of pine than pine itself. The pine of cleaning, not of nature. This fits the decor, which is very orderly. It almost feels to Avery like a series of those rooms you see in museums, where the furniture is correct to the period, but it doesn't look like anyone's ever sat in it. In this case, the period could be thirty years ago, or maybe sixty. If it weren't for the flatness of the TV in the den or the lack of cords on the phones, there'd be no sense of the current century.

Ryan lets go of Avery's fingers, scratches his head as he looks around.

"I don't think I need anything from these rooms," he says. "Just my bedroom. All my stuff is pretty much there. Which is pretty weird, when you think about it. I guess I didn't trust it to be anywhere else."

This statement makes Avery sad, down to his core. But he doesn't say anything. He's here to listen, not to comment. Not unless he's asked. He's figured out that much.

Ryan's bedroom door is closed. When he sees this, he says, "That's strange." And when he opens it, he goes, "Jesus!" Avery is expecting to look in and see it's been trashed. But instead it's . . . neat. Right-angles-no-clutter neat. From Ryan's reaction, Avery is guessing this is not the room's regular state.

"They couldn't leave it alone," Ryan says. "Seriously. I bet that's the first thing she did after I left—made the bed, cleared away all signs of me."

There are still plenty of signs of him, Avery thinks. But he can see how it might not feel that way. All the old toys are arranged with military precision, the shirts folded beyond recognition. There are a few posters on the walls—an Ansel Adams tree, a Scott Pilgrim. But the white walls create large gaps between them, as if there'd be too much trouble if they congregated close.

"Okay," Ryan says. "Let's do this." He takes the duffel from his shoulder and hands Avery two boxes of trash bags from inside. "I'll tell you whether something should go in a green bag or a black bag, okay? Let's start with the clothes."

Not "my" clothes, Avery notices. *The* clothes.

Avery is sentimental about his clothes. There are some shirts of his that might as well have their own names, since what Avery feels toward them is almost like friendship. They've been through a lot together, good and bad. Some shirts marked his elevation into the person he was meant to be. Even some shirts from his earlier life, the ones he didn't give away once he made clear to his parents what he wanted to wear and what he didn't want to wear—he has an attachment to them even if he'll never wear them again.

Ryan doesn't seem to have any such attachments. He goes through his drawers like he's operating a weed whacker. He takes out each shirt, barely looks at it, and says either "green bag" or "black bag." Quickly enough, Avery realizes black means *keep* and green means *trash*. (One or two also end up in the duffel, but Avery's not sure what *that* means.) Sometimes Ryan will hold up a shirt to see if it still fits. But mostly he judges them without unfolding them. Same with his shorts. Socks. Underwear.

It's definitely going quicker than Avery expected. And Ryan doesn't even seem to find it weird that he's handing over his old underwear to his new boyfriend.

I guess he's comfortable with me, Avery thinks. And also he thinks, *Ryan is throwing too many things away.*

Avery wishes they were stopping to talk about some of the clothes. Maybe Ryan would offer him a shirt or two. He's seen a couple that went in the green bags that he'd totally wear. But at the same time, he wouldn't want to wear something Ryan never wants to see again.

Once the drawers are empty, Ryan turns to the closet. Or, more accurately, he turns against the closet, pulling shirts and pants off their hangers as if they were toilet paper some prankster had thrown in a tree. Some are clearly too small for him now—this is a childhood cleanup that has waited years to occur. When Ryan green-bags a fiendishly soft flannel, Avery risks a "Hey, this would probably fit me." At first, he doesn't think Ryan hears him . . . but then Ryan shrugs, says Avery can take it if he really wants it. Avery puts it aside. Ryan green-bags another nine or ten shirts in a frenzy. Avery remembers what those frenzies were like, when panic would wind his nerves tighter and tighter. He didn't take it out on his clothes, but he did take it out on himself and the people around him, because it felt like if they didn't see him exactly right at that moment, if he didn't show himself as exactly right at that moment, then he'd never get anything he wanted.

Ryan stops. Stares at the near-empty space he's created.

Avery waits.

"What am I doing?" Ryan asks.

Avery waits some more.

Ryan turns. Whatever has been fueling him is running low.

"I thought I'd keep what I wanted to keep and get rid of the rest. Leave no trace. But now that doesn't feel right, either. It feels like I'm taking everything out on my room, and my room didn't do anything to deserve that, you know? So what do I do?"

"You stop."

"Just like that."

"Yup. You're having what I call a claustrophobic moment. I used to have them all the time. It's when you get so caught in a moment, you lose all sense of its actual size. It squeezes in on you with really high walls, so it's hard to see past. You think everything needs to be decided. You think if you don't do something this very moment, you'll never do it. But nine hundred ninety-nine times out of a thousand, you actually have time to stop. To look over those walls. Or maybe realize they're easy to move aside. Like now. I don't know that much about your parents, but I don't think they're going to change the locks as soon as we get out of here. I don't think they're going to come in here and burn your clothes. Tidy them up, sure. But I don't think you need to decide everything today. Take what you want, and leave the rest for another day. It's not going anywhere. And you're only going to the other side of town."

Ryan puts his palms together and moves his hands so his thumbs cross his lips. Then he puts his hands down. He takes a breath, releases it. His eyes never leave Avery.

"Thank you," he says. "You're right."

"Let's leave all the green bags here. You can go through them another time."

"Okay."

"And let's focus on what's important to you. What do you need?"

Ryan picks up the duffel and heads to his bookshelf, taking down a set of notebooks and putting them safely inside. He doesn't explain what they are, and Avery doesn't need him to. Then he gets his laptop and all the wires for his laptop. His phone charger. A few books that were sitting by his bed, and a few more schoolbooks from his desk. A couple of photos of him and Alicia and their friends. One of him and Caitlin. He leaves the one of him as a kid with his parents. Avery is pretty sure it would have ended up in a green bag, before. He thinks this is probably better.

Ryan picks up a teddy bear from the same bedside table from which he took the books. "Allow me to introduce you to Bartholomew Bear," he says to Avery.

"Nice to meet you, Bartholomew Bear," Avery replies.

Bartholomew Bear nods to Avery, then Ryan turns him for a talk.

"I'm leaving you in charge," he tells the bear. "If Toucan Charlie starts to pull his old tricks, you know how to reach me. And don't forget to feed the socks. You know what happens if they're not fed."

Bartholomew Bear nods.

Avery watches as Ryan smiles, puts Bartholomew Bear back in his place. He wants to stop time, seal off this room, let the day lift away so they could be here together without any pressure, without any concern. Avery wants the full tour, the relaxed tour. He wants to get to know Bartholomew Bear and all the rest of the animals. He knows this will only welcome him to love Ryan more, because he will know more of Ryan to love.

"It wasn't all bad here," Avery says to Ryan.

"No," Ryan agrees. "It wasn't. Not even close. But the best times were when I was alone. Or when friends were over."

"Well, I'm a friend. And I'm over."

"Yeah, well." Ryan looks a little sheepish. "There was one thing I never did with any of my friends."

Avery moves a little closer. "What was that?"

Ryan erases the rest of the distance, leans in, and whispers, "This."

They kiss and kiss and kiss. Then Ryan pulls back and, in a move profoundly endearing to Avery, takes off his sneakers before lowering onto the bed. Avery follows both actions.

They roll around and kiss for a while. Then Avery stops, pulls back, and says, "You know . . . you're a liar."

Ryan raises an eyebrow. "Am I?"

"You said there was only one thing you never did with your friends. But I think there are lots of things you've never done in this room."

Ryan holds up his hands in defeat. "You're right. I lied. But I swear, it was only to get you into my bed."

"Looks like your plan worked."

They kiss again.

There is a part of Ryan that thinks: *It's about time.*

To be in this bed with someone he cares about. To have his room witness who he's become, what he is capable of doing, who he is capable of loving.

It feels amazing, and it also feels like part of the goodbye.

Yes, there's a part of him that can be here with Avery and enjoy the heat of their bodies, the humor of their words, and the fact that the world feels right-sized for once.

But the other part of him . . . well, the other part of him is still listening for the first sign of the garage door.

The kissing grows intense, but then it slows. They lie there facing each other, Ryan running a hand over Avery's arm, up to touch his face, to confirm he is, in fact, here. Avery runs his hand under Ryan's shirt, rests his palm on Ryan's heartbeat as it, too, slows back to its everyday rhythms.

No music is playing, and no music is needed. All Avery hears is breathing and thoughts, breathing and thoughts.

"We should bring the things to the truck," Ryan says. "Before they get back."

Avery says okay, but they take another minute to lie there, to exist in that twofold space, before sitting up, putting their sneakers back on, and resuming their task. When Caitlin texts to say things are wrapping up soon with Ryan's parents, Ryan and Avery move even faster. In truth, it doesn't take long, since they're leaving all the green bags behind. They're only taking the things Ryan wants to take.

Once the truck is loaded, Avery asks Ryan, "Are you forgetting anything?"

And Ryan smiles and says, "I'm sure I am. But that's okay, you know?"

* * *

The whole week, when Ryan was imagining this moment, it was a big cleave, him planting his flag on the side of After and banishing all vestiges of Before. But that's not how he feels, now that he's gotten to it. He may never live here again, but he'll be back. Right now, it's just him closing the door, locking it, and driving off.

They arrive back at Caitlin's house around the same time she does. The three of them empty the back of the truck, and then she says they need to sit down at the kitchen table and have a talk. Ryan and Avery both appreciate that Avery is automatically included.

"How did it go?" Ryan asks.

"It went better than I expected," Aunt Caitlin reports. "I might even say much better than I expected . . . although that probably says as much about my expectations as it does about what actually went down."

"What did they say?"

"Well, the strange part is that they seem more confused than angry. They genuinely don't understand what they did to make you want to move in with me. I told them it wasn't my place to explain—that's between the three of you, and it's not something that can be resolved second-hand. But I told them it wasn't a whim or a phase, and it wasn't you 'acting out,' which is a phrase my sister likes to use for anything that doesn't conform to her standards of behavior. That's nothing new. I said, from what I can tell, there was a time they could have made it right, but that time passed without any effort on their part. They say they didn't see it, they didn't know for sure . . . and I can't honestly say whether they were telling me that, or just telling themselves that, if you know what I mean. They want you back, but they didn't talk about any changes that would happen on their end if you returned. They just want it to be like it was."

"According to them."

"Of course. Their version of like it was. But, in fairness, they also recognize that isn't going to happen, and they said they were grateful that you could come here, and that you haven't gone any farther or done anything else." Caitlin turns to Avery now. "I won't lie—they definitely think you had something to do with this."

"It was a Big Gay Brainwashing!" Ryan proclaims sarcastically.

Aunt Caitlin chuckles, but she also shakes her head. "I'm sure that's part of where they're coming from. But they also know this is your first time. And everyone, gay or straight, can be a fool when it comes to their first time."

Avery and Ryan blush a little. Caitlin chuckles again, and pats Avery on the hand.

"Don't you worry," she says. "It seems to me you're erring on the side of good foolishness, not bad foolishness. To which I say: Carry on."

"Do you mind if we wait until you leave the room?" Avery asks.

Now Caitlin swats at him. "Respect your elders!"

Both of them laugh, but Ryan wants to finish the conversation from before.

"So how did you leave it?" he asks. "With them?"

Caitlin becomes serious again. "I promised them you'd go to school every single day, get your work done, and stay out of trouble . . . which, from what I've seen this past week, is a pretty easy promise to make. I also promised I'd try to get you to talk to them . . . and I want to try, not just for them, but for you. They also offered to give me some money for your room and board, which was a decent thing for them to do. And I took it, because let's face it, Ryan—I'm a one-slice-of-pizza person and you are an only-one-slice-left kind of guy, and while that is very complementary, it also means buying a whole lot more pizza than I was planning to buy."

"You know I'll chip in," Ryan says.

"No, sir. You weren't paying your way with your parents and you're not going to pay your way with me. Your money is still your hard-earned money. Spend it on something besides room and board."

Now Ryan is tearing up, which makes Avery tear up, too.

"Okay, okay," Caitlin says, standing up and looking away before it's three-for-three. "Go unpack your things. Last night while you were asleep, I cleaned out the small dresser by the washing machine. You can use that for now, until we can get you something bigger."

Ryan and Avery retrieve the dresser, which used to hold sewing scraps and other odds and ends. It doesn't quite fit in the den, near the couch, but Avery figures everyone's willing to be a little odds-and-ends right now.

Ryan starts the unpacking with his duffel bag. The couch still has his sheets on it from when he slept there, made like it was a bed. Now, instead of moving things to the dresser or anywhere else, Ryan puts the contents of the duffel bag out on the sheet one by one, as if taking an inventory. His laptop, the cords. His charger. The unexplained notebooks. The books from his bedside table and his schoolbooks. A few pens Avery didn't notice being thrown inside. Then some of the clothes that he consigned to the duffel instead of the black or green trash bags.

As he does this, Avery realizes he left behind the comfy flannel he put aside.

"Oh man," he says out loud, and when Ryan asks him, "What?" he explains.

"That's okay," Ryan replies. "There's something else I wanted to give you."

He reaches in and pulls out a shirt so tightly rolled up that Avery didn't even notice it when it was passed into his hands to put into the duffel.

"It's my secret shirt," Ryan says. "I always kept it in the back of my drawer."

Avery has no idea what he's going to find when he unrolls it; from the outside, it looks like a regular blue T-shirt. But once he opens it up and takes a look, he laughs at how obvious it is: On the front of the shirt, there's a rainbow jumping from a cloud.

"I know, I know—it's so corny. But picture this: I'm in sixth grade, and Mom and I are at Target. I'm bugging her to go to the toy section, like I always do, and I've worn her so far down that she tells me to go ahead, that she'll meet me there after she's done getting hairspray or dishwashing gloves or whatever. So I prance my way down the aisles, and along the way I see this shirt in with all the Star Wars shirts and the Pokémon shirts and—well, you know the kind of shirts they have at Target. And my first thought is that someone's made a mistake, that this shirt should be in the girls' section and not the guys' section. I tell myself I should probably just move it back to the girls' section, so I pick it up . . . and I realize, no, it's a guy's shirt. And I kinda like it. I'm not making the connection here between rainbow and gay, right? Not consciously. But that connection is inside somewhere, because I can't put down the shirt. It's a men's extra small, so it can fit me. A little big, but it fits. But just as sure as I know it's a shirt I need, I also know there's no way in hell my mom is going to buy it for me. So I grab a couple other shirts along with it, and I go into the changing room. And while I'm in there—I'm not proud of this, but I'm not *not* proud of it, either, you know? While I'm in there, I take off the shirt I'm wearing, put on the rainbow shirt, tuck it into my pants, and then put the original shirt on right over it. I button to the top button so you can't see underneath. Then I walk back out and put the other shirts I brought in on the

I'm-not-going-to-get-this rack, real smooth, so no one will be able to tell there's one shirt missing. The shirt's not nice enough to have one of those electronic sensors.

"I rush to the toy aisle, where my mom is already looking for me. Because she has the laser-stare thing down good, I figure she'll spot what I've done right away. But she doesn't! Not then, not when we're checking out, not when we're driving home. I'm wearing an extra shirt and she can't even tell. It's like, not only is the shirt invisible, but it makes me invisible in a very good way. That's how it became my secret shirt. Every now and then I'd wear it under something else; it looked a lot like a Superman shirt I also had, so I think my parents assumed it was that shirt. I told my mom I wanted to do laundry as a chore, and she thought I was being a good son, but really it was so I could sneak in my secret shirt every now and then without her noticing. There were a few close calls, when she told me she'd help me fold, et cetera. But it's stayed a secret all this time. Eventually, I didn't fit into it anymore. But I still liked knowing it was there, keeping all my other shirts company."

"Wow," Avery says. "This is a very powerful shirt."

"Yeah. And I guess what I'm saying is, I'd like you to have it. I think it will fit you. It won't have to be a secret shirt anymore. It can just be a shirt that I love."

Avery's first reaction is *Oh, no, I can't . . .* and that's exactly what he says, making to hand Ryan the shirt back. But Ryan won't take it.

"Really," he says. "It's yours."

Avery's second reaction is to accept it, to accept it for what it is, for what it means. Accept all of it. And instead of pushing it away, be grateful.

"Thank you," he tells Ryan. Then, "I just need you to hold it for a second."

Ryan takes it, and Avery, right there in Caitlin's den, takes off the shirt he is wearing, puts it down on the couch, takes the secret shirt from Ryan's hands, and puts it on. It's not a perfect fit, but Avery likes it even more for that, that it keeps some of Ryan's shape.

"Nice," Ryan says, taking in the sight of Avery in the shirt. He didn't realize how much this would mean to him, too. When you wear a secret openly, it stops being a secret. It starts being something you can take pride in. It's hokey for this particular shirt to make him feel that way, but he respects that his sixth-grade self wouldn't find it hokey at all. His sixth-grade self would be scared and maybe a little ashamed and definitely a little intrigued by this turn in Ryan's life. But most of all, at the most essential level, he would be astonished.

Aunt Caitlin doesn't see Ryan's sixth-grade self as she walks into the room. At least not separately. When she sees Ryan now, she's always seeing his younger selves and how they've all added up into this near-man. Which is its own astonishment, truth be told.

She's come in to suggest they all go on an excursion. She

clocks that Avery has changed his shirt, and that Ryan has just done something he wasn't sure he could do. She knows this from a glance. But the rest of it is a mystery to her, and she is fine with it remaining a mystery. She wants Ryan to have mysteries under her roof, as long as they aren't harmful ones. And this one is clearly the opposite of harmful. Risky, yes, in terms of how much Ryan is giving his heart. But not harmful.

"I thought," she tells the two boys, "we'd go out and buy an actual sofa bed."

Ryan and Avery don't have to choose.

They can have the destination and the detours.

Neither of them expected to spend part of their afternoon at a place that proclaimed itself to be a "sofa emporium"—when they walk in, Avery asks Ryan, "Do you think the Emperor of Sofas is actually here today?!?" and both Ryan and Caitlin crack up. When the salesman asks Caitlin if these are her two sons, she says a simple no, and then when the salesman is out of hearing range mutters, "Wrong on so. Many. Levels," which cracks the boys up again.

Ryan hasn't forgotten where he's just been or what he's just done. He's aware of what kind of check his parents must have given Caitlin if she's in the position to get a new sofa bed. But he decides not to swim in those currents. He decides to swim instead on the surface, in the sunlight. The salesman has given them free rein to try out whatever bed they'd like, so Ryan and Avery are hopping from one to the next, giving each a rating of one to five stars. Sometimes the mattresses are too thin; sometimes Ryan and Avery can feel the bars beneath, like they're in a bear trap waiting to spring rather than a place for dreaming. Those get one star.

Caitlin wishes they could see themselves like this, the ease with which they share their space, the lightness with which they move. They're not her sons, and they've been through plenty that has required them to grow up faster than many of their peers. But right now she can see them clearly as kids. Kids, playing. Kids, knowing the task isn't asking for any responsibility on their part. There is something sublime in seeing them goof around. Standing there, waiting for them to figure out which sofa deserves five stars, she wishes them nothing less than a future of endless goofing around.

Maybe they share the same wish, because they spend much more time in the sofa emporium than any other customer that afternoon. They narrow it down to three sofa beds. Then two. They pull Caitlin onto each, so she can help judge. Lying there, snuggling in, staring up at the ceiling, it feels like home. The particular sofa bed becomes immaterial. The three of them bouncing, laughing, pretending to sleep—that, more than anything, is five stars.

Ryan still wants it to be a date. They stop for a late lunch, get back to Caitlin's. His stuff is everywhere, and he knows he needs to sort it out. But Avery doesn't have to be here for that.

Ryan wants them to go somewhere, to do something, to share something besides the new logistics of his old life.

He wants them to go somewhere they've never been together. Do something new. Discover new things about each other. Because building a love is not like building a house. You still add to the foundation even as you live in the rooms.

He gets an idea and checks the weather on his phone. It looks like it might work. When Avery's in the bathroom, he tells Caitlin about it. She smiles and tells him to go ahead. It doesn't matter if he leaves his possessions all over the den. They can figure out where everything goes soon enough.

Avery returns to the room and knows something's up.

All Ryan needs to say is "Let's go" and Avery follows.

They secure the canoe in the back of Ryan's truck. Ryan puts the destination into his phone, but won't tell Avery where they're going.

"Now it's a date," Ryan says.

Avery shakes his head and says, "It's always been a date."

Date. From the Latin, traced to the word *dare,* which means:

To give.

To grant.

To offer.

＊＊＊

When it goes right, this is what Ryan and Avery do.

They give. They grant. They offer.

They do this when they show up for the hard parts. They do this when they drive off toward the destination. They do this when they veer on the detours.

They do this when they kiss.

They do this when they sing along to the radio, as they are doing now.

They do this when they share their thoughts, their lives, their bodies, their hopes.

They give.

They grant.

They offer.

And they receive.

It takes them two hours to get into the park, then twenty more minutes to get to the lake. On the map, it's a blue patch in a green expanse, separate from all the streets and cities of the world. At some point, it was set aside as national land, and a hundred years later, Ryan made his first trip here, not as a driver but as a passenger, Caitlin taking them on a long hike. He's always meant to return.

It is nearly dusk, and the park closes at dusk. Avery doesn't notice the sign that says this, and Ryan has chosen to ignore it.

The lake sits beautifully indifferent to the time of day. Its surface is still, reflective.

"We have the place to ourselves," Ryan observes. Which is exactly what he'd been hoping for.

"Just us and the bears," Avery says. He makes it sound like a joke, but he's definitely scanning the woods for bears.

They bring the canoe to the water. They get in.

Ryan passes a paddle to Avery, who takes it with confidence.

They push off from the shore.

Avery has no idea where he is. And he knows exactly where he is:

He's with Ryan.

The only sounds are the wind and water. They could be anywhere in time. Because there have always been the sounds of wind and water, and there will always be the sounds of wind and water. The personal part, the intimate part, comes from the fact that right now they are the ones hearing this particular whisper, this particular score. They are the ones living in the space between the tide and the breeze.

It is cold on the water, bracing. They ride into it, through it.

* * *

The sun shows them which way is west. No matter where they paddle, its glittering trail points their way. It shares some warmth, the closer it gets to the horizon. It fills the air with honeyed light, landing gold on the forest surrounding the lake. Avery and Ryan stop paddling. They know they will only have this light for a very short time. They breathe it in, and the honey spreads through their lungs. Contentment is breathing; breathing is contentment. They touch their knees. They hold their hands. They look in each other's eyes, and also at the world transforming around them.

The world grants. The world gives. The world offers. Because he is with Avery, Ryan accepts it. And because Avery is with Ryan, he accepts it.

The sun bids them adieu, leaving behind a satisfaction of pink and orange, followed by a deepness of blue.

Ryan reaches up and touches Avery's cheek. Avery reaches out, pulls Ryan closer. The boat rocks back and forth. But at heart, it's steady.

Avery kisses Ryan. Ryan kisses Avery. After the first few kisses, it all blurs.

The stars come out to see. First one, then four, then seven, then countless. Ryan and Avery don't notice . . . until they do. They feel the peaceful immensity of the stars, the lake, the wind. They marvel together at what they are seeing.

There will be more dates. So many more dates, until it's simply days, until it's simply life. Dates and days as countless as the stars. Memories more a blur. Detours and destinations debated. The world acting cruel, the world acting generous. A tide that always goes forward isn't really a tide. There is always need for navigation. There is always need for steadying.

To ride together in a boat until the dead of night. To ride beneath the stars and attempt to recognize their patterns. To share what you see with the person you most want to see you. To stare into the peaceful immensity and understand how beautiful and small and remarkable your own existence is. To want to share, and share, and share.

To give.

To offer.

To grant.

To receive.

To arrive.

Acknowledgments

Ryan and Avery first appeared in my novel *Two Boys Kissing*, which is narrated by a chorus of gay men. This book is not narrated by that chorus, but they have been with me the whole decade I've been working on the story, marveling.

Thank you, as always, to my parents.

Thank you to the rest of my family, especially Adam, Paige, Matthew, and Hailey.

Thank you to Noah Lee, who asked me at a reading in London whether I was going to keep writing about Ryan and Avery. It wasn't until I answered yes that I realized I would. This book is the result.

Thank you, Avery, who told me at another reading that the character was the reason he'd chosen the name for himself. Thank you to all the Averys and all the Ryans I've met over the years.

Thank you to my friends. Many of the chapters in this book started as valentine stories I shared with my friends. If you ever received one of them, and especially if you sent me encouragement in return, you have not just my gratitude, but also my heartfelt appreciation. Particular thanks to Billy, Nick, Andrew, Zack, Nico, Mike, and Gabriel, who've been in the room at various times as I've written this book. (For example, right now Gabriel is in the kitchen sipping coffee, having no idea I am typing this.)

Speaking of coffee, thank you to everyone at City of Saints.

Thank you to all my author friends, with a special shout-out to Stephanie, Nina, and David for periodic Zoom check-ins while I was writing this. Also, to Tiernan, Ben, Brian, Ned, and Ben for other meaningful conversations at that time.

Thank you to everyone at Random House Children's Books, including but in no way limited to Marisa DiNovis, Mary McCue, Melanie Nolan, Barbara Marcus, and Adrienne Waintraub. A special shout-out to Barbara Perris for her copyediting and to Artie Bennett, who has now shepherded my books into grammatically correct pastures for two decades. (I know he will correct this statement if it is factually inaccurate.)

Thank you to everyone I work with at Scholastic.

Thank you to Bill Clegg and everyone at The Clegg Agency.

Thank you to Nancy Hinkel, for always coming back from San Francisco, time after time.

And thank you to two decades' worth of readers. You're all somewhere here in this book.